SEAL CATCH

Book 3 of *The Fearless Trilogy*

T R Schumer

SEAL Catch, Book 3 of the *Fearless* Trilogy
Copyright © 2017 by T. R. Schumer
All Rights Reserved Worldwide

Published by T. R. Schumer
ISBN-13: 978-976-95924-7-6
Printed Edition v1.0 - March 2017

Cover Design by Damonza
Editing by Scribendi

SEAL CATCH

T. R. Schumer is a writer and adventurer, an instrument rated pilot who once copiloted a single-engine aircraft around the world, an avid scuba diver, and sailor. The author is currently sailing around the world. After departing from Palma de Majorca in the Balearic Islands, in December of 2014, she's passed the halfway mark of New Zealand. As of February 2017, T. R. Schumer has reached the shores of Australia. The author's first novel *Death Catch* was written while sailing Tahiti and the Society Islands, and then published from New Zealand. Book two of The Fearless Trilogy, *Drone Catch*, was written entirely in New Zealand, while the author traveled both the North and South Islands. Part three of the trilogy, *SEAL Catch*, was mostly written during time spent in the islands of Fiji and then completed in Brisbane.

For Murray, thanks mate

I and my clan against the world
I and my brother against the clan
I against my brother
— Somaal proverb

Chapter 1

The Rendezvous

Ex-Navy SEAL Alex Moss braces against the chill while he stands on a rain-slick jetty at the edge of the North Sea. A light shower of sleet stings his face. The conditions could be better, a lot better in fact, but this day, this moment, is actually one of the best of his entire life.

Moss cracks a smile as he watches the wife of his boss steady herself atop a large metal platform directly in front of him. The woman is currently fifteen feet above him and standing beneath the prow of the ship. The ship is a newly completed, ninety-seven-meter-long research vessel, and she is the state of the art in every way.

The gleaming vessel is perched broadside above the water and on an elaborate arrangement of launch sleds. Even as he looks at her outside on the pier, resting right in front of him, Moss still can't believe she's actually finished. His ship to command . . . He's still getting used to the idea, despite the past two years he's spent working to reach this point, and now, finally, it's time to get this girl wet.

"Is the microphone working?"

Moss nods in agreement while the crowd packed in around him responds cheerfully to the question. Despite the fact that they're all freezing their asses off, everyone's in a celebratory mood. They wait in anticipation while they stomp their feet, and rub their hands in a futile effort to stay warm on this gray, October morning in Bremerhaven, Germany.

The magnificent profile of the brand-new vessel being prepped for launch is an impressive one—even to the most seasoned of seamen who've gathered to witness the event. Moss tries hard to take in every detail and to absorb every moment. His eyes pass slowly from bow to stern in admiration while his employer, Marcus Waverley, addresses the crowd of invited guests on behalf of the foundation that financed the project.

Waverley then hands the microphone to his wife. She grasps the microphone with a delicately gloved hand while she tugs at the collar of her full-length fox coat with the other. She turns to face the crowd, then flashes a perfect smile at her audience just before she begins to speak.

"For thousands of years, we have gone to sea. We have crafted vessels to carry us and we have called them by name. I christen this ship Fearless; may God bless her and all who sail aboard her."

A buzz of energy connects the onlookers as the woman passes the microphone back to her husband. Then the ship's designer steps in; he hands her a festively decorated bottle of Dom Pérignon wrapped in burlap. Moss chuckles at the look of determination on the woman's face as she grips the neck of the magnum-sized champagne bottle with both hands, draws it back, and then smashes it across one of the ship's twin anchors.

Cheers and applause erupt when the bottle explodes on impact. The resulting shower of frothing champagne sprays across the leading edge of the ship's steel hull, as well as the first row of onlookers.

Thirty minutes later, with the last of the preparations completed and the final safety checks made, Alex Moss is uncharacteristically filled with excitement, and an all-too-rare moment of pure joy, as the launch warning alarm sounds, followed by a bellowing command from the launch director—LOOSE!

The crowd is hushed by the movement of the massive vessel balanced above the water in front of them. Her motion is subtle at first, but soon becomes more obvious as she rapidly gains momentum.

With well-choreographed precision, the electronically triggered hydraulic rams send her sliding broadside down steel sleds, and into the sea. She hits the water perfectly. The impact sends a wave crashing up, and then over, the empty jetty on the opposite side. Fearless rolls sharply away from her audience before she rocks back, then gently rights herself.

Moss is still grinning and clapping as he glances around at his fellow crew members. Some he has known for years, while others are new acquaintances. Mixed among them are special operations forces veterans like himself. Men in search of a new chapter in their lives, and all of them now shouting and cheering as Fearless gracefully begins her life of service to science.

Malcolm Rafferty, the ship's newly minted first mate, and one of Alex Moss's closest friends, is still clapping when he turns to Moss. "So, Captain," he says, "what do you think of her now that she's finally afloat?"

"I think she's the most beautiful woman I've ever seen," Moss responds. "But, you know, Razz? I've been thinking about this whole Captain thing, and I'd prefer something a bit different: How does Chief of Operations sound to you?"

"I like it," Rafferty agrees. "So, Chief, how soon before we can move on board and get out of here? As far as I'm concerned, we can finish fitting her out once we reach the Caribbean—this place is colder than a witch's tit."

Moss smiles. "I wish we could leave today, but we still have to complete the sea trials, and then Pete has his own list."

"Ain't that the truth!" Pete interjects, "I've been a ship's engineer long enough to know that launching a new vessel isn't the end of the project, not by a long shot. This is only the beginning, fellas; the fun part's over. Now we all have to get to work if we want this ship to be the best she can be."

. . .

Three weeks later, light snow skips across the broad spread of reinforced laminate windows on the bridge of Fearless. Moss gazes out at the gray, frozen haze billowing across the ship's foredeck before he shifts his focus back to his officer of the watch.

He's an Australian, and a top notch seaman, but Murray also happens to be a former member of Australia's elite, Special Air Service Regiment. In his previous life, he was a small arms specialist and an explosives expert. Today, however, his job is to insure the ship's safe departure from port.

Moss steps over then takes up a position next to Murray. "It's your call," he says.

Murray looks up from the twenty-six-inch flatscreen that displays the ship's conning system. The thin-film-transistor, liquid-crystal screen is currently reporting a myriad of sensor inputs coming in from all over the ship—heading, course, rudder angle, turn rate, and turn velocity.

Then there's speed forward, astern, and athwart ship, thruster pitch, RPMs, and propeller pitch. Added in with this data is her environment—true and relative wind speed, wind direction, air temperature, water temperature, and depth.

All of this information is important, vital even, as far as the safe operation of the ship is concerned, but at the moment, Murray is mainly focused on only two key factors—tide and traffic.

The tide in the North Sea can vary by as much as three and half meters. It's the only reason it's now three in the afternoon, and they're still in port, but not for much longer. Murray looks back at Moss. "Tide's just now coming up to peak, Chief; winds are steady at six knots—we're all go."

Moss nods in response, then he reaches for the ship's comm. "All hands, prepare for departure."

Moss leans forward over the instrument panel; he peers out of the front windows and searches the foredeck for his first mate. The flurries billowing across the bow shroud the deck crew in a frosty haze. All are bundled inside full foul weather gear, with heavy deck boots, while the hoods of their jackets have been pulled down tight.

Moss can see them all hustling to prepare to cast off. Then he spots Rafferty walking across the helipad. He switches radio channels, and then clicks the receiver again: "Razz, are we all go?"

Rafferty stops in his tracks and then grabs his handheld out from his coat pocket. Moss sees him lift the radio up near his face, then he hears him: "Ready to slip lines, Chief—we're all go."

Moss glances over at his helmsman, then back at Murray. "She's all yours; take us out."

The radio clearance from harbor control signals the final green light for departure. Moss works alongside Murray to coordinate between Razz, who's in charge of the nine men outside on deck, and the bridge. Then the moment everyone's been waiting for finally arrives as Fearless smoothly maneuvers away from her berth, motors out through the Bremerhaven channel, and then turns south into one of the world' s most congested shipping routes.

With the deck secured, Razz heads below with the rest of his crewmen. He shakes off the chill as he peels away layers of frozen storm gear. Then he heads up to the bridge. Ten minutes later, he's standing beside Moss. He's finally beginning to warm up as he takes a sip from a steaming mug of coffee, and looks out at the view of the frigid North Sea in late November.

The ship is currently making way at a conservative twelve knots. Razz takes another sip from his coffee mug and notes that the snow flurries have shifted back to sleet. He can feel the subtle motion as he watches surging black swell roll beneath the prow of the ship. Her bow steadily rises and then falls with the waves in a lumbering, methodical, rhythmic beat. It's as if the ocean itself were slowly breathing in, and then slowly breathing out.

Razz steps over for another look at the radar, then he scans the instruments—Wind's still holding steady at ten knots . . . He shifts left for a glance at the chart plotter. The LCD screen in front of him displays a thick, and largely indiscernible, jumble of small digital triangles. Each signal represents a vessel transiting the designated shipping lanes. Razz grimaces at the level of congestion: "Geez that's a lot of traffic, Chief . . . even in this weather this place is a zoo . . ."

"I agree," says Moss. "I wish we could've left sooner." He steps over and glances at the plotter. "Conditions only get worse from here." He shifts back to the view in front of him. "What you're looking at is our best possible weather window, so unfortunately, we'll need to push to stay on schedule." Moss pauses as he turns back to Rafferty. "We still have sixty-seven nautical miles between us and the rendezvous point off Borkum."

• • •

Germany's East Frisian Islands hang off the coast of Upper Saxony like a row of dull teeth. Borkum lies at the bottom of the chain, and right along the border with the Westerems Strait, which belongs to the Netherlands. Borkum happens to be the largest, and most westerly, of the East Frisians. The island has a centuries-old and widely varied history, having served once as a base for whaling, then piracy, and later as a military outpost. Wernher von Braun even used the island as a testing ground for his earliest V2 rocket prototypes.

Today Borkum is known as a summer holiday spot. But what Moss is actually aiming for is a preplanned rendezvous point just beyond the three-mile limit off Borkum's west coast. A set of GPS coordinates that lie directly over the Geldsack plate, in fact. It's here that the crew of Fearless are due to pick up a special delivery. A selection of items both Moss and his employers would rather keep off the books, and out of the sight of German customs officials.

By the time Fearless maneuvers into position at a point precisely three point four nautical miles due west of Borkum, what was a gray, cold day has now become an even colder, rain-soaked night.

Malcolm Rafferty reaches up and then switches on the small light strapped to his forehead. He yanks down hard on the hood of his foul weather jacket, then draws in a final warm breath before he pushes open the hatch in front of him. He steps outside into the damp, freezing night air. He can hear the rain pelting the hood of his jacket as he deftly unsnaps the safety line attached to his life vest with a gloved hand and then clips in. Then he proceeds to make his way down the ship's wet, rolling deck.

Eleven more crewmen follow close behind him. The men all brace against the numbing cold and freezing rain as they steady themselves in the swell. Razz leans against the icy railing as he waits, and watches, for a signal that can't come soon enough. The urban glow from the coast of Saxony, and the island three miles away, is barely visible. He searches the blackness alongside his crew mates as the seconds that slowly tick by drag into minutes. Then, finally—There . . .

Rafferty grips the rail alongside his crew mates while he waits for the brief series of flashes to repeat . . . "That's it!" he calls out. He turns back to his deck crew. "Get those lines ready, let's make this quick."

The men move rapidly to lower ropes over the side as a small fishing trawler emerges from the darkness. The boat motors in close and then takes up a position alongside—just beneath the point where the twelve men wait on deck. The trawler bobs in the sea beside the research vessel for only a few minutes. Long enough for six, large, and unmarked crates to be hastily hauled up and then systematically moved below deck. The men work in near total silence. The moment the final crate leaves the deck of the trawler, her skipper doesn't hesitate, he simply moves off without a word, and turns back toward shore.

Fearless resumes course, and then continues on with her maiden voyage. She heads south along the Dutch coast, before she enters the English Channel. She manages to navigate four hundred nautical miles before the weather closes in, and she is forced to make port in Southampton, in the south of England. After a brief weather delay, she sets off again, this time on a six hundred and twenty nautical mile passage across the treacherous Bay of Biscay.

The sun finally breaks through for the first time in weeks, as Moss guides his ship into her final port of call in Europe. He observes closely from the bridge as Rafferty works with the deck crew to secure lines. Then he glances back at Murray, and then over to Rich, his helmsman, but what Moss sees is not merely a group of capable men; he sees the vital elements of a successful operation.

He's running a twenty-seven-member crew that have progressed to the point that they function together like the inner workings of a Swiss watch. He plans to keep it that way. With the ship secure, Moss quietly lets out a relaxed sigh as he gazes through the bridge windows at the historic, north-western Spanish city of A Coruña.

A weekend of R&R is followed by a week of solid work to clean, provision, refuel, and prepare Fearless for the next leg of her journey—the Atlantic Ocean. Moss and Rafferty are on the bridge running a test of the ship's radar systems when Murray walks through the door. "Hey Chief . . ."

Moss looks up from the radar screen at his officer of the watch. "I opened those crates we picked up off Borkum," Murray reports. "You guys ready to have a look?"

Moss and Rafferty trail behind Murray as the three men head down three flights of aluminum grate stairs, and then stride to an auxiliary storage area just aft of midship. It's a cramped room with a low overhead located beneath the ship's radar and communications array. Moss scratches his forehead as he stares down at the contents of one of the opened crates. "Well that's certainly interesting . . ."

Murray reaches inside the container and pulls out a police grade Taser sealed inside a clear plastic bag. "They sent buckets of these things, Chief." Moss warily eyes the stun gun as Murray holds the bag up in front of him. "Must have been on special, but no worries," Murray adds. He tosses the Taser back inside the crate. "I'm sure we can make use of 'em. You never know, they might come in handy."

"Yeah, you never know," Moss says as he sighs then raises his hands to his hips. "So what else did Marcus Waverley's connections get us?"

"Oh right, have a look at these beauties." Murray steps over to the next crate and then lifts the lid.

"Now we're gettin' somewhere." Rafferty reaches down and gently lifts up a Sig Sauer P226 MK25 9mm pistol. The small anchor engraved into the side of the barrel is a familiar sight; the P226 has long served as the official sidearm of the U.S. Navy SEALs.

"What about spare clips and ammo?" Moss asks.

"No worries, Chief, we got heaps. But you haven't seen the best bit." Murray walks over to another one of the six crates and opens it.

Moss immediately recognizes the fully automatic capable, 9mm parabellum submachine guns neatly lined up inside as the Heckler & Koch MP5K-N-PDW.

What at first glance reads as an excessive amount of lettering to tag on to such a compact weapon, in reality, signifies quite a bit to a man with Moss's history. The "K" stands for Kurtz, the German word for short, while the "N" stands for Navy. The P, D, and W at the end translate as personal defense weapon. Which is exactly what Moss had in mind when he requested the armaments in the first place.

"Well done, Marcus . . ." Moss quickly assesses the weapon's perfect condition before he replaces the unit back inside its cradle. Then his attention returns to Murray. "How about carbines?"

"Oh yeah," Murray answers excitedly, "we got those too." He shifts two steps to the right and then opens the last crate. "Four H&K G36Ks complete with all the fruit."

Murray lifts one of the short-barreled assault rifles out from the crate and then hands it to Moss. "The SOPMOD kits came courtesy of the German KSK Kommando Spezialkräfte. Oh, and, 5.56 x 45mm NATO standard ammo."

Moss is in the process of examining the compact assault weapon when he hesitates. He hands the G36K back to Murray before he shifts right, and then picks up something different.

"That one's the pick of the litter, Chief." Murray watches Moss as he lifts up an H&K G28 DMR—designated marksman rifle.

Moss takes note of the fruit, which in this case, includes a folding bi-pod, a Schmidt & Bender PMII 3-20 x 50 daytime telescope with laser sight, plus an optoelectronic night vision adapter, a telescoping shoulder stock with adjustable cheek rest, and a sound suppressor.

"They only sent us two of those," Murray adds. "Fires 7.62 x 51mm NATO, which is similar to your Winchester .308. It's a sure bet somebody pulled some strings to get their hands on this pair, too. What you have there is a brand-new design."

Moss hands the DMR back to Murray. "Pete thinks the port at Colon, Panama, will be our best option to lay up and make the modifications for the armory. Until then, I want all this stuff locked down tight." Moss then shifts his focus over to Razz. "We gotta get back to work; we've got an ocean to cross."

Chapter 2

Only a Moment

"My work is so critical, Mr. Moss, and I must admit, I feel somewhat inadequate in my ability to express my gratitude toward you and your crew."

"Dr. Ingham," Moss responds, "it's been an honor to have you aboard. I'm pleased we were able to facilitate your research in a meaningful way."

The fastidious climate scientist's thin face forms a meek smile. "I will of course be mentioning the foundation's generous contribution toward climate progress in my report to the United Nations." Dr. Ingham pauses just long enough to look past the line of crewmen standing shoulder to shoulder on deck. He admires Fearless one last time before he looks back at Moss.

"Mr. Moss," he continues, "as an IPCC lead scientist, I must tell you that having access to a ship of this quality from which to conduct my surveys of the Maldives archipelago has made all the difference."

Moss nods and smiles pleasantly, as he listens intently to the scientist. He stands alongside Razz and the rest of his crew, while just in front of him, the ten members of Dr. Ingham's team file by in a steady line as they depart the ship. The vessel is currently moored alongside the commercial fuel jetty adjacent to Ibrahim Nasir International Airport on Hulhulé Island, one of twelve hundred that make up the Maldives chain.

The string of twenty-six low-lying atolls dangles four hundred and fifty nautical miles off the southwest coast of Sri Lanka in the Indian Ocean. The departing science team, headed up by oceanographic climatologist Dr. Phillip Ingham, has been aboard for the past six weeks taking minute measurements and making detailed surveys of key islands the team previously selected.

Ingham's thin smile remains placidly fixed as he once more looks up at Moss. "Of course it is tragic how quickly the islands are succumbing to rising sea levels," the climatologist continues, "but my research will figure prominently in the next UN assessment. My team's modeled projections are going to generate a lot of media buzz. I must admit it's been wonderful to work in the field again, but now that I have the data I was looking for, I'm afraid I will have to hit the ground running once I return. My agent tells me my press tour is already fully booked; he's actually had to turn down interview requests."

Moss reaches out and shakes the PhD climatologist's hand. "I'm glad to hear it Dr. Ingham. We hope to have you aboard again some time."

Ax and Razz maintain their polite expressions as the last of the climatologist's team, and Dr. Ingham himself, depart the vessel. Razz waits until the last of the members have climbed into their waiting cabs and the cars have pulled away before he turns back toward Moss. "Ax, wow, what a blowhard. I thought that guy would never leave."

Moss smirks. "Hey, Razz, we're helping to save the planet. Besides, this is what we signed up for, right?"

"Sure, I get it," Razz answers. "But I gotta admit, I liked the whale doctor a lot better. How about when we tagged that fin whale and her calf? Now that was a rodeo. And how about the giant squid doctor? That guy was cool."

The sudden reminder triggers a single image to flash through Moss's mind—that of a ten-meter-long squid, with its tentacles wrapped securely around the acrylic viewing dome of the ship's C-Researcher 3 Submersible. Moss grins. "You're right," he says, "bringing up that squid from a thousand feet down was pretty incredible. Those expeditions were a lot more fun." Moss takes a moment to look over his crew as they break formation and head back to work, then he shifts back to Razz. "Do you know what day it is?"

"Is that a trick question?"

Moss smiles. "Today's the ship's one-year anniversary, can you believe it? It's been a year since the launch in Bremerhaven."

"A year already?" Razz is genuinely surprised. "We should celebrate somehow. What do you think?"

Moss smiles again. "Absolutely, that's exactly what I've been thinking. We've all been busting our asses, and we've earned some R&R, so I arranged for a schedule change with Marcus. Rather than head straight for Reunion and then Cape Town, how does a week in the Seychelles sound?"

Rafferty's eyebrows go up as a grin spreads across his face. "Some French islands for a change? You bet I like it. I can organize our paperwork and get us cleared out of Maldives in a matter of hours. How soon do you want to cast off?"

• • •

République des Seychelles lies just over nine hundred miles east of the African continent in the Indian Ocean, and some one thousand three hundred nautical miles southwest of the Maldives. Named for Jean Moreau de Séchelles, Louis XV's Minister of Finance, the islands later fell under British rule until the tiny African nation eventually gained its independence in 1976. For the crew of Fearless, traveling at a steady twelve knots boat speed, the one hundred and fifteen mountainous, tropical islands that make up the Seychelles archipelago will come into view in about three and a half days.

• • •

At half past six in the morning, on their second day out from Maldives, Alex Moss grabs a plastic cafeteria tray, a thick ceramic coffee mug, and a bundle of standard, crew-grade cutlery as he moves through the breakfast chow line inside the ship's bustling crew mess. His command style on board has been informal from day one.

Moss wears the same uniform as the rest of his crew, which, in the tropics, means a white polo with the Fearless Research Foundation logo embroidered on the upper left, navy blue Bermuda shorts, and lightweight deck shoes. He eats with his crew, keeps his office door open, and he's always ready to take up the slack for any job that needs doing—no matter how menial.

His morning routine never varies. He's up at four, then it's off to the ship's gym for his daily workout. Hit the shower, then his first cup of coffee, black, no sugar, as he reviews the day's duty roster and maintenance schedule. He'll address any complaints or other issues that may have popped up during the night watch before he checks for any email that may have come in from the foundation's headquarters in Long Beach, California.

The routine keeps him organized, and organization keeps him focused. As ship's chief of operations, Moss is responsible for a two-hundred-million-dollar, state-of-the-art science vessel, twenty-seven souls, and up to a dozen more when a science team is aboard. Keeping everyone safely on task has his full attention, twenty-four hours a day, seven days a week.

As Moss makes his way down the steaming buffet line, he can see by their faces that his crew are in need of a break, and, truth be known, he's looking forward to a week off as much as anyone.

"Chief! Top of the morning."

Moss grins at the sight of his cheerful, senior galley chef. "Same to you, Bob. I'll have one of your famous homemade buttermilk biscuits, some of those scrambled eggs, and a plain yogurt."

"Coming right up, Chief."

As Moss moves down the line toward the coffee station he quizzically eyes his crewmen as they eagerly load their plates with chef's hot fluffy biscuits and piles of fried bacon. Chef's biscuits stuffed with crispy bacon have become a coveted crew favorite.

The guys go through ten pounds of bacon each and every morning, in fact. A big chunk of storage space inside the galley's huge walk-in freezer is devoted to it, and as much as Moss would love to get his men eating something healthier, he gives his crew's high ratio of bacon consumption a pass in favor of a strict no smoking policy. After breakfast, Moss heads straight for the bridge to relieve his first mate.

"Morning Chief, how's the bacon holding up down in the galley?"

"Going fast, as usual." Moss lifts the log book lying open on the mahogany chart table and quickly scans the night's entries. He stops when he sees the notation of a radio exchange between Fearless and a passing NATO frigate. "I see we heard from that NATO ship we spotted last night. Did they report any pirate activity in the area?"

"Not a peep," Rafferty responds. "They gave us the all clear. As a matter of fact, they haven't seen or heard anything in weeks."

"That's good news." Moss snaps the logbook shut and then stows it. "I have the bridge. You better get down to the galley."

"Aye aye, Chief," Razz answers cheerfully before he heads out the door.

Twenty-four hours later, at three in the morning local time, and with the light of an intensely glowing full moon to help guide the ship in, Fearless drops anchor just inside the breakwater of Port Victoria, off the main island of Mahé, in the Seychelles. The next day, Moss is working on deck with the rest of his crew to clean their ship after the passage when he spots the NATO frigate they had radio contact with returning to port after her patrol.

"So that's the Alvaro De Bazan . . ." a crewman comments as the sleek, modern warship glides past Fearless. "That's some ship."

"I get a warm fuzzy feeling just looking at her," Murray adds.

"She's armed to the teeth, fellas," the crewman continues. "She's got all the latest toys. That there's an F100 class, guided missile frigate—the flagship of NATO's counter piracy fleet running Operation Ocean Shield and Operation Atalanta."

"Well in that case I think I'm in love," Murray quips.

Moss stops what he's doing and looks at his crewman. "Hey Mike, how do you know so much about that ship?"

Mike swivels away from the frigate and looks straight at Moss. He then shifts a bit nervously. "Sorry, Chief," Mike answers. "I didn't mean to spout off like that."

Moss steps closer. "Hey, Mike, it's okay, don't apologize. I'm serious, how do you know?"

Mike looks around at his crew mates, then he sighs and walks closer to Moss. "I spent some time out this way is all. I still got friends in this neck of the woods, you know how it is."

Moss eyes the guy more carefully. "Yeah Mike sure, no problem. Maybe later we can talk."

Mike's expression relaxes. "Sure thing, Chief, anything you wanna know."

• • •

The icy chill coming off the frosty green bottle feels good in Alex Moss's hand. He takes another sip of his beer then examines the label. "Sey Brew . . . not bad."

"Not bad at all," Malcolm Rafferty chimes in just before he takes another long pull from his own frosty bottle. Razz steps over to the edge of the beach bar's covered deck and looks out at the streaks of fiery orange and scarlet that fill the evening sky beyond Port Glaud, then he looks at Murray. "This is a nice place. Good pick."

"Thanks guys," Murray responds. "I hear the tucker's good, but if you ask me, the scenery's even better."

Moss looks out at the striking sunset sky. "Nice view. Not as good as the sunsets we have at sea, but not bad."

"Oh, I don't mean that sort of scenery, Chief, I'm talkin' Sheilas."

Moss flips back to Murray with a smirk as the fit and muscled Australian SAS veteran nods toward a group of young women chatting near the bar. "If you'll excuse me, gentlemen," Murray adds, "I'm gonna go introduce myself."

Moss tips his beer back and checks the girls out. Then he observes as Murray boldly joins their conversation. By the way they're speaking, Moss can tell the three young women clustered at the far end of the bar are also Australians, and most likely university students on holiday—Too young for my taste . . . he quickly concludes.

Then one of the young women looks past her friends chatting with Murray and stares right at Moss. And in that moment, her stunning gaze catches him totally off guard. Her long blond hair is swept up into a loosely tumbled twist behind her head as her pale blue eyes make a direct connection. Moss can't help but stare back at her . . . She's a knockout . . . and you're way too old for her . . . The young woman holds eye contact with Moss for only a few seconds, then she smiles softly before she shifts her attention back to her friends.

"Hey Ax, our table's ready. You want something to eat? I'm starved."

Moss shifts away from the bar to look at Razz. "You bet, lead the way."

Chapter 3

A Smart Boy

"Maggie wake up . . . come on, we're on breakfast duty, remember?"

The slim brunette draws her knees to her chest as she lies on her side in her bunk. She lets out a groan, then pulls her pillow over her head and tries to turn away. "Oh god no," she mumbles from beneath her pillow. "Please, I'm too hungover . . ."

Her cabin mate frowns, then snatches the pillow away. "Get up!"

"Trish, stop!" Maggie squeals. Then her ragged voice shifts to an angry tone. "Dammit I'm serious! I feel like shit." She looks up at Trish with red eyes and colorless lips before she turns away once more and folds back into a fetal position.

Trish sweeps back loose strands of her blond hair, then she grips the pillow with both hands and hits Maggie with it. "Get up!" Trish shouts.

Twenty minutes later Maggie stumbles into the galley of the seventy-two-foot ketch Ellie Marie. She finds Trish busily cracking eggs into a plastic bowl, while directly behind her, a cast iron pan stuffed with sausages crackles on the stove. Trish pauses to evaluate her friend. "You do look like shit," she says, before flashing a smile. "So, was he worth it?"

Maggie yawns, rubs her eyes. "I don't know," she says. "I guess so, he wants to hook up again. He seemed nice enough, you know?"

Trish eyes her friend with a mix of sympathy and irritation. "Here," she says, "finish cracking these eggs. I need to turn the sausages."

"Ah! So, the party girls are finally awake!"

The booming, heavily accented voice startles Maggie to the point that a partially cracked egg slips from her hand and plops into the bowl in front of her. She looks down as the broken egg's shell sinks out of view. "Shit! Angelo!" The girl plunges her hand into the pool of raw eggs and fishes out the broken shell.

The sailing yacht's Italian captain leans in close to Maggie and peers down into the bowl, "Make sure you get it all yes? I don't like my eggs crunchy."

"That is disgusting."

Trish briefly looks up from the gas stove to see another of her ship mates enter the sailing yacht's narrow galley. "Hey Niklas, so where were you guys last night?" she asks. "We waited for you guys. We never saw you."

"That's because we did not want to be seen," Niklas responds flatly. He eyes the frying pan stuffed with sizzling sausages. "At least you know how to cook sausages correctly."

Trish playfully elbows the twenty-three-year-old German engineering student in the ribs as he pushes by her. "Thanks, Niklas . . . no, really," Trish taunts, "your sensitivity is touching." She turns to look at him. "If you didn't want to meet up with us you could have just sent a text."

Niklas raises an eyebrow at the suggestion. "I am not the type to text girls, you know? And besides, it's too expensive."

"You're being an ass, Niklas," another voice comments as a second young German enters the galley. He squeezes between Maggie and Trish. Then he playfully reaches back and pinches Maggie in the side. "I heard you got some action last night?"

Maggie crinkles up her nose. "You better cut it out, Jannik, my hands are covered in raw egg." She sneers at Jannik as she lifts her dripping hand up from the bowl of yellow goo. "Shall I pinch you back?"

"Bambini!" Angelo quickly intervenes before his galley gets trashed, yet again, by his adventure-seeking, budget-priced, back-packer clientele—"Basta!" he shouts. Then he claps his hands together to get everyone's attention. "Am I about to sail for Cape Town with this pathetic crew?" He places his hands on his hips and stares at the students gathered in front of him. "We have work to do, okay?" He first points at Jannik. "You, go make sure everyone is up; tell them they have thirty minutes to finish breakfast, then I want all of you on deck for the safety briefing."

Trish stares back at Angelo with a startled look. "Safety briefing? Are we leaving already?

"But we just got here!" Maggie complains. "It's so lovely. I thought we'd have more time."

Angelo folds his arms in front of him as he leans back against the stainless steel door of the galley's fridge. "Look, ragazzi, it is like this, okay? I've been watching the weather. There is a low-pressure system moving in, so the wind will increase. If we leave tomorrow, we can take advantage of the low. We will have a good wind angle, and fast sailing. If we wait, we miss the window, and we could be stuck."

Angelo sighs at the disappointment on his client's faces. "Look, I'm sorry, but she is a fickle bitch the wind, so when she wants to give to you, you take it." He leans away from the fridge and then straightens. "I've made the decision. We are going, so get ready, and I don't want any bullshit from you people, okay?"

• • •

Moss is working at his desk inside his personal office when he looks up and finds Mike's rugged frame filling his doorway. "Mike, come in, have a seat. I just got some fresh coffee. You want a cup?"

"Sure Chief, thanks," Mike answers as he pulls up a chair and then sits opposite Moss.

Moss twists back and grabs an empty mug off the shelf just behind him. Then he opens the thermos sitting on his desk and pours a steaming cup for Mike. "Sugar?"

Mike silently shakes his head as he takes the mug of black coffee from Moss.

Moss evaluates his oldest able-bodied seaman with a fresh eye. Mike was the last hire before leaving Bremerhaven, and although his military record appeared spotless at first glance, it was also incomplete. So much seemed to be missing in fact, that Moss asked Razz to do some digging just to be sure the guy was legit.

Turns out Mike Corwin's record was more than legit. Razz discovered he's a twice decorated veteran of the first gulf war. Mike had enlisted in the Navy back in the mid-eighties at age nineteen, got recruited for SEAL training. He graduated BUDS—basic underwater demolition school—and then advanced to become a top tier sniper. He saw action for the first time in December of 1989 during Operation Just Cause, otherwise known as the United States invasion of Panama. Then came Operation Desert Storm in January of 1991.

His official record dried up sometime during the gulf war, and Razz found out why. Turns out Mike wasn't only a U. S. Navy SEAL, he was a member of the elite, of the elite—The United States Naval Special Warfare Development Group, otherwise known as DEVGRU, but colloquially referred to by news media and the public as SEAL Team Six.

That bit of information by itself was enough to explain why so much of his record had been redacted. Moss has always made it a policy not to ask questions, or otherwise discuss, his crewmen's past special ops missions. Just like his own, they're classified. But Mike's last deployment was almost twenty years ago, and Moss knows Mike needs to tell him something, so he has his full attention.

Mike takes a big swallow of the coffee, then he sets the mug down and looks directly at Moss. "Chief, look, I know this NATO Operation Ocean Shield is giving everyone a solid sense of security and all, but based on my own experience in this region, I don't feel it's wise to let our guard down."

"How so?" Moss leans in toward Mike. "I had a one on one with the NATO mission commander earlier this morning, and he says pirate activity has dropped off the map."

Mike smiles. "Please don't take this the wrong way, Chief. I'm sure those guys are doing the best they can, but they can't be everywhere." Mike lifts the mug and swallows down another gulp, then sets the mug down. "Like I said, I spent time here, and sure, it was some years ago, but things haven't changed all that much. I know how those pirates operate, and these days, they're better organized, better funded, and better equipped. All I'm saying is that keeping our guard up won't cost us anything more than some extra shifts on deck."

The creases in Moss's forehead deepen. "You think we should go fully armed all the way to Cape Town? Mike, I appreciate your concern, I do, but that's a lot to ask."

"You're right, Chief, it would be, so I have an alternative in mind."

The furrows in Moss's forehead relax. "I'm listening."

"In my experience all we need is a minimal, visible deterrent in place, and nothing more. Two guys outside on deck with carbines, and two more as support. We go with a staggered rotation at thirty-minute intervals to keep everyone fresh and focused. We use the old mark-two eyeballs by day, and the forward infrared radar at night, but we need to go dark, Chief: no AIS and no radio transmissions."

Moss takes a sip of his coffee then leans back in his chair. "Thanks, Mike, I appreciate your input. I'll have to get approval, but it's a good plan."

. . .

"Crank that winch!" Angelo yells. The slim Italian stands at the helm of the Ellie Marie as she cuts through the Indian Ocean in light seas, and under the bright sun of midday. His hands lightly dance over the wheel as the yacht smoothly gybes. He looks up as the boom passes overhead, shifting from port to starboard. Then he glances over again at Trish manning the genoa sheet winch. "Faster!" he shouts again. He watches as Trish rapidly cranks the winch. "That's it, good girl, keep going until it's tight."

He shifts back to his first mate on the mainsheet winch. "Tirarlo in stretto Fabri, adesso per favore," then Angelo focuses on his second paid crewman, another Italian, now managing the smaller mizzenmast aft. "Andiamo Andrea."

With the maneuver completed, Trish locks off the Genoa sheet then climbs back inside the yacht's cockpit. Angelo pats her shoulder as she passes the helm. "You're okay, you know? If you get sick of law school you come find me, you can join my crew anytime."

Trish smiles. "Does this mean I get a discount on the passage?"

Angelo chuckles. "You're too smart, you know?" He wags his finger. "No more compliments for you. Now go get some rest, I need you fresh for tonight's watch."

• • •

At three in the morning, and four days out from the Seychelles, Trish steadies herself as she zips up her storm jacket. She grabs a life vest and then makes her way aft for her watch duty. She tugs at the nylon straps of the life vest as she enters the galley. Then she stops at the gimbaled stove that steadily swings with the constant motion of the sea passing beneath it.

She reaches past the side rails that surround the stove stop and lays her hand against a small Bialetti coffee pot—it's cold. She sighs. She lifts the small Italian espresso maker, pops the lid and looks inside. There's a shot left. She reaches above the stove, grabs a small cup, pours off the last of the strong, stale liquid, and then gulps it down.

"You just drank the last of the coffee, didn't you?"

Trish spins to see Jannik enter the galley. "Hey, beat you to it, I guess." Then she sees the fatigue in the young German's eyes. "I can start another pot if you like; it'll only take a minute."

Jannik looks back at her as if he's about to answer, but then he purses his lips. He stands in silence for a few more seconds before he says, "I'll do it; you go relieve Niklas. He's always so grumpy when he gets the night watch, and to be honest, I'd rather you saw him first."

Trish flashes a reassuring smile. "Yeah, I know what you mean, no worries."

Jannik grins. "I'll start a fresh pot for us."

Trish climbs out on deck and a fresh wind hits her face. She looks up at the solid blanket of stars that fill the night sky. The uninterrupted mass of light only ends at the ocean's stark, seamless horizon. The only sounds she hears are the gentle moan of the rigging and the sea rushing past the yacht's hull. Trish gazes at the yacht's full sails bathed in the pale light. "What an incredible night," she mutters softly.

"Ah it's you." Niklas stands up. "So Jannik sent you out first? He's such a pussy."

Trish says nothing as she steps over to the helm. She checks the autopilot's course and speed. Then she looks at the small electronic chart plotter.

"Everything is correct," Niklas assures her. "You don't have to do a thing." He turns away and then shakes his sleeping crew mate. "Shelly, get up, we've been relieved."

Trish looks up from the plotter and then scans the eastern horizon. "Niklas, what about that ship out there? I don't see it on the chart plotter. They must not have their AIS on either."

"Nobody does out here," he answers. "You know where we are, right? Angelo's not stupid. He's sailed this route a dozen times; he knows what he's doing." At that moment, Jannik silently emerges from below deck. Niklas sees him. "At last you show up, huh?" Jannik says nothing as he steps aside to allow Shelly to go below. Then Niklas starts to push past him, but pauses to whisper in Jannik's ear. "You shouldn't be late, it makes us both look bad."

• • •

A sharp flash of bright sunlight pierces through the hatch above Trish's bunk and rudely wakes her. She shields her eyes from the glare just as the deck overhead rattles with the sounds of pounding feet and the grinding of winches. She senses Ellie Marie gybing again . . . It's too soon . . . something's wrong.

Trish quickly pulls on some clothes and makes her way out into the passageway. She moves down the narrow, mahogany-paneled gap that runs past the main mast. Then she steps through the saloon on her way aft. She finds everyone crowded into the galley, with Angelo and Niklas in the midst of a heated argument.

"We will be fine as long as you all stay below and out of sight!" Angelo fires back.

"We use the radio, we call someone, right?" Niklas shouts. "We must call for help!"

Angelo shakes his head. "You don't get it, do you?" His tone is now so agitated it borders on shrill. They're only shadowing us. They've done this before; it means nothing. It's only window shopping."

"This is ridiculous!" Niklas screams. "We can't just ignore them! We radio for help! This is the only responsible measure.

29

There are military ships close by, we've seen them. They can chase them off; it's their job."

Angelo takes a step back, exhales loudly and then looks at the five students crowded in front of him. "Look, ragazzi, it's like this, and what I am telling you is true, okay? You are the thing of value. They are shopping for hostages, and your rich, white, asses are exactly what they want." Angelo looks directly at Niklas. "So are you scared now? Are you ready to trust me yet? Because I know what I'm doing here."

"Of course I am afraid," Niklas answers calmly. "Anyone would be. This is why we must radio for help. Are you stupid? We radio for help!"

Angelo folds his slender arms in front of him and stares at Niklas. "I am glad that you are frightened; you should be. But if I pick up that radio and issue a distress call? We are all fucked. This is exactly what those shits out there want. They want to hear us make a radio distress call, and then they will listen to the emergency channel as we communicate how many people we have on board. They will keep listening as the military responds, and then they will know exactly how much time they have—they will know everything."

Niklas sighs. "I didn't understand." He stares back at Angelo. "Okay then, you're right, so what do I do? How do I help?"

Angelo pats Niklas on the shoulder. "Smart boy." The captain then turns his focus toward the rest of his passengers. "Ok, ragazzi, I've done this before and it always works. Fabri and Andrea have already gybed the boat and altered course southeast. We have good wind, so we sail hard and fast away from the coast. We hold this course for only a couple of days at most. Those pirates out there are lazy bastards okay? They're following us in open skiffs, they have no protection, and only a few provisions. They want an easy, juicy target, they don't want to burn up fuel and supplies chasing an old sailboat with only a couple of skinny Italians on board."

"So in the meantime what do the rest of us do?"

Angelo locks eyes with Trish. "You are going to keep your pretty little blond head out of sight."

Chapter 4

Good at Something

Malcolm Rafferty quietly lifts a G36K assault rifle and then slips the 7.3-pound weapon over his shoulder. The pre-dawn air blowing across the deck of the ship feels good even if having to carry a gun on patrol doesn't. Razz gives a silent nod to Cal, a signal to his fellow, special-ops veteran that he's now been relieved. Razz then shifts back to his watch partner, and for this rotation, he'll be with Seth.

The ship is less than forty-eight hours out from Seychelles, and en route for Cape Town, but already, everyone on board has fallen back into their scheduled routines. The only two things out of place are the extra watch rotation, and the loaded carbine currently hanging off Rafferty's shoulder.

It's not what he signed up for, but he understands the reasoning behind it. It's the same reasoning that brought the weapons on board in the first place. It's why they spent three weeks in Colon, Panama, converting what was originally spec'd as an extra fuel tank into its true purpose—a weapons compartment. But now that the armory's been opened for the first time to defend the ship,

Razz finds he's having second thoughts. But like everyone else, he'll keep his opinions to himself, and follow orders.

He and Seth have the port side of Fearless, while Murray and Rich are over on the starboard side of the ship. Seth is a former SEAL, just like Razz, but Seth also happens to be the ship's medic, a good friend, and a damned handy guy to have around. Razz has known Seth for a long time. They served together in the same squad in Afghanistan, along with Moss, who was squad leader.

Ax was in charge then just like he is now. He's also been Malcolm Rafferty's closest friend for a lot of years, but, to be honest, Razz likes him better these days—He's much more relaxed.

Aboard Fearless, Moss is still known to his friends as Ax, but it's more out of habit than the reason he earned the handle in the first place. Back then, Alex Moss was both feared and respected by friends and enemies alike; back then, even his commanding officers would often refer to him as The Ax.

Seth lifts a pair of night vision binoculars and scans the black horizon before he turns back to Razz. "You want a look?"

"You use 'em," Rafferty responds. "We'll have first light in a few, and I've got the daylight binos. Besides, I have the infrared scope on the carbine."

During the next twenty minutes on deck, Razz observes in awe as the first hints of morning begin to fill the vast horizon of the Indian Ocean. Then he watches a thick jumble of distant cumulus clouds gradually shift from stark gray to fiery pink.

The current sea state is merely a gentle roll, with wave heights only topping out at two meters. It's nothing for their ninety-seven-meter-long ship as Fearless steadily motors at twelve knots boat speed. Against the rising sun, Razz can make out sharp outlines of the wave tops clearly. He methodically scans from north to south and then back again.

"I got something."

Razz spins back toward Seth. "Point it out to me."

"Seven o'clock and less than half a klick."

Razz shifts the rifle further behind him as he lifts his binoculars. "I got it, looks like an open skiff . . . no wait, I see two."

· · ·

"We need to reef; winds are twenty-two knots and building."

Angelo flashes an irritated glance at his first mate. With both hands on the helm, he leans forward and squints at the electronic instruments in front of him. He then looks up at the fully raised sails, now stretched tight and trembling under the stress. Angelo looks back over his shoulder at the pair of open skiffs tailing a few hundred meters behind his boat, before returning his gaze forward. "We can't risk it."

Fabri glares at his captain. "We can't risk losing the rig either."

Angelo sighs calmly. "She can take it; I know my woman. She can take it; she won't let us down."

"What about those kids down below? They've been stuck down there for almost two days, Angelo. They need some relief."

Angelo's expression hardens even further. "Being sick is nothing compared to getting hijacked by those bastards out there. We keep going; we hold this course."

· · ·

Alex Moss stands on the gusty aft deck of Fearless. He raises a pair of binoculars to his eyes and focuses on the two high-speed skiffs that dip and bob at the tail end of the wake behind his ship. Each boat carries three men—one driver, and two shooters, each with an old, Soviet-style Kalashnikov rifle. From what Moss can observe, the two boats are sparsely equipped with what appear to be extra fuel tanks, and not much else.

"It's been four hours and no change," Razz reports as the building wind buffets against his body. "There's no sign of a mothership on radar either."

"There has to be a mothership within range somewhere," Moss responds. He lifts the binoculars for another look at the threat. "We're too far off shore. These guys are opportunists; they're scouting us, so that means they have to be in communication with their base." Moss lowers the binoculars and looks at Razz. "Nobody's heard them on the VHF, so my guess is they're most likely using a satphone."

"So what do you want to do about it?" asks Razz.

Moss sighs. "Nothing for now." He looks at Razz. "They've already sized us up and reported back to whoever they take orders from, but I won't play their game. We're not deviating from our planned course. If they make any attempt to board this vessel we blow a few of their heads off, and that should be the end of it."

"You sure about that, Ax?"

"Yes I am." Moss raises the binoculars and takes one more look at his opponents. "We stick with our current program, and if these guys don't leave soon, we'll do something different."

• • •

"I can't take any more of those things," Maggie whines. "They just make me sleepy and I still feel awful. They aren't working."

Trish looks down into her friend's damp eyes as she braces herself against the edge of the upper bunk. The two girls' narrow cabin is located port side of the yacht's main mast. Normally it's a good position to be in, but with the seventy-two-foot yacht going flat out in crossed seas, there's no longer any such thing as a good position on board. It sucks no matter where you are. Ellie Marie creaks and complains under the stress, and her rigging whistles in the strong wind, as the sunlit, azure sea rushes past the cabin's tiny port.

The forces generated by the boat's constant motion try to pull Trish to the floor. She resists the inertia by grabbing the bed frame with one hand, while she holds out a bottle of seasickness pills in the other. "Maggie," she says, "you only have motion sickness; it's not like having a virus. Your body's just reacting to the environment. Other than that, you're perfectly healthy."

"Easy for you to say . . ." the girl grumbles,

"Take the medication, please? You can't stay hydrated if you're vomiting." Trish allows two of the pills from the bottle to drop into Maggie's trembling hand. She watches her friend shove them into her mouth, before she reaches for a water bottle poking out from the pocket mounted above Maggie's bunk. "Here," Trish says, "and keep drinking, okay?"

Maggie tips up the plastic bottle and takes a few gulps of the tepid water inside. Then she wipes her mouth with her other hand. "I need fresh air badly. It's so bloody hot and disgusting down here. If I could just get my head out the hatch for a moment."

Trish frowns at the suggestion. "We can't, they will see us." Trish bends down and looks Maggie in the eye. "Angelo knows what he's doing. He said that's just the sort of thing the pirates are looking for. If we can keep hidden long enough they'll leave us alone. It can't be much longer, so seriously, Maggie, promise me?"

"Yeah, whatever . . ." Maggie groans as she flops back onto her bunk. "I just need air."

Trish eyes Maggie laying her bunk like a discarded doll. "Promise me you won't do anything stupid."

"I promise . . ." the girl whimpers.

Trish straightens. "I'm going to the galley. Can I bring you something?" Trish makes an honest attempt to smile and sound pleasant. "I'll bring you some dry toast, okay?"

"Okay . . ." the girl answers meekly. Maggie watches Trish leave, then immediately shifts her gaze to the square hatch above her head. Trish hadn't told her anything she didn't already know; Angelo's orders were very clear—Nobody goes outside . . .

She also knows this means nobody can show themselves in any way. Which means no open hatches, and no cabin lights at night—she knows this . . .

Maggie searches the small square of blue sky framed inside the plexiglass hatch. She can just make out part of the rigging and a section of sail—a sail full of wind . . . A sail full of fresh, clean air.

"What the hell are you doing?"

Maggie snaps back toward the cabin's entrance to find Shelly leaning against the open door frame in front of her. "Nothing," Maggie sighs. "I was just thinking is all."

"Is that so?" Shelly peeks back into the passageway behind her, then she steps inside the cabin. She braces momentarily as a wave knocks against the boat before she closes the slender door. She steadies herself, looks directly at her friend's pallid face, and flashes a devious smile. "You want some air?"

Maggie pushes herself upright. "We can't, Shelly, it's too dangerous."

"Oh please." Shelly takes two tenuous steps forward then grabs for the edge of the upper bunk. The floor beneath her bare feet shifts and lurches in the bumpy seas. She giggles at her own awkwardness, and then smiles again. "I've been opening my hatch since yesterday and nobody's noticed."

"What? Shelly—are you . . .?" Maggie catches herself. "How?"

"Just like this, darling . . ." Steadying herself, Shelly reaches behind her head and pulls a lemon yellow scrunchy from her curly, strawberry blond hair. She waves the hair band in front of Maggie's face. Then she steps up onto the edge of Maggie's bunk. "If you hook it properly . . ." She slips the fabric-covered elastic band around the handle of the spring-loaded hatch, then stretches it across to the nearest corner of its wooden frame. She uses her slender fingers to expertly wedge it in between the frame and the ceiling panel. "There, now we can open it just a bit."

Maggie gasps as the hatch pops open slightly and a waft of fresh air hits her face. "Oh my god! Shelly, you're a genius!" She leaps to her feet, grabs the bed frame and stands directly under the slim opening. "It's simply delish!"

. . .

Mike rubs his thumb across a 7.62 x 51mm round. The partially exposed bullet will be the first to be fired from the ten-round magazine he holds in his right hand. Mike clicks the magazine into place and then cocks the G28 DMR. He opens the rifle's bipod, before he drops down and lies flat on the upper aft deck of Fearless. He leans into the rifle's telescopic scope and begins making adjustments. "Just the outboard, right Chief?" he says without moving his eye from the scope.

Moss kneels down next to his crewman. "Yeah, just the motor," he answers. "Can you do it?"

"Sure can."

"Okay, take the shot."

Moss watches silently as Mike calmly exhales. The DEVGRU sniper allows his pulse and respiration to drop to near zero as he blocks out everything but his target. The two ragged go-fast boats, clearly visible off the stern, bob and dip and trade positions like a pair of drunks on a dance floor. They crisscross the wake of Fearless in an erratic, zig zag pattern, approximately four hundred meters from the flash guard of the G28.

Mike's been observing these clowns for hours, just like everyone else on board. And just like the rest of his crew mates, he's sick and tired of 'em. More out of ingrained habit than for any other reason, he's been studying and evaluating his potential targets at every opportunity. And now that he's been given the green light—he knows exactly how to hit his mark.

Mike waits in silence for his chance, then he gets it. One of the boats hits a wave, slows, and then cuts back at a near perfect, ninety-degree angle. The sniper's actions are now on automatic. It's as if he's transformed physically into the weapon itself, instead of being merely the man in control of it. The profile of the boat's high-powered outboard motor fills his crosshairs, and in that instant, a series of minute calculations simultaneously fire off inside the sniper's head as Mike squeezes off a single round.

A momentary delay follows the discharge before the NATO standard bullet rips through the engine's plastic outer cover. The impact is hardly dramatic, only a dull pop, but it's quickly followed by a brief clatter as the outboard motor mechanically disintegrates. A sly sneer crosses Mike's face as he watches an initial puff of black smoke rapidly expand into a thick cloud. The smoke cloud then quickly envelops the rear of the skiff, and the three Somali pirates inside descend comically into full panic.

Moss folds his arms in front of him and looks on with bemused satisfaction as the men in the second skiff abandon pursuit and turn back to the aid of their countrymen. The two open skiffs quickly fall back and then drift out of sight as Fearless motors onward.

Mike says nothing as he methodically stows the G28 DMR back inside its tactical soft case and then zips it shut. He grabs the case by its handle and then stands up. "I'll clean this weapon and return it to the armory, Chief."

Moss knows a guy like Mike can make a shot like that in his sleep, but he's still impressed. Mike straightens and then he eyes Moss more closely. He can read what the chief's thinking just by looking at him. "It's just my job, Chief," Mike says. "We all gotta be good at something or we wouldn't be here, right?"

Moss grins. "Sure Mike, but thanks anyway." Moss takes in a relaxed breath and looks out at a sea now free of menacing pirates. "I don't think we'll be seeing those guys again."

Mike slings the bag over his shoulder. "Probably not."

Chapter 5

Bat-Shit Serious

Diric Abdirashid Abshir listens in abject frustration to the flurry of tangled explanations that only serve to pollute his mind and obstruct his thinking. The gang leader listens until he can't take it anymore. "You are all idiots," he tells them. "Get back here now." Abshir folds away the antenna of his satellite phone and then stuffs the vintage, bulky unit back inside a side pocket of his cargo shorts.

Abshir stands outside in the scorching, Indian Ocean sun, and on the foredeck of a rusted, one-hundred-and-fifty-foot-long, formerly Taiwanese, tuna trawler. The dilapidated fishing boat has served as his seagoing base of operations for the past year. It's a ship he is actively working to replace. Abshir has his sights set on obtaining a new vessel—a modern ship capable of taking his operation to the highest possible level.

The goal has been in his thoughts for some time, but only recently has its possibility come within his reach. Ever since he saw the photo and read the detailed report his paid informants in Seychelles emailed to him ten days ago, and as a result, he's become obsessed with achieving his goal—I will have her . . . he tells himself repeatedly. She is the perfect ship; even her name is appealing—Fearless.

Abshir's phone rings again. He groans with disgust as he yanks the satphone back out from his pocket and looks at the incoming call. He reluctantly answers: "What is it?"

He listens for a few moments as his second team complains bitterly of their conditions. He can hear the whine of the skiff's engine in the background; he can tell by the sound that it's not getting enough oil. He listens some more, and as he does, he once again evaluates the costs versus the potential payoff of taking on more hostages.

If his informants' report is accurate then the vessel his second team is currently shadowing is indeed worth taking. He has to be certain before he fully commits his resources. He only has the word of his informants to go on; they didn't send photos of the second target, and they've been known to exaggerate.

Abshir holds the satphone to his ear and listens while his men argue that they must take the yacht immediately. But he knows they also want relief from their current conditions. He listens some more while he considers the loss of an expensive outboard. He can't afford any more costly mistakes. He has his own bosses to answer to. "Do you know for sure?" Abshir demands. "Tell me the truth." He waits for an answer. "Keep tailing them and don't lose them. Do you hear me?"

He stuffs the satphone back inside his pocket and then grabs the cheap walkie-talkie clipped to his belt. Abshir uses the small handheld to alert his crewmen manning the deckhouse of the mothership. "Start the engines," he orders. "We are repositioning; we move on the target tonight."

. . .

Moss stands on the aft deck of his ship at midday. He lifts his sextant and takes his daily noon-sight of the sun's position. He measures the angle at three consecutive intervals over the course of twenty minutes. He carefully records the degrees of latitude in a small notebook and then heads back to the bridge, so he can plot the numbers out on his chart of the Indian Ocean.

"I've got the revised watch schedule and duty roster worked up, Chief." Razz smiles as he lays the clipboard down on the chart table. "That was some shot Mike made; everyone's been thanking him for it."

Moss lays his pencil and navigation protractor down and then picks up the clipboard. He straightens as he flips through the pages. "You're not gonna to be happy about this, Razz," Moss sighs, "but I want to maintain the extra watch on deck, at least for a few more days."

Rafferty frowns at the news. "You sure about this, Chief?"

Moss lays the clipboard down, then he turns, and leans back against the chart table. "Look, Razz, we just experienced an incident that confirmed we're under threat. And as much as I'd like to believe we sent a clear message, there's nothing that says these guys won't be back, and possibly in force."

Razz grimaces at the thought. "Sure Ax, I get your point. How do you want to proceed?"

"We stick with the old schedule for now, and in three days we reevaluate. Maybe then we switch over to this new one."

Razz picks up the clipboard and tucks it under his arm. "You got it, Chief, I'll inform the crew."

• • •

"Minchia! Che cazzo!" Angelo marches down the deck of El-lie Marie and angrily stomps down on the partially opened hatch. "Che cosa fai?" He flashes an exasperated look back at Fabri who only shrugs in response. Then Angelo continues to rant in Italian while his colorful hand gestures reinforce his equally vibrant language. "You didn't see this?" he demands. "I told you to watch the deck, Fabri, and you didn't see this?" He marches back to the cockpit still waving his hands as he continues to complain. "These stupid fucking kids! Don't they know I'm trying to keep them alive?"

Trish bursts into her cabin to find Maggie and Shelly cowering together on Maggie's bunk. "What the bloody hell are you two doing?"

"It was only open a crack, Trish," Maggie argues. "Come on, give us a break!"

"Yeah Trish, seriously!" Shelly shouts. "We're suffering horribly down here, and who put you in charge anyway?"

Trish moves in close to Shelly's face. "I'll tell you who you don't want in charge, and it's those pirates out there." Trish's face is red with anger. "Do you know what you've risked by opening that hatch? Do you understand the danger we're all in?"

. . .

Abshir bites hard into the thick bundle of fresh khat leaves wedged in the side of his mouth. The naturally narcotic stimulant suppresses hunger, wards off seasickness, and leaves the user with a feeling of euphoria. The first surge of energy jolts through his brain. He leans forward into the wind and steadies himself as the high-speed skiff he's riding inside bounces over the waves.

"We have it! We have it!"

Abshir listens to the excited voice coming from the walkie-talkie that dangles off his neck. He lifts the handheld and clicks the receiver. "Are you sure?"

"Yes, yes, we have it."

He lets go of the handheld and then reaches for another piece of equipment. This time, an inexpensive, night vision monocular. Abshir moves to the bow of the long, slim fiberglass skiff and then scans the night horizon for his prize—There she is . . . The pale green outline of Fearless lies only a few kilometers ahead. Abshir shifts position and then looks back at the armed men clustered behind him. He shouts a rapid series of orders before he draws a forty-five caliber, Czech-made, semi-automatic pistol, then turns to face his target.

• • •

"These guys are bat-shit serious, Chief." Murray scans the sea in front of him using a military grade, L3 binocular night vision device. "I have three skiffs in sight . . ." Murray adjusts the electronic zoom on the BNVD. "I count four men in each boat . . . all of them armed."

"I confirm," says Moss as he squints through his own BNVD. "They're carrying Kalashnikovs and wearing ammo belts." Moss lowers the BNVD and then snaps the hand-held radio from his belt. "Cal, report."

"We've spotted two boats approaching from the south, Chief; both are heavily armed, and moving fast."

Moss glances over at Murray as his mouth forms a tight line, then he clicks the radio. "Wait for my signal."

"Wilco Chief."

Moss clips the radio back onto his belt. He swings a G36K off his shoulder and sets the select fire for a three-round burst. The armed fleet of five skiffs is just coming into range, but he wants them closer. Gripping the carbine in his right hand, he lifts his BNVD and eyes the enemy one more time, then he calmly pulls the radio from his belt. "Mike."

"Yeah Chief?"

"You're up."

"Roger that."

From his vantage point just below the ship's radar and antenna suite near the top of the ship's superstructure, Mike aims the DMR at the occupants inside one of the skiffs and then fires three measured rounds in rapid sequence.

The first round strikes a man in the chest. The bullet rips through the man's left lung, severs his aorta, and then exits his body just to the right of his spinal column. The second plows through a man's forehead. The bullet compresses on impact before it exits with the back of the man's skull and a large chunk of brain matter along for the ride. The third shot hits inside the boat near the engine mount, ricochets, and strikes the driver in the back of his right knee.

Moss watches through his BNVD as the one man left standing inside the skiff Mike just fired on ignores his fallen comrades, appears to yell at the wounded driver, then returns fire with a pistol. "Fuck . . ." Moss grabs his radio. "Fire at will—fire at will— fire at will." The response is immediate as the overlapping trill of multiple automatic weapons ignites from the deck of Fearless.

Abshir stays low as the skiff takes more fire. He then looks back at the bleeding man crouched behind him and crying out in pain. "Drive, you fucking bastard!" Abshir shouts in Somali. He stuffs his pistol inside his belt, yanks a Kalashnikov from the hands of a corpse and sprays the research vessel with bullets.

Murray yanks a spent clip from his MP5 and quickly replaces it. "A grenade launcher would be handy about now."

"You said it," Razz barks back just before he unloads his G36K into another of the attacking skiffs. The volley of rounds sends two pirates tumbling overboard while a third drops inside the boat. Razz smiles when he sees the driver spin away in retreat.

Moss, Murray, and Razz fire on the last two skiffs until the two boats break off their attack and run. Moss watches and waits until he's certain the retreat is legitimate, before he slings his rifle back over his shoulder and grabs his radio. Report, guys. Is everyone okay?"

"Chief, it's Seth. Dan got grazed, nothing serious, no other injuries."

Abshir's failure only fuels and ignites his rage. He looks back at the fading lights of the ship, as Fearless motors on. Then he jerks the satphone from his pocket and calls his men still shadowing the sailing yacht. "Take the boat." He listens to their response. "You heard me, take the boat; take it now."

Chapter 6

Amphetamine Chaser

Angelo exhales nervously as he loads hollow-point rounds into a Smith & Wesson, nickel-plated, .357 revolver. He won the garish handgun from an American in a poker game three years ago, but he's never fired it. Truth be known, he's hardly touched it. Somehow, just knowing he had the gun on board seemed to be enough. The thought that he would actually need to use it had never crossed his mind.

Even the single box of twenty-four bullets that came with the gun has never been opened—it still had the factory seal. Angelo slides the rounds one by one into the six chambers of the revolver, while the brutishly simple instructions from the gun's previous owner echo inside his head, from a far corner of his scattered past: "It's easy," the guy said. "Cock the hammer and fire, but in a pinch, just point and squeeze the trigger."

Angelo loads the last of the six rounds and then closes the revolver. He stuffs the loaded pistol inside his belt, then hastily dumps the rest of the bullets out from their molded plastic tray and into one pocket of his cargo shorts. Angelo turns. He starts to reach for the handle of his cabin door but pauses at his reflection in the mirror tacked to the back of it. After a momentary evaluation, he's satisfied that his loose-fitting T-shirt sufficiently hides the gun. But the sensation the chunk of metal leaves against his skin only adds to his anxiety.

Outside, the night air is clear, and the sky is once again lit with stars, as Angelo climbs out on deck. He can see his own fear reflected in the faces of his two exhausted crewmen. A reflection just like the one in the mirror on the back of his cabin door. In seven years of sailing this part of the world, he's never had pirates tail him for this long. His vessel has been shadowed, and scouted before, of course, but only for a day at the most, never like this— Never this long.

Fabri looks at his captain. "Angelo, they're coming for us."

As Fabri's words register, Angelo's hand reflexively brushes against the gun hidden under his shirt, but the confidence he had hoped it would give him isn't there. Then the whine of two outboard engines registers, and even though he can't yet see them, he can tell the two skiffs are coming in fast.

"Get below," Angelo orders. "Fabri, Andrea, get below now."

Fabri grabs Angelo by the arm. "Angelo, no, we all get below, and we close off the hatch behind us. We lock ourselves inside, we make a radio distress call, and we wait."

Angelo listens to his first mate before he lifts his shirt, and reveals the gun. "It's too late for that; I'm staying here."

Andrea spots the wood-finished grip of the revolver poking out from Angelo's belt. "Are you crazy?"

Fabri releases his grip on Angelo's arm and steps back. "Shit . . . you are crazy."

"Get below," Angelo repeats. "Lock the hatch behind you." He then glares at his stunned crewmen. "Do it now!"

Below deck, the high-pitched whine of the skiff's outboard engines wakes Trish. She sits up in bed and focuses on the sound growing louder—It's them . . . this can't be happening. She feels a sudden flush of numbing fear wash over her body. "Maggie!" she calls out. "Maggie, wake up!" Trish drops down from her bunk as shouting erupts outside in the passageway. She grabs Maggie's arm. "Get up!"

Trish opens her cabin door and sees Fabri standing in front of her. He's exasperated and flustered; he's also clearly terrified. "They're coming for us, aren't they?" Trish asks flatly, and as the words leave her mouth, the fear trying to control her suddenly shifts to resolve.

Fabri quickly nods in response before his expression goes cold. "Change your clothes," he orders. "Dress well, cover your hair, and—"

The sudden eruption of gunfire outside cuts Fabri off mid-sentence.

"My god!" Maggie screams. "They're shooting at us!"

Trish spins back toward Maggie. "That wasn't an automatic weapon; that was a handgun." She turns back toward Fabri. "Where is Angelo?"

. . .

"Ah ha! You bastards! You weren't expecting me to shoot at you!" Angelo pulls a handful of bullets from his pocket. He kneels down inside the cockpit of Ellie Marie and frantically works to reload the .357.

The first shot he fired from the pistol felt so powerful he nearly dropped it. But with his second shot Angelo hit one of the skiffs. The impact from the hollow point round left a grapefruit-sized hole just under the bow of the boat's fiberglass hull, and now the skiff is taking on water.

The startled pirates inside cut their engine. They were less than fifty meters away when Angelo saw his chance and emptied his pistol. His fifth shot managed to hit one of the pirates. Angelo watched with a mix of shocked surprise, then horror, followed by elation, as the man was knocked overboard.

He slides the sixth round into its chamber. "You fucking bastards," he mutters as he closes the gun and then cocks the hammer back with his thumb. Angelo climbs to his feet, aims the revolver, and then opens up with a second harried flurry of hollow points.

A pirate inside the second skiff points his AK-47 at the synchronous muzzle flares coming from Angelo's pistol and returns fire. The full automatic spread of 7.62.39mm rounds light up the aft section of the yacht. The bullets explode through the cockpit and also into Angelo.

The second skiff rapidly motors in alongside the yacht and three armed pirates leap onto the deck of Ellie Marie.

Trish can hear their feet on the deck just above her head. The pirates shout in Somali as she rushes to pull on a pair of jeans. She digs into her backpack and grabs her running shoes. "Get dressed!" she shouts at Maggie. "There's no time! You've got to move faster!"

Trish turns away from Maggie and continues to rip through her backpack. She locates a printed cotton scarf. As she hastily pulls it out she spots her pocket knife. She reaches for the small blade and then grabs it.

Trish glances at her friend with pity. Maggie has only managed a pair of hiking shorts, sandals, and a long-sleeved T-shirt. Trish quickly glances around the tiny cabin until she spies the bright yellow scrunchy still dangling from the handle of the overhead hatch. She snatches it down and then uses it to bundle up her hair. She wedges the small knife inside and then wraps the scarf tightly around her head as if it were a hijab, as the cacophony of angry shouting on the other side of the cabin door rapidly grows louder.

Jannik's heart pounds inside his chest; it throbs up through his ears as if it were a bomb about to go off—They're just outside the door . . .

A few seconds later, the young German holds his trembling hands over his head as he enters Ellie Marie's saloon.

"Get to the floor!" one of the pirates shouts in accented English. "Now!"

Jannik silently complies. Then he looks up and sees Niklas walk into the saloon. Jannik has never seen fear on his partner's face before—this is the first time.

His final instructions just before they were both taken hostage were classic Niklas behavior. Words spat out with concerned immediacy, but also cold, and painfully practical. "We are no longer a couple," he whispered to Jannik in German. "I no longer know you, and you do not know me."

Trish can hear Shelly sobbing behind her as she enters the saloon. Be gray . . . she tells herself. Just be gray . . .

Trish walks slowly, one step at a time. She looks down at her feet; she keeps her fingers laced together behind her head. She can sense the knife still hidden in her hair, and knowing it's there somehow gives her comfort. She kneels down next to Niklas, but she doesn't look at him.

Trish forces herself not to look up at her captors—she turned her face away when they burst into the cabin. She tried not to react when they pointed their guns at her, but the shock was horrifying, and even now, the reality of what's happening hasn't quite sunk in. She sits, and focuses on the floor panel directly in front of her. She tries to breathe, and also tries to concentrate on what her dad taught her.

Trish can just make out the flash suppressor at the tip of an assault rifle's barrel. It's right at the edge of her peripheral vision. While the saloon itself is consumed in a constant eruption of sound. The three Somali pirates holding them all captive appear to be jacked up on something. They repeatedly shout random orders in rapid succession, then nonsensically scream them again and again.

They shove Maggie to the floor next. Trish can see her bare thigh, and she can hear her crying, but she stays quiet. She concentrates instead on her list, methodically running through it again and again, as if it were a mantra. In the hope that she has remembered every detail—You're just a member of the group and nothing more. Do as you're told. Don't speak. Don't look at anyone. Never make eye contact with your captors. Don't let your captors think you would ever be able to identify them—you're not a threat. You're nobody, you're just part of the background, you're gray, nothing but gray . . .

• • •

Abshir holds his satphone to his ear and listens to the rapid stream of Somali coming from the leader of his second team. "Patch the hole so that the boat does not sink." He paces the open air, aft deck of his mothership as he continues to listen. "Do not kill anyone else . . . Do you understand me? Get rid of the body and wait for me . . . Use your knives to lower the sails; it will stop the boat faster that way. Do you understand? Repeat everything to me so I know you understand."

Abshir listens carefully to the strung-out voice at the other end of a dim satellite connection. He carefully evaluates the information coming from the man. He has to be certain his orders will be followed precisely. He listens until he is satisfied the man fully comprehends what is being demanded of him, then . . . "We will be there soon," Abshir assures him. "We arrive in four hours."

· · ·

As dawn breaks, Alex Moss stands on the bridge of Fearless and grimaces at the star-shaped, white depressions the previous night's firefight left scattered across the front windows. He places his hands on the edge of the instrument panel, leans forward, and closely studies the seven impacts contained within three of the ten, specially laminated, and hurricane-resistant window panels. Then he begins adding up the cost of repairs—his employers will not be pleased.

Malcolm Rafferty walks in, and in that moment, Razz doesn't see his ship's chief of operations, he sees his friend. "Have you informed the foundation yet?"

"No . . . not yet." Moss continues to stare at the pockmarked windows for a few more seconds, then he turns toward Razz as he folds his arms in front of him and sighs. "I don't want to contact the board until I have a complete and detailed assessment of the damage. I have to be fully prepared to answer their questions accurately; they'll be expecting it."

"If it's any consolation, Ax, I would've made the same call. I mean it. In your shoes? I'd have done exactly what you did last night."

Moss grimaces once more. "Are you sure about that Razz?"

Razz braces at the thought. "Yeah, I am." Rafferty walks over to the damaged windows and examines the bullet marks up close for the first time. Then he shifts back toward Moss. "We took a risk last night, and we took some hits for it, but it'll pay off big time Ax, I'm sure of it."

Moss frowns. "I wish I had your certainty, Razz."

"Look, Ax, the ship only took some surface hits, but as far as we can tell, that's it. It's nothing some paint and filler won't fix. We can have these damaged window panels replaced in Cape Town. In my mind, it's nothing compared to what we've gained here."

Moss ponders Rafferty's words before he answers: "We successfully defended the ship."

"We did a hell of a lot more than that, Ax; we kicked ass last night. We sent a clear message that we're a hard target, but more than that, we've just cemented our reputation in this region." Razz leans back against the chart table. "Taking those guys out was the best move we could have made, Ax. Word travels fast; they'll think twice before they ever hit us again."

• • •

Jannik's arms ache. He's spent hours in the same position but he dares not move—he's still too terrified. Prolonged fatigue hasn't dulled his fear. He sits cross legged on the floor of the saloon and packed in tightly amongst his shipmates. He worries about Angelo; he hasn't seen him.

Then Jannik's thoughts return to his parents before he stops himself. He tries to think of something else, school, equations, anything at all, but his parents keep resurfacing in his mind and with a result that is beyond painful. He focuses back on his own condition. It's been hours with no relief; he's hungry, thirsty, he would like to use the toilet, but he knows the men holding him captive are completely without compassion.

The student of advanced hydraulic engineering catches himself, and sneers at the idea—Compassion . . . how ridiculous . . . The demands of the privileged western class hold no weight here. Look at these men? They followed us for two days in small open boats. They've never experienced compassion themselves, so how can they possibly express it to someone else? Suffering for crumbs is their life. We are simply commodities to be transacted, like a cow, or a goat.

Jannik then decides to occupy himself by mentally assessing the hijackers, along with every facet of his captivity. With each incremental advancement in his detailed evaluations, however, Jannik finds himself circling back to his original premise—They will kill you without a single thought to the repercussions. You have no leverage . . . your status is meaningless, if not a clear detriment.

He then shifts the focus of his methodical observations to the condition of his fellow captives—Where is Angelo? Jannik doesn't want to dwell on that thought for too long, like thinking of his parents—it's too painful.

He knows he will be able to count on Niklas, despite his partner's stark pronouncements. Niklas will stand by him; that goes without question, and also the two Italians, but Jannik sees the three women as a problem—Useless, as usual . . . another burdensome issue rather than any sort of asset . . . Then Jannik's eyes settle on Trish—At least one of these girls isn't whimpering like a baby . . . He can just make out the back of her head tightly wrapped in a hastily improvised but effective hijab—Smart girl . . .

Chapter 7

Show of Force

In rapid, angry Somali, the voice at the other end of the satellite connection shouts into Abshir's ear. "You cost us money last night, Diric," the voice says, "money that is difficult to replace. Our backers in London expect a return on their investment. You said you were going to take the ship. You told us it was going to happen, and now I learn that, not only did you fail to do this, you lost boats, you lost weapons, and you cost us men. So, tell me Diric, how can I trust your judgement when you did not deliver on your promise?"

Abshir grits his teeth in frustration as he listens silently to his employer. He waits a few more seconds before he answers: "Last night was not a failure," Abshir responds calmly, "we took the second target."

"There was a second target? What are you speaking of? Explain this to me, Diric."

Abshir shields the satphone from the wind in order to be heard as he stands just outside the deckhouse of his mothership. The old trawler lumbers along under intense sun as she steadily closes in on the Ellie Marie. "I did make a promise to you, Ahmed," Abshir continues. "Haven't I always delivered? You should not be surprised. We attacked two targets last night, and we have captured the second; the boat is ours, and the hostages we took are worth a lot of money. I can assure you, the backers will be pleased with their investment."

. . .

Trish lowers her arms and stands as ordered. She hasn't spoken since she was taken hostage, and like everyone else, she's exhausted after being forced to sit in a cramped and uncomfortable position for nearly five hours. The gunmen yell for everyone to move from the floor to the saloon's settee.

The five students and two Italian crewmen do as they're told. As Trish and the others are finally allowed to sit, the settee's stiff, vinyl cushions come as an incredible relief. Meanwhile, Jannik continues to carefully observe every detail of the pirate's actions. Especially when a man he's never seen before suddenly enters the saloon. From the way he carries himself, and by the manner in which he's being treated by the others, Jannik is certain this man is the gang's leader.

Abshir briefly looks over his merchandise before one of his men hands him a stack of passports. He quickly flips through the documents. He notes the nationalities of the students, then the yacht's crew, and he is pleased, but he will keep this to himself. Then Abshir opens Angelo's passport. He turns to his crewman, and asks in Somali, "This is the dead man?"

"Yes," the man answers. "We dumped the body as ordered."

Abshir stuffs the stack of passports inside a large duffle that's been packed full with an assortment of valuable items his men recovered after a thorough search of the yacht. Among them are Angelo's nickel-plated .357, and the remaining hollow-point rounds.

Abshir pulls a cellphone from his pocket and then proceeds to make a video recording of his captives. He says nothing as he slowly walks from one end of the settee to the other. He's careful to clearly capture the details of each of their traumatized faces. After a few minutes, he completes his video and ends the recording. Abshir turns off the phone and slips it back into his pocket, and then he leaves.

Outside the sun is hot and high. Trish and the others try to shield their eyes from the harsh glare as they're forced at gunpoint onto the rolling deck of Ellie Marie and then into waiting skiffs. It's the first time in nearly three days that either she, or Maggie, Shelly, Jannik, or Niklas have been outside. And in that instant, as a strong, fresh wind washes over her, Trish takes in the brief comfort, but the moment is all too brief. It vanishes when she catches sight of the bleak and rusted mothership.

The greasy hulk slowly rolls in the swell just off the yacht's port side, and the view fills her with dread. The old trawler's belching diesel exhaust leaks a stain of black smoke against the clear sky. It trails off with the wind, and all hope seems to be going with it. The sight is incomprehensible to her, as her own raging denial shouts inside her head—How can this really be happening?

Abshir oversees the transfer of his property from the deck of the yacht into waiting skiffs. He waits until he is certain his orders are being followed, then he drops back down below deck.

• • •

"I completed the damage report, Chief."

Moss looks up from his desk at his first mate with an uncomfortable, and uncharacteristic, sense of dread. "How bad is it?"

Rafferty holds up the thumb drive in his right hand before he pauses, and nervously taps it against his left palm. "Well, let's just say it could have been worse."

Moss sighs. "That bad, huh?"

Razz steps over to Moss's desk, sheepishly lays his thumb drive down, and then quickly steps back. "Turns out we'll be needing a bit more than paint and filler, Chief."

Moss grimaces as he stares down at the flash drive and unconsciously scratches at his forehead. "Shit . . ." He reaches for the flash drive, looks at it briefly, then his eyes return to Razz. "It's the Doppler radar dome, isn't it?"

Razz winces. "Yeah . . . turns out it was hit pretty bad. Pete took a look at it; he thinks the entire outer shell will have to be replaced."

Moss scowls and looks back at Razz. "That's a half-million dollar piece of equipment, Razz."

"You wanna take it out of my pay?"

Moss stares back at his friend for a few more seconds before he suddenly cracks a smile. "Fuck it," he says. "I've already scheduled a secure satellite video link with the foundation's board of directors for this evening at 18:00 hours. I'm not holding anything back, Razz. What's the point? I'll give them the full report, and they can decide how they want to proceed."

Razz sighs as he folds his arms. "Sure, Ax, I get it, but those suits back in Long Beach aren't out here getting shot at, you know?"

"Knock, knock, Chief."

Moss and Rafferty each swivel in the direction of the open office door, and find Murray standing just beyond it.

"Sorry to disturb you, Chief, but we just received a radio call; it came over the emergency channel."

Moss stands up from his desk. "Is it a distress call?"

"We're not sure, Chief," Murray responds, "but the guy is calling us directly, and he's asking to speak to you."

Moss enters the bridge to find a cluster of his crewmen listening to the VHF while the radio call repeats: "Fearless, Fearless, Fearless, this is sailing yacht Ellie Marie, Ellie Marie, Ellie Marie, respond . . . We wish to speak to the captain . . . respond."

Moss walks over to the navigation station. He lifts the VHF receiver from its cradle, and then responds to the call: "Fearless to Ellie Marie, please state your request, over."

"Ellie Marie to Fearless, I will only speak with Captain Moss."

Moss shoots a concerned glance at Razz, while Rafferty is just as shocked. Moss turns back; he waits a few more seconds before he clicks the receiver. "Fearless to Ellie Marie, this is the captain speaking, please state your request."

"Captain Moss, I will to tell you that our fight is not over . . . I have taken the sailing yacht Ellie Marie; her crew and passengers are now my captives. The yacht is not far away, you will need to find her, she is southwest of your current position. I repeat, you should look for her because the clock is ticking, and our fight is not over, Captain Moss."

The muscles in Alex Moss's jaw tighten as he listens to the man's threat, and the deep well of anger he keeps buried inside himself begins to overflow. He clicks the receiver once more. "Fearless to Ellie Marie; who am I speaking to?"

Abshir silently congratulates himself as he switches off Ellie Marie's VHF radio—his informant's report was detailed…and correct. He lets out a brief sigh of satisfaction before he nimbly climbs up, and then out, onto the seventy-two-foot yacht's weathered, teak deck. He looks around briefly, then strides to the yacht's stern where more of his men wait with skiffs. "Strip this boat," he orders. "Take all you can." Abshir then glances across the narrow gap of rolling sea between himself and the hostages now being loaded onto his mothership. "She is no use to us; we have what we came for."

• • •

Trish has pulled her scarf up enough to cover her mouth and nose but the rotting stench of the mothership's interior is impossible to escape. Shelly and Maggie are now both so weak and dehydrated from vomiting that they've stopped speaking. Trish hasn't seen or heard Jannik, Niklas, Fabri, or Andrea for hours, not since they were separated, which was just after they arrived on board.

Trish stands up inside the dank, hot, windowless store room that is now her prison cell. She steadies herself against a moist steel wall as the ship's movement tries to knock her off balance. She waits for the wave to pass, then she steps to the locked door once more and pounds on it with her fists. She yells out as loudly as she can for her captors to bring water. She waits, and then someone, a man's voice coming from the other side of the door, shouts a stream of rude expletives in return. Trish yells again, pleading for water, but this time, she hears nothing.

• • •

Malcolm Rafferty stands on the bow of Fearless, and squints as he focuses his binoculars. "It could be her, but we won't know for sure until we get close enough." He allows the binos to dangle from the strap around his neck as he rests his hands on his waist. He then turns toward Murray. "What do you think?"

Murray stares out through his own set of lenses. "It's definitely a sail boat."

"I'll go inform the chief; you stay here and keep watching. Let me know if you see any activity on board."

"Sure thing, Razz, no worries."

On the bridge, Moss is in the midst of a satphone conversation with the commander of the Seychelles coast guard patrol boat Sapphire. The commander's information is sobering, and much more detailed, than the sterile briefing Moss received from NATO back in Victoria. Moss listens carefully to the coast guard commander's advice. He asks a few more questions, and then finishes the conversation by expressing his gratitude for the commander's time.

Rafferty walks onto the bridge through the room's steel-reinforced door just as Moss ends the transmission. "So what did you find out?"

"A lot, actually," Moss responds. "Well, more than what I got from NATO."

"So the pirate situation is worse than we were led to believe?"

Moss sighs. "Yeah . . ." He stares back at Rafferty. "The NATO ships are out here mainly as a show of force. Their primary mission is the protection of ships carrying relief supplies. Their orders of engagement are highly restricted. When they're out on patrol, the local pirate gangs keep clear, and so the NATO patrols rarely see them."

"I'm guessing the coast guard sees a lot more action, am I right?

"Yes they do," Moss answers flatly. "I was just speaking with the commander of their lead patrol ship. He said they've experienced four lethal engagements in just the past three months. He also advised that we leave the area immediately."

Moss pauses. "The commander wasn't surprised when I told him we were forced to repel an armed attack. Apparently, we're smack in the middle of an area that's controlled by a Somali pirate named Abshir. He runs a gang the coast guard's been trying to take out for the past three years, and according to the commander, this guy's a real piece of work. "

Razz grimaces at the news. "So what do you think the odds are that the wacko who called us on the radio was this guy Abshir?"

Moss frowns. "My gut says nearly one hundred percent."

Chapter 8

We Gotta Talk

Murray strains to make out the letters painted in Gothic script across the stern of the yacht as she rolls in deep swell—E . . . LL . . . I . . . E . . . MA . . . R . . . IE . . . He unclips the handheld radio from his belt and calls up to the bridge. Within minutes, Moss, Murray, and Seth have a six-meter RIB launched from the equipment bay of Fearless and are en route to intercept.

"She looks abandoned," Seth shouts back over the roar of the engine as Murray navigates the rugged inflatable boat across two-meter ocean swells.

Murray slows the RIB as he motors in closer. It's clear to Moss her passengers and crew left in a hurry—Or were forced to. The foresail, mainsail, and mizzen of Ellie Marie lie collapsed in rumpled disarray across her deck, while a tangle of ropes and loose rigging hang from her gunnels and drag in the sea. Moss grimaces at the scene—No sailor would ever leave their boat like this willingly . . .

As her dire condition comes into full view a flash of raw anxiety sends a familiar chill through Moss. The last time he felt it he was in Afghanistan, and it's a feeling he's come to respect, as much as loathe, because it's always signaled that things are about to get a lot worse.

Murray maneuvers the RIB alongside the yacht and then bumps up against her hull. Seth tosses a rope over and hooks onto one of the rolling yacht's mooring cleats. Moss draws his sidearm from its holster before he steps aboard. Murray and Seth quickly secure the RIB, before they each draw their own weapons, and then follow after Moss.

The deck of the seventy-two-foot yacht is a cluttered mess. The three war veterans pick their way cautiously over the jumble of sails and ropes as the stricken yacht pitches and rolls in the swell until they reach the cockpit.

Moss stops short at the sight of a large swath of dried blood smeared across the yacht's aft deck. Murray bends down and then grabs up one of the spent shell casings still clattering back and forth across the teak planking. He briefly examines the shell and then sniffs it. Then he looks back at Moss. "Three fifty-seven," he says, "fired within the last twenty-four hours."

Moss studies the scene more closely. "Someone strafed the back of this yacht with automatic weapons fire."

"They sure did," Seth adds. The veteran combat medic crouches down for a closer look at the blood stain. "Whoever took this hit is dead, Chief." Seth straightens, and then turns back toward Moss. "I say we complete our recon, and get out of here as soon as possible."

"I agree," Moss answers. He swivels back toward the cockpit's open main hatch, holsters his weapon, and then unclips a flashlight. Moss approaches the hatchway, and shines the light inside. "It looks deserted . . ."

He starts to step through the opening just as Murray reaches in and blocks him from going any further. "Sorry, Chief, but I'm going down there first." Murray eyes the scowl forming on Moss's face. "Oh you could try, Chief, but it ain't gonna work, so you might as well step aside." Moss reluctantly takes a step back and then allows Murray to pass in front of him. Murray shines his light through the opening, raises his P226, and then goes below.

The small circle of light first passes over what was once the yacht's navigation station. Now looted and stripped of equipment, only loose wires dangle from the empty panel. Murray advances through the narrow galley and then into the saloon.

He quickly sweeps his light across the yacht's darkened interior until it lands on a white sheet of printer paper with a handwritten note, left tacked to a hand rail. Moss moves past Murray, steps over to the scrawled message, and then yanks it down—For Captain Moss . . . Then, noticing something taped under his name, he peels back the tape.

Seth leans in and looks at the small flash drive in Moss's hand. "Shit, Chief, this just got real personal."

• • •

Jannik tries again to force water into Niklas but he only pushes the bottle away. "I am not well," he mumbles in German. "Stop trying to help me."

"What do you think these guys will do to you when they find out?"

Jannik's eyes flip from Niklas to Fabri. "I don't know what you mean," he answers in English. "I am only trying to help my friend."

Fabri smiles. "Oh really? Is that all?" He shoots a knowing glance over at Andrea, then he focuses back on Jannik. "Look, I'm a liberal guy, okay? I don't hold prejudices against anyone, and Andrea here, I can tell you, he doesn't care one way or the other."

"It's true," Andrea shrugs.

Fabri moves in closer to Jannik. "We don't care who you fuck, it's your business, but let me tell you something, if you truly love this man, then you will pretend you don't know him."

Jannik lowers his head. "When we realized we were going to be taken hostage," the young man whimpers, "Niklas said he no longer knew me, and I thought . . ."

"You thought what?" Fabri interrupts. "You should have listened to Niklas; he's a smart guy, he knows. So now you will listen to me, okay?" The middle-aged Italian points his finger at the young student. "You're a pretty little rich boy, and where do you think you are right now? We've been hijacked by a bunch of fucking, third-world drug addicts, and now we're stuck in medieval hell." Fabri rises onto his knees then leans in closer while he continues to point his finger, but now, it's right in Jannik's face. "If these bastards find out who you really are?" he hisses. "They will kill you both."

Fabri allows his hand to drop back in his lap. He rolls back off his knees, then plops himself back down as he sighs. "Look, it's like this, okay? I just don't want to see anyone else getting killed. So please, for Niklas, for all of us . . ." Fabri pauses momentarily before he suddenly lifts both hands in exasperation. "Jannik, please? Do as I am telling you."

• • •

It's late in the day when Moss walks into the ship's main science lab to find Cal and Seth still hovering over the lab's central computer. "Did you guys find anything on that flash drive?"

Seth pops his head up from behind the flatscreen monitor. "We think we have the file reconfigured, Chief; we were just about to try to open it."

Moss takes up a position next to Cal and looks down at the monitor. "Good, let's see it."

Cal types in the final commands and opens the file. "It's a video file, Chief." He taps on the keyboard. "Let me see if I can start it."

At that moment, the video begins playing and all three men flinch in anger. It opens with a vanity shot of the pirates themselves. A common tactic employed by terrorists and designed to intimidate, to instill fear, but in Moss's case, it only ignites a desire to kill.

Checkered keffiyehs hide their faces, fully loaded ammunition belts hang across their chests and AK-47s are held up boldly in front of the camera. Moss recognizes the yacht's interior. His pulse accelerates as the camera moves away from the pirates and then slowly pans across the faces of the hostages.

Then the camera doubles back for another pass, and this time, it pauses briefly on each of the captive's faces. Moss closely observes each one of them, then the camera stops once more in front of the young woman wearing a hijab. She's still trying to keep her head down, like she did in the first shot, but this time an accented voice demands she look into the camera, and in that moment, Moss blinks.

"Cal, play that back. Can you freeze the shot of that girl for me?"

"Sure, Chief." Cal taps the space bar, scrubs the video back, then pauses it. "How's that?"

The beautiful young woman he encountered at a beach bar in Seychelles stares into the camera. Moss looks once more at her pale blue eyes before he shifts back to Cal. "Okay, let's see the rest."

Cal hits the space bar and the video continues. After the camera records all seven of the hostages' faces, it then moves to a table where each of their passports is systematically opened in front of the camera so as to positively identify each one of the captives.

The camera is then lifted and turned around to show the man who has been holding it. Moss sneers at the face of his opponent as the man begins to speak. "My name is Diric Abdirashid Abshir, and these are my hostages. My demand is simple. I will take your ship in exchange for the lives of the people you see here. You will give me Fearless, Captain Moss, and I will give you these people unharmed. There is no negotiation, Captain Moss. These are my terms. You will sail to the coordinates I have written. You have twenty-four hours to arrive at the point of exchange, the clock is ticking remember? If you do not meet my demand, if you make contact with anyone else, I will guarantee to you that these people will die."

• • •

At 18:00 hours Moss logs onto the foundation's secure server and establishes a satellite link. He rubs his eyes as he waits for the connection to initialize and then sighs as the image of his employer, Marcus Waverley, appears on the laptop screen in front of him.

"Chief! Looks like we have a good connection, so let's get down to business, shall we?"

"Yes sir. Did you have the opportunity to read my report?"

"Yes I did Alex, and I would like to express my concern. It sounds like you guys hit a rough patch out there."

"Yes sir, we did, but—"

Waverley leans in closer to the camera. "Look, Chief, I had to call an emergency board meeting over this, and we've fully reviewed the situation."

Moss looks directly at the camera. "I'm sure you have a lot of questions for me, sir, and I am ready to answer them; anything you wish to ask, just fire away."

"We do have a lot of questions, Alex." Waverley then pauses. He glances down at his hands folded in front of him, then says, "But we feel it would be better to wait until the ship safely reaches Cape Town. Two of our senior board members will be waiting at the dock when she arrives."

"I understand sir, but we have a number of serious issues happening right now. We—"

"Alex, I hate to have to inform you like this, but the board feels it would be best to turn command of the ship over to Malcolm Rafferty."

"What?" Moss concentrates on Waverley's expression while what his boss just said slowly registers. "Sir, if you would allow me to explain, we've just experienced events that—"

"Alex, the board has made their decision." Waverley lifts his hands to convey a gesture of hopelessness. "It's out of my hands at this point. You've been suspended until further notice. We'll meet with you in Cape Town, and we'll conduct a thorough and detailed investigation at that time, but until that time, Malcolm

Rafferty is in command of Fearless. Have I made myself clear, Alex?"

"Yes sir, very clear."

A brief smile crosses Waverley's face. "Alex, look, I'm in your corner on this, but you know the rules, so just wait until the ship reaches Cape Town, and we'll get this worked out. Can you give me that much?"

"Yes sir," Moss responds flatly. "I will see you in Cape Town."

"Thank you Alex, I appreciate this very much."

• • •

The next morning, Moss finds himself sitting silently inside the clamorous crew mess. He stares down at his untouched breakfast tray. Then he looks up to see his first mate standing in front of him, and the guy looks pretty steamed. "I just got off the satphone with Marcus Waverley," Razz huffs. "Ax, we gotta talk."

Walking into his personal office, Moss starts to head for his desk, but then he stops himself, and, instead, sits down on the couch. Rafferty says nothing as he follows Moss inside. Razz closes the door behind him and then leans back against it. "Ax, what the fuck is going on here?"

Moss looks up at his friend. "I've been suspended without pay until further notice, and you're now in command of Fearless."

"Yeah," Razz huffs again, "that's what Marcus told me, so let me ask you again." Razz straightens. "What the hell is going on?" He turns away and paces the floor in front of Moss. "I tried to explain to Marcus what happened."

"So did I."

"The guy's got a one-track mind; I couldn't get a word in edgewise."

Moss reaches up and pinches the bridge of his nose as his head pounds. "Me neither."

Rafferty stops in his tracks and stares at Moss. "I'm under orders to put you ashore in Kenya. Can you believe that shit?"

Moss lets his hand drop to his lap. "Yep, I can believe it." He looks up at Razz. "It's standard procedure when the commander of the vessel has been relieved of duty. It's in the foundation's bylaws, Razz. That way the new captain has full autonomy to command the ship without hindrance or undue influence."

Razz places his hands on his hips as he searches Moss's face in the hope of finding more answers than he's getting. "So what do we do about this? I mean, we've got a serious situation happening here," he says as he leans against the desk. "Cal showed me the video you guys recovered from that yacht. Ax, we can't just ignore this, we have to do something. People's lives are at stake here."

Moss looks up at Rafferty. "What you're going to do is follow orders, and take command, that's what you're going to do, and that's all you're gonna do."

Razz sighs. "Yeah, okay then, but what about you?"

"I'm working on it."

Chapter 9

No Promises

A sharp lurch wakes Trish. The movement startled her, but not as much as the realization that she was, in fact, asleep. She slowly pushes herself upright from the floor while her eyes quickly search for Maggie and Shelly. She sighs in relief when she sees them. The two girls lie next to each other, and both seem to be still asleep.

Trish slowly scans across the dim, squalid room while a storm of emotions churns inside of her—fear, outrage, disbelief, regret . . . Her head pounds, and her body aches. She's hungry, dehydrated, but mostly she's worried about what her family back home in Sydney are going through—Do they even know what's happened?

A muffled rise of sound grabs her attention. She freezes, and then listens to what she recognizes as a growing, shouting mob. Then Maggie and Shelly suddenly awaken to the horrible sound. Both girls begin to cry before they shriek in terror and then desperately grab for Trish.

The girls cling to each other as the shouting outside rapidly increases and the deafening mob is just beyond their door. In that moment Trish senses a searing pain burning in her throat, and only then does she realize she's screaming in panic as the the door flies open, and the mob explodes into the room.

A flood of dark figures obscured against the intense morning light rushes in through the opening. Trish is still screaming as she tries to hold on to Maggie and Shelly, but the mob quickly fills the room and dozens of rough, hard hands grab her arms and legs.

She kicks and fights as several men drag her out through the doorway. Outside the sun is blinding. Trish shuts her eyes as more hands grab at her body. She senses herself being lifted up and then sharply lowered down.

It's as if she's falling, but the mob still has her in its grip when a splash of warm water suddenly washes against her. It soaks into her clothes before another wave hits her back and she opens her eyes. She looks down at a patch of white sand beach just in front of her face—We've made landfall . . . they're taking us ashore.

. . .

Malcolm Rafferty is on the bridge and in the midst of studying a chart of the Kenyan coastline when Murray walks in. "Cal said to tell you he was able to get that video uploaded to the Seychellian coast guard's server."

Razz looks up from the chart. "That's good news."

Murray walks past Razz and then over to the broad spread of windows and looks out at the setting sun. "Yeah, I guess you could say that."

Razz turns around. He leans back against the polished mahogany chart table. "Murray, hey, you know none of this was my choice."

Murray turns to face Razz. "I know it wasn't, and don't take this wrong way, but this whole situation stinks worse than a dead goanna."

Rafferty sighs as he folds his arms in front of him. "Yeah, I agree, but we don't have a choice, and I can't run this ship without you. I need you, that's why I asked you to fill in as first mate."

Murray frowns. "So is that what you're doing then? Filling in?"

Razz smirks at the thought. "That's all I can do, right?"

A grin crosses Murray's face. "Right, so I guess that makes two of us."

• • •

In the fading remnants of dusk, Moss walks out to the farthest corner of the upper aft deck. He steps to the railing and then gazes down at the churning wake. He only waits a minute or two before Razz walks up and then takes a position along the railing right beside him.

"I was able to speak with the Seychellian coast guard commander," Razz says calmly. "He looked at the video; he's passing it directly to NATO headquarters. He'll mark it as a top priority, but that's about all he can do."

"Why am I not surprised."

Razz rests his elbows on the railing. "Yeah, well, he did tell me a few more things."

Moss turns and looks Razz in the eye. "Anything I should know?"

Razz straightens as he stares back at his friend. "He told me that NATO regularly shares their satellite surveillance images as part of the joint cooperation initiative. He said this morning's sweep picked up Abshir's mothership beached on the southern Somalian coast."

Moss sighs before he turns back to the ship's churning wake. "They've moved the hostages inland."

"That's my guess too," Razz answers as he too turns back to watch the steady stream of white froth trailing off the stern of the ship. "The commander said it's a standard tactic this guy uses. He knows that neither the coast guard nor NATO can touch him once he's on his home turf."

"And no government authority will go after him either."

"What government authority?" Razz scoffs. "The whole country's practically a lawless war zone." Shifting toward Moss, Razz briefly places his hand on his best friend's shoulder. "Look, I'm not at all excited about you moving ahead on this without me. We've always had each other's back, Ax—always."

Moss stares at his friend. "There's nobody I'd rather have next to me in a fight, but your responsibility to this ship and her crew has to come first, and if you truly have my back, Razz, then that's what you'll do." Moss pauses while he studies the face of a man he knows is trying to save him from himself. "Your job is here," Moss ends, "and that's how it has to be."

Razz drops his head as he lets out a brief groan. "This shit sucks . . ." He looks back at Moss. "Okay, you win, but officially? I don't know a thing, and I don't want to; just promise me you'll come back still breathing and in one piece, okay?"

Moss looks back at Razz. "I can't promise anything, but I'll certainly do my best." He leans in and hugs his friend. "Thanks for the help, buddy."

"You bet, man." Razz steps back, then he quickly reaches into his pocket. "Shit, I almost forgot." He pulls out a piece of paper and hands it to Moss. "The coast guard commander passed along the GPS coordinates of that beached ship."

Moss looks at the numbers of longitude and latitude written out by hand, then he carefully folds the paper and slips it into his pocket. "So how long until we reach the coast of Kenya? Do you have a port of entry planned yet?"

"Well, you know how it is," Razz responds. "Mombasa is our best choice, but arranging for a berth on short notice is a bitch. Then there's the paperwork and all. I'm estimating three to four days before we can get in there."

Moss smiles. "I better get packed and ready to get off the ship then."

Razz chuckles. "Sure, Ax, you do that."

• • •

Moss stands in the center of the engine room of Fearless while the low, smooth hum from the ship's twin, two-thousand-six-hundred kilowatt marine diesel engines send gentle vibrations up through the floor panels. Moss likes the sensation—it helps calm his simmering rage. He checks his watch before he looks up to see Mike coming down the steps toward him, and just by reading his expression, Moss knows Mike's on board.

Mike walks up to Moss. He stops in his tracks, and then places his hands on his hips. "Go ahead and brief me, Chief," he says, "but whatever you've got planned, I'm in."

Moss nods in approval. "I appreciate this, Mike, more than you know, but, I have to be honest: this mission is extremely high risk, it's well outside of any legal authority, and once we're in, we'll have no backup."

Mike flashes a brief, thin smile. "Good to know." He lifts his hands from his waist and then folds his arms in front of him. "What about Intelligence?" he asks. "We'll be needing all we can get our hands on."

"I've already tapped my own sources," Moss responds, "but I'm guessing you still have some connections."

"I do," Mikes answers calmly, "and they're current. I'll gather what I can." Mike moves his hands back to his hips. "So who else do you have in mind for your team?"

Moss draws in a long breath before he answers. "At the moment it's just you and me, but a few of the other guys have expressed interest."

Mike reaches up with his right hand and scratches at the gray stubble clinging to the end of his chin. "Any of those other guys happen to be Seth?"

The corner of Moss's mouth turns up slightly. "As a matter of fact . . ."

"Well then." Mike allows his hands to drop to his sides. "In my opinion, one more man is all we'll need."

Moss nods in approval. "Go in light and tight."

"Absolutely, in and out, no muss no fuss." Mike shifts his weight and then gestures in the direction of the weapons compartment. "Have you given any thought to equipment yet?"

"I have," Moss says, "but I could use your input, so let's have a look, shall we?"

"Lead the way, Chief."

Moss steps over to a utility box sitting near engine one. He reaches inside and pulls out an oversized grab hook. Then he walks across the perfectly uniform checkerboard of the engine room's diamond aluminum floor panels until he reaches a specific point. As Mike looks on, Moss kneels down beside one of the square-meter-sized panels, and then slips the hook into a grommeted hole located at one end. He then takes a firm hold of the hook's handle and lifts up the panel.

Mike steps in to assist with the heavy, sound-insulated floor panel. The two men shift it aside before Moss pivots back toward the opening. He removes a second layer of rubberized insulation to reveal a glowing digital keypad. He rapidly types in the eight-digit security code and then opens the compartment. Mike looks on as Moss leans in and then reaches down inside. He flips on the lights, then Mike watches as the chief climbs down inside.

It's a tight squeeze down a narrow, welded aluminum ladder to the painted steel floor of the ship's weapons compartment. The room has six square meters of floor space and is three meters deep. Mike follows Moss down the ladder, then he turns around and views the candy store of lethal wares neatly arranged in front of him.

Moss looks back at Mike as a sly grin crosses his face. "Okay, where do we start?"

Mike walks over to a wall rack that holds four Heckler & Koch G36K carbines. "We'll need the SOPMOD kit with this one, but Seth will be packing his medical so I think we should only take the one." Mike then steps over to the pair of G28 DMRs. "As for me, I'll take this lady right here . . ." He briefly touches the sniper rifle before he turns, and steps to the rack that holds the MP5K-N submachine guns. "These are essential in close quarters."

Moss's eyes follow Mike over to the rack of MP5s. "I agree, and with sidearms, we'll be covered. So what about edged weapons? Any preferences?"

"For myself?" responds Mike. "I like a good field knife, Chief, but I know you probably have something special in mind, am I right?"

Moss smirks. "Yeah . . ." He turns and then walks to the far end of the compartment, where he kneels down and unzips a soft black storage case. He then lifts out the twin sheaths that contain his custom-made Kukri blades. The long-handled, axe-like blades were hand forged from Damascus steel by a master sword smith in Afghanistan under Moss's personal direction.

Mike's eyebrows go up at the sight of them. "Now those things have a reputation all their own," he quips. "Mind if I see one up close?"

Moss draws one of the blades out from its sheath, and then he passes the handle over to Mike. "Be my guest."

Mike grips the leather-wrapped handle as he closely examines the distinctively shaped, razor-sharp blade. He studies the compressed patterns that are a hallmark of Damascus steel. The intricate, swirled lines dance across the blade's surface like the waves of a distant sea. "This is top-quality work, Chief." Mike hands the blade back. "So this is why they call you The Ax, am I right?"

Moss's expression goes cold. "Something like that . . ."

. . .

At 22:00 hours, Alex Moss is alone in his cabin. He's propped up in his bunk with his laptop open in front of him as he replays the video file Abshir left for him. Moss runs through the video over and over while he waits. He studies each frame for clues, as he gleans all he can from the actions and behavior of his opponents—especially Abshir.

He familiarizes himself with each of the hostages' faces . . . but then he sees her, and with every replay, Moss finds himself pausing at the same frame in order to linger a bit longer on the girl with the pale blue eyes.

He knows her name. He's memorized all of the hostage's information from the passport shots. But the young woman he briefly encountered at a beach bar in the Seychelles, is named Trisha Louise Peterson, and she's from Sydney.

Moss even went on line and looked up her family. He found out her father runs a prominent law firm in the city. Moss did some more digging and discovered that Trisha's dad is a former member of the Australian SAS.

As he passes the time, Moss brings up the law firm's website. He locates the site's contact page, and there, he finds an email address for Trisha's father. Moss lets out a sigh as he stares at the screen. He considers the potential for blowback, but then proceeds to tap out a carefully worded message. His finger hovers over the keyboard for a moment before he presses Send.

He clicks away from the website and opens a personal file. He skims through the document briefly, and sees no reason to make any changes, so he sends it over to his printer. Moss listens as the printer spits out the last page. He shuts down his laptop, stands, and then walks over to his cabin's small desk. He starts to pick up the loose pages but then pauses.

Moss reaches across the desk and picks up a pen, then he signs and dates his will. He leaves the printed pages face up inside the printer's catch tray and in plain view of anyone who would need to enter his cabin in the event of his death.

A soft knock on his door grabs his attention. Moss spins back toward his cabin door. He opens it and sees Seth's face on the other side.

"We're good to go Chief," Seth says assuringly. "You ready?"

Moss squares his jaw. "You bet, let's head out."

Chapter 10

Five Mike

Moss trails behind Seth as his medic heads down the crew quarters passageway before he hangs a left, then up a flight of stairs to the ship's central corridor. The two men walk in silence as they move forward toward the double hatchway that leads to the ship's helipad.

Meanwhile, the ship's interior is totally silent, and Moss can't help but wonder why. Then again, he figures, everyone would know full well that what he, Mike, and Seth are about to do is hardly legal. The crew have most likely chosen to avoid the chance of being implicated—A smart move, actually . . .

As Seth pauses at the hatchway, he glances back at Moss, flashes a confident grin, and then he turns the handle. The chopper's engines are just starting to turn over outside as Seth pushes the hatch open. Moss takes two steps beyond the opening before he suddenly stops short. What lies in front of him stuns him as he gazes out at the entire crew complement of Fearless.

Moss lifts his hands to his hips and grins as he scans across the field of familiar faces gathered in front of him. Then he looks ahead through a cleared path, and on toward the Bell 429 Global-Ranger. Her twin turboshaft engines now spool steadily at idle as she waits on the helipad. Moss can see Mike and Razz standing beside the open door of the chopper. Seth looks back once more and winks, then the two men stride forward.

Alex Moss looks into the faces of his crewmen as he heads for the helicopter. He pauses briefly in front of Razz as his first mate extends his hand. Taking a firm grip, Moss stares his friend in the eye before turning to climb inside.

Seth slides the door shut behind him, then he takes a seat and straps himself in. Flip, the ship's chief pilot, radios Razz that he's preparing for takeoff. Razz and Murray clear the helipad as the rest of the crew quickly disperse and head back to their posts. Then Razz and Murray watch from a distance as the Bell 429's navigation lights begin to flash and the helipad lights up with bright, sequential pulses of red and green.

"GlobalRanger, ready for takeoff."

Razz lifts his radio. "Roger that; stay safe out there." He sees Flip briefly wave from the cockpit just before the chopper lifts off from the ship's helipad. The Bell 429 gains altitude, smoothly pivots, tips forward, and then flies off toward the Somali coast. Almost immediately after taking flight, the helicopter's nav lights are switched off, and she disappears into the moonless night.

• • •

Jannik sits with his legs stretched out in front of him as he leans back against a rough, bare, cinderblock wall. He nervously pushes his hand into the ground beside him and lifts a handful of sand. Then he concentrates intently as he allows the dry desert granules to sift smoothly between his fingers. Across the darkened room he can just make out Niklas curled up in a far corner. Fabri and Andrea seem to be sleeping as well.

At least we are no longer rolling on the sea . . . As Jannik lifts another handful of sand, he focuses on the calming sensation as the grains smoothly flow through his fingers. Then he leans his head back against the rough block and takes in the stillness—Is it not better to be on dry land? Yes it is! At least the horrible rolling has stopped!

. . .

Seth hears Flip's voice over his headset as the Bell 429 skims low over the waves. "Five mike, final checks . . ." The veteran combat pilot then holds up five fingers as he repeats his previous announcement. "Five mike." Seth glances at his watch. He removes his headset, pulls the hood of his dry suit over his head, and then grabs his mask and snorkel. He briefly locks eyes with Moss, and then Mike, before the three men ready themselves for the helocast.

Flip sits right seat in the Bell's cockpit as he flies toward a desolate stretch of beach located along the southern Somali coast. He scans the sea in front of him and the shoreline ahead through the green glow of night vision goggles as he rapidly closes in on the insertion point. The insertion point is only five hundred meters off the beach, but Flip is counting on steady offshore winds, and low altitude, to mask the sound of his approach.

Flying an unarmed, civilian chopper into hostile territory and inserting a fully armed team, so they can attempt a hostage rescue, is not what he signed up for. But when the Australian veteran of the special air services regiment got word of what the chief was planning to do, and when he learned that Australian citizens were among the captives, Flip insisted on flying the mission. He also knew that if he didn't step up, Ax would just improvise; he'd find another way, and, no doubt, at much higher risk.

Flip reduces forward airspeed to under ten knots as he approaches the insertion point while the three special operations veterans sitting behind him prepare to helocast. For Mike, Seth, and Moss, accustomed to 3K swims for shore, helocasting five hundred meters is a cakewalk.

Flip reduces altitude as he moves into position, then he feels someone tap his shoulder. Flip reaches up and pushes the left side of his headset away from his ear. Then he hears the chief's voice.

"Safe flight back, my friend; thanks for the ride."

"I'll see you guys in Kenya," Flip shouts back.

Flip then senses the aircraft shift as the passenger doors are slid open. Then his bird slightly jumps as, one by one, the three frogmen secure their gear, step off the chopper's rails, and then plunge five meters into the black sea below. The moment he's certain the team has been successfully deployed, Flip increases altitude and then spins back toward Fearless.

• • •

Malcolm Rafferty squirms uncomfortably as he stares at Marcus Waverley's reddened face through the computer screen in front of him. Razz forces himself to listen patiently as Waverley chews him a new one over a secure satellite connection.

It's currently one o'clock in the afternoon California time, while, by Rafferty's clock, it's midnight. Waverley's expensive, tailored suit, and perfect white teeth, only add to Razz's unease.

"We're on a schedule here, Malcolm," Waverley barks. "Fearless should be halfway to Cape Town by now. Each day we delay costs the foundation tens of thousands of dollars that, frankly, we can't afford to spend. I shouldn't need to remind you that we're a nonprofit, and this is just the sort of thing that will bleed us dry, Mr. Rafferty."

"We're doing our best to resolve the situation as quickly as possible," Razz responds, "but to be perfectly honest, sir, the Kenyan customs and immigration authority doesn't give a flying crap about our schedule."

Waverley's red face leans in closer to the camera. "Look, Malcolm, I know you're doing the best you can, but I've got the rest of the board breathing down my neck on this. The decision's been made: this issue needs to be resolved; we want Alex off the boat ASAP."

Then Waverley sees the reaction his words just left on Malcolm Rafferty's face. He leans back, relaxes, then, "You have to see my position here . . ." he says as he tries to calm his tone. "I'm on your side, Malcolm, but you have to give me something concrete to pass on to the other board members. And excuse my language, but I'm in the middle of this shit storm, and it's you guys who put me here."

"I understand, sir, I'll have an answer for you by end of the day tomorrow."

Marcus leans forward in his chair once more. "I'll be expecting it, so let's move on to the next issue. How is Alex? Is he giving you any trouble at all? Is he behaving himself?"

Razz looks directly into the camera. "To be honest, Mr. Waverley, I haven't seen him; he's keeping a low profile."

Waverley smiles. "That's good news, Malcolm, very good news, but Alex has always been a standup guy. I would have expected nothing less from him."

"You and me both."

A five-hundred-meter, night swim to illegally infiltrate a hostile country without backup may sound insane on its face, but truth be known, it went off like a training exercise. The three-man team emerged from the surf with their gear intact, NVGs engaged, and their MP5K-Ns raised and ready. If a single word were used to describe the operation up to this point, that word would be textbook.

Moss, Seth, and Mike then moved quickly across open ground and found cover amongst a cluster of sandstone boulders and low scrub. The team shed their drysuits to reveal the full tactical clothing underneath. The dry sacks that had been used to transport their gear and supplies were then refilled with the swim gear, and promptly buried.

With the first phase of their mission now behind them, Moss and Seth find themselves looking over Mike's shoulder as he unfolds a laminated map. He'd printed it out from an electronic file while still on board the ship, and then pieced it together using a roll of clear packing tape.

"How much do you trust your source?" Moss asks.

Mike chuckles at the thought. "Well, Chief, you know how it is, you get what you can get, and you hope what you got is good enough."

Seth gazes quizzically at the map. "You know we have the plugger."

"GPS is a great tool," Mike answers as he continues to stare at his map using his NVGs, "but bear in mind that the unit you have there uses our military's precise positioning service. Which means it has secure coded deferential, and that level of encryption will be noticed." Mike glances over at the precision lightweight

GPS receiver Seth is holding. The military acronym being P-L-G-R, or plugger for short.

Mike then shifts his gaze to Seth. "Best to leave that turned off, or we could end up with JSOC breathing down our necks." Mike's gaze then returns to his map. "Or worse . . ." he grumbles before he clears his throat. "Anyway, my navigational aid doesn't need batteries."

Mike studies the map through the green glow of night vision as he runs his finger across it. "At the moment, we're here," he says as his finger stops, and then points briefly, before setting off again, "and this small village over here, this is supposedly right in the middle of Abshir's territory, which is about thirty klicks north-west of our current position."

Mike lowers the map and looks up at Moss. "My source tells me this is Abshir's preferred location when he brings in hostages. He also said this region is, more or less, controlled by his clan, and that Abshir's uncle is the local warlord."

"More or less?" Seth asks. "Who else do we need to be worried about?"

Mike grimaces as he stares back down at the map. "You can pick your poison in this part of the world, son. According to the intel, we need to stay clear of the Al Shabaab jihadis. It won't be easy though because they've laid claim to most of southern Somalia. What's worse is the fact that Joint Special Operations Command flies regular drone strikes on the Al Shabaab positions out of Camp Lemonnier in Djibouti. So, getting anywhere near Al Shabaab could mean getting in the way of JSOC's Reapers."

Moss frowns. "The sooner we get moving the better." He reaches for his pack. "Let's head out and scout for transportation; we need to get our hands on a vehicle."

The three men cover slightly more than three kilometers on foot before they reach a small settlement. The tight cluster of low-roofed houses sits amongst livestock pens and a mud brick storage shed containing a sparse collection of dilapidated vehicles. After a brief recon, a vintage, Datsun pickup is pushed out from under the shed. They roll the battered truck about three hundred meters down a dirt road before they pop it into gear, and get it started.

At just past 0400 hours, Moss, Mike, and Seth find themselves lying flat on their stomachs in sandy gravel at the crest of a scrub-covered hill, which, in reality, is little more than a slight rise in the terrain. The men watch, and wait, as they size up the village that was previously marked only as an inked dot on Mike's hand-made map.

Moss trains a pair of night vision binoculars on a small cinderblock building. With the aid of the BNVD, he can clearly observe the structure's lone guard armed with a vintage Kalashnikov. First impressions tell him the guard is most likely in his late teens, and of low rank within Abshir's organization. He wears long, dingy trousers, flip flops, and a tattered T-shirt.

Moss watches as the kid rounds the far corner after taking a piss out the back. He waits until the guard returns to his post adjacent to, what he's guessing, is the structure's lone entrance. Moss observes the guard sit back down on a plastic crate, and then rest his gun across his lap. Ax lowers the BNVD, shifts his position, and slides back over to Mike.

"What do you think?" he whispers.

Mike's been studying the guard same as Moss, but he's been using the DMR's night vision adapter. He knows his target is precisely three hundred and forty-seven meters away. There are no obstructions, the air is clear, dry, and wind is practically nonexistent. He also knows discharging his weapon won't attract attention.

The G28's sound suppressor has been attached to the carbine's barrel since the beach.

"I've got a clean shot . . ." Mike answers without looking up.

Moss glances over at Seth, and gets a nod of approval, so he shifts his attention back to Mike. "Take him out," Moss says calmly.

The former DEVGRU sniper's breathing slows as he moves his finger to the trigger, and then centers the man's head inside the crosshairs. A few more seconds go by as the pure mechanics of Mike's skill and concentration take over, and in that moment, the thought of what he is shooting disappears—only a target remains.

He waits until he's certain before he squeezes the trigger.

Moss has his BNVD focused on the target when he hears a single, muffled round leave the chamber of Mike's G28 DMR. The bullet is now traveling at more than twice the speed of sound and will take a mere .45 seconds to cover the distance between Mike and his target.

Moss is still looking at the man's head when the impact vaporizes half of it. The remnants splatter across the cinderblock wall he was leaning against. Moss lowers the infrared binoculars. "Let's move out."

The sleeping inhabitants of the village remain undisturbed, as Moss, Mike, and Seth approach the small, windowless, cinderblock building. Without a word, Mike and Seth move directly toward the guard, and right into the ugly business of removing the body. Meanwhile Moss powers up a tiny LED flashlight taped to his MP5 and enters the building.

"What's happening?" a voice suddenly calls out in English. "Who are you? Where did you come from?"

The former SEAL, fully armed and dressed for combat, is hit with a pang of self-conscious embarrassment as the light attached to his MP5 shines into the startled faces of two elderly pensioners in their pajamas. The shocked couple each struggle to sit up in their bed, while Moss lowers his weapon, "Uh . . . excuse me, please," Moss stammers, "uh . . . sir, mam, we're here on a rescue mission."

The old man's eyes quickly widen as the commando's words resonate. He then smiles broadly up at Moss. "A rescue mission?" he says excitedly. "That is wonderful news, sir! You are American, right?" The man then turns to his aged wife. "Elsa, did you hear that? We are to be rescued!"

Chapter 11

Out of Time

Seth's jaw is still clinched, the knot in his gut still throbbing, when he steps back, and then turns away from the thicket of dry brush ahead of Mike. The two men then quickly return to the front of the small building and to where they left the Chief.

Seth rounds the front corner first and is once again confronted with the still moist stain of fresh blood and brain matter that clings to the structure's outer wall. He pauses in front of it, but then feels a nudge at his back. Seth spins back to find Mike's cold stare. Mike doesn't need to say a thing; the message comes across clear as day—Don't clog up the mission . . . keep moving.

The two men then take up positions on either side of the building's rough plank door. Seth reaches up and gently knocks. Moss immediately opens it and the two men enter.

Seth lets out a disappointed sigh at the sight of the elderly European couple smiling up at him. "Thank you young man!" the woman says as she reaches toward Seth and then grasps his hand. "Thank you!"

Moss briefly flashes his small light on the two eager faces in front of him. "Allow me to introduce Lars and Elsa." Ax then catches sight of Mike. The SEAL team six veteran is currently straining to hold a straight face, and the smirk on the chief's face isn't helping. Moss regains his composure. "They're from Gothenburg, Sweden," he says, "and they've been held here for—"

"Eighteen months," Lars hastily interrupts before his trembling voice trails off. "Yes, it's been eighteen months."

"Eighteen months," Moss confirms.

Mike is still snickering, but the moment of levity is short lived as his smile quickly fades, and his eyes return to Moss with renewed concern. "We need to get out of here."

"You came for the others then, am I right, Mr. Moss?"

The sudden confirmation grabs Moss's attention. He swivels back toward Lars. "Yes sir; I apologize, we didn't know you were here." He steps closer to the elderly Swede. "What can you tell us about the others? Do you know where they are?"

"Yes of course," the old man eagerly answers, "they just brought them in. They're being held on the other side of the village; I can take you there."

"No," Moss responds, "it's too dangerous." He then gestures toward his medic. "Seth here will guide you and your wife out. Just tell us exactly where the rest of the hostages are."

. . .

Jannik isn't sleeping. He reaches up and rubs his aching neck after what seems like hours spent leaning against the rough, block wall behind him. An attempt to lie across the sand floor and hold his eyes shut produced nothing, and now he's disappointed. At no time has true sleep taken over, but then again—Just look at where

you are . . . His head still hurts from the rough treatment he received when he and the others were dragged from the mothership
and forced ashore.

His initial relief at being back on dry land has been short lived,
and an all-consuming melancholy has returned. As the reality of
his situation takes hold, so too does a suffocating weight of constant dread. He is a prisoner by mere circumstance, being held for
no just reason, and his jailers are criminal drug addicts.

The building bothers him. Jannik attempts to distract himself
by launching into a detailed critique of the structure that surrounds him. The dim light only seems to highlight the structure's
flaws more vividly. The pale glow outside easily slips through the
myriad gaps and cracks in the small building's four block walls.
Jannik's evaluation only leaves him with a feeling of contempt for
the builder. He can see nothing inadequate in the quality of the
basic materials; only a lack of skill, and a complete disregard for
the principles of construction, would produce such a brutally care-
less result.

The young engineering student is still scrutinizing the sloppy,
uneven rows of cinder block that make up the wall directly in front
of him when he notices something odd. The subtle light filtering
through the gaps appears to be in the process of being steadily,
and briefly, blocked. And it seems to be occurring due to something moving outside. Jannik sits up and stares intently at the two
large shapes. They progress toward the door but stop short. He
hears a faint sound, sudden, yet also soft, like a burble, but it only
lasts a few seconds.

Jannik is on his feet when he hears the bolt outside lifted, and
looking right at the door when it is opened. In that instant, he
finds himself face to face with two fully armed commandos. They

enter in darkened silhouette, and close the door behind them before one flashes a small light in his face.

Jannik lifts his hands to shield his eyes. "Leuchte nicht dieses Licht!!" he commands in a gruff whisper. "Sie werden dich sehen!"

Moss stops in his tracks just beyond the doorway. "Do you speak English?" he asks.

At that moment Mike puts his hand over the tiny LED light. "He says to douse the light, Chief."

Jannik lowers his hands. "You are Americans?" he asks in English.

Niklas slowly rises to his feet and then steps over beside Jannik. He pauses for a few seconds in order to size up the rescue team. "What is happening?" he demands in German. "Has the KSK come to save us?"

"Nein," Jannik responds in an irritated tone, before he switches back to English. "It is the Americans."

Niklas folds his arms in front of him and scowls at the two armed men before he continues in perfect English: "Are you certain?" he asks, "Look at them, they look like our German KSK."

Fabri pulls Andrea to his feet, then he turns to face Jannik and Niklas. "Only you two idiots would argue over what kind of commando has come to liberate us." Fabri then looks up at Moss. "Whoever you are, we thank you. Now let's get the fuck out of here, okay?"

Focusing on Fabri, Moss points his finger at the Italian. "You," he orders, "you're with Mike here." Then he looks at the others. "You three are with me; let's go."

Moss leads the men outside, but then Mike grabs Fabri by the arm. "You're with me, remember?"

Mike pulls Fabri back toward the doorway. "Help me with this."

Fabri reluctantly shifts back and then follows Mike. The two men backtrack only a few steps before he's confronted with the fresh corpse. The body is just visible in the pale glow of predawn light. The sight stuns him. "Madonna . . ." Fabri whispers under his breath.

"Grab his feet," Mike orders.

"But . . . all of this blood?" Fabri gasps as he catches a glimpse of the deep laceration across the man's throat, a vicious strike that appears to have nearly taken off the man's head entirely. He grimaces at the gruesome sight, then looks away.

"His feet, goddammit," Mike grumbles. "Move it."

Fabri bends down and grips the body by the ankles. "But the blood?" he asks again, "There is so much."

Mike slips his hands under the shoulders of the corpse and then lifts the upper torso. "Kick some sand over it," he growls.

Fabri can still feel the warmth of the dead man's body as he lifts the corpse by the ankles. He steps back, and then awkwardly sends two kicks of sand across the blood-soaked ground where the body fell. "Americans . . ." he complains, "you all think you're Rambo."

"We get the job done," Mike answers flatly.

The two men quickly move the body behind a nearby jumble of rocks and then lay it down in between a pair of large boulders. Fabri then reaches for the Kalashnikov assault rifle still strapped across the chest of the corpse.

"What do you think you're doing?" Mike snaps.

Fabri doesn't answer as he rapidly checks the chamber and then pulls the clip.

"Put that thing down," Mike orders. "Don't waste time."

Fabri flashes an irritated glance Mike's way then continues to efficiently evaluate the assault rifle's condition. "I was three years Esercito Italiano," he says softly. "I know what I am doing."

"Italian army, huh?" Mike answers, while in his mind, this guy's just moved up a notch. "Good," Mike says, "now get rid of that thing; we gotta move out."

Fabri drops the rifle, then he looks Mike in the eye. "It wasn't even loaded."

• • •

"This is your vehicle?"

Seth opens the passenger's side door of the old Datsun pickup and then helps Elsa inside before he looks back at Lars. "Well sir, at least we have wheels."

Lars rests his hands on his hips. "I know your Pentagon has received budget cuts," he says, "but this?"

"We aren't with the US military anymore," Seth responds. "We work independently." Seth gestures toward the truck's worn and rusted bed. "You mind getting in, sir; we need to be ready to move out."

Lars obediently climbs into the back of the pickup and sits down, but before Seth can move out of reach, the old man suddenly grabs him by the arm. "what happened to Cabdullahi?" he says.

Seth feels his gut twist again. He lets out a brief sigh before he turns and looks into the pleading eyes of the old man. "Who?"

"The boy who was guarding us," Lars answers. "His name is Cabdullahi. He would not have left us willingly; what happened to him?"

Seth looks away from the old man and then at the ground as he sighs once more.

Lars frowns. "You killed him, didn't you?"

Seth doesn't say anything at first. He slips his arm away from the old man's grasp. "We're getting you and your wife out of here," he answers. "It's best not to ask too many questions about how we're doing it."

Then Seth hears a familiar voice break the tension. "Okay people, load up," Moss orders. "We're moving out."

Seth spins back toward Ax and Mike, but they only have four of the seven known hostages in tow. "Where's the three women?" he asks.

"They weren't there," Moss answers flatly. He sheds his gear and hands it to Seth, opens the driver's side door, then folds his six-foot, four-inch frame inside behind the wheel.

Moss pauses, then gestures in back of him, toward the two Italians and the pair of Germans. "None of these guys have seen them since they were first taken captive." Moss then closes the door of the truck. "Let's get this thing going." He then looks up at Seth and Mike through the truck's open window. "We don't have any more intel, and we've got no time."

• • •

As the hot morning sun beats down, Abshir silently stands with his arms at his sides in front of the open door to an empty building. A building that once held his hostages. He bites down hard on the ball of fresh khat leaves wadded in the side of his mouth while a tempest of anger rages inside of him.

He nervously fingers the trigger of his newest trophy—a shiny, .357 magnum revolver that dangles from his right hand. The bloodstain in the sand at his feet, and the second bloody mess on the other side of his village tells him all he needs to know—he has been robbed of his property, and the men responsible will pay.

"Do you know the men who did this, Diric?"

Abshir looks into the eyes of his uncle. "Yes," he says, "I know who they are."

His uncle sighs. "I am ready to help you, Nephew."

Abshir folds his arms in front of him. "Many thanks, Uncle. I will go by sea today, but we must also search by land."

"I will leave right away," the warlord answers. "We will search for the hostages and bring them back. What would you have me do with the thieves who took them?"

Abshir's eyes turn to ice as he stares back at his uncle. "Cut them into small pieces . . . begin with their feet."

Chapter 12

Ten-Round Clip

The normally boisterous crew mess of Fearless is dead quiet. Malcolm Rafferty sits alone at an empty table while he picks at his lunch. The basic, institutional, yet seaworthy tables that surround him are all lined with crewmen seated on benches, which, like the tables themselves, are permanently fixed to the floor.

The crewmen busily eat, yet none make any attempt to speak to their new skipper. Razz isn't taking it personally. He knows the rest of the guys are just giving him space, but then again, if he were in their shoes, he wouldn't know what to say either.

It's been over twelve hours since Ax, Mike, and Seth left the ship. Razz hasn't heard from them and everyone knows it. The last thing Ax said is still buzzing inside Malcolm Rafferty's head—I've got the sat, but if you don't hear from us, don't come looking for us. Razz shoves the thought aside; the welfare of the ship and her crew are priority one, and Ax, more than anyone, would agree.

The noise level inside the crew mess unexpectedly jumps. Razz looks up from his lunch tray and spots Murray heading his way. He can see by Murray's expression that lunch is over. He is already on his feet and moving before Murray even makes it halfway across the room.

"We've got company." Murray's announcement sends the room into action as crewmen push their trays aside, stand up, and then head for their assigned duties.

Razz strides toward Murray. "How many? How far away?"

"Six skiffs," Murray answers, "less than four miles out and closing fast."

Razz stops in his tracks. He rapidly swivels around and scans the faces of the men gathered around him. "Cal, Dan," he calls out as the two men each give a brief nod in response, "you guys are with me." Razz then points at Rich. "You're with Murray, we've got ten minutes—suit up."

Before leaving the crew mess, Razz grabs the ship's comm and then calls up to the bridge: "Increase our speed . . ." he orders. Razz then listens a moment before he answers: "Yeah, give me all of it . . . call down to Pete, tell him what you're doing." Razz listens some more, then, "You bet," he says, "right now."

Murray and Rich are already waiting on the aft deck when Razz arrives with Dan and Cal in tow. The three men each carry a large black nylon duffle, each one filled with weapons and ammunition. Razz lowers the heavy bag to the deck as he locks eyes with Murray. "Where are they now?" he asks.

"Five o'clock." Murray then shifts and points off the ship's starboard rear quarter. "A thousand meters and closing."

"Still?" Razz flashes a rare look of shock. "Jesus, they don't give up."

Murray hands Razz his binoculars. Razz lifts the lenses to his eyes and focuses. "Shit."

"It's worse than that," Murray answers. "Have a look at the farthest skiff to your right."

Razz scans across the ragtag armada of battered, go-fast boats trying to chase down his ship. The slender open skiffs leap and bounce over the waves on a direct course with their high-powered engines at full throttle. Each boat carries four men including a driver. The shooters all brandish Kalashnikovs, and most wear fully stocked ammunition belts across their chests—Nothing new . . . Then his eyes land on the last boat, and what Razz sees raises the hair on the back of his neck.

Razz lowers the binoculars and turns toward Cal. "Here, what do you think?"

Peering through the lenses, Cal steadies himself as he zeros in on the outside skiff. "Fuck . . ." he utters softly before he lowers the binoculars, and looks back at Razz. "That's an RPG."

"Can you hit it?" Razz asks.

"Whoa," Cal says as he takes a step back. "Honestly? That would be one hell of a shot . . ." Cal reaches up and then nervously runs his hand through his close-cropped hair. "I mean, if it was Mike out here instead of me? I'd say maybe, but . . ."

Razz steps in close and then looks into the eyes of his remaining veteran sniper. "We don't have a choice, Cal."

Cal lets out a small groan before he stares back at Razz. "I'll make it work."

• • •

Abshir welcomes the surge of chemical amperage as he balances at the bow of a speeding skiff. He stares out at his prize once more before he shifts his attention back to his fleet. He lifts an AKSU-74 high above his head to signal his men. He glances back and forth at the full throttle go-fast boats that flank his own. He then lowers his weapon, clicks the receiver of the walkie-talkie hanging from his neck, and draws it up close to his mouth, "Wait . . ." he orders, "wait . . ."

Abshir releases the walkie-talkie to dangle again in the wind. He's staring straight ahead at Fearless when he feels his satphone buzzing inside his pocket. He slings the carbine back over his shoulder and snatches the phone from his pocket. He looks at the number before he spins back out of the wind, and then ducks down to answer it. He listens to the excited voice of his uncle, and as the warlord's message crackles inside his ear, Abshir smiles broadly. "Many blessings, Uncle."

. . .

Moss jerks his elbow up across his eyes to shield them from the shards of rock shattering off the ledge above his head. He allows the dust to clear a bit more before he peers out, and then catches sight of Mike returning from recon. Moss lays down another volley of suppressive fire and then withdraws as soon as Mike reaches him. Ax then briefly swivels back for another look at Seth. He's relieved to see that Seth's conscious, and the two Italians already have his med kit open. His eyes then dart from Seth over to the Germans. They're keeping low, and for once, are doing exactly what they've been told to do—shut up and look after the old folks.

Mike scrambles in close to Moss as the thunder of high-caliber bullets pounds their position near the peak of a small bluff. Mike's winded, but Moss can tell by his face that Mike's recon was worth the effort . . . And the risk.

"They've got three technicals," he reports through heavy breaths, "six men total, three with AK74s." Mike takes in some more air. "Two trucks mounted with old Soviet Dushka fifty-cals," Mike continues before he pauses to take in another breath. Then his eyes narrow. "The third technical's mounted with anti-aircraft, and it's a big fucker."

"They haven't fired it," Moss observes.

Mike smiles. "No, they haven't."

The ledge just above their heads is pelted with more heavy machine gun fire. The two men cover their eyes once more. Moss opens his eyes just as the dust clears, and then he looks back at Mike. "How much fifty-cal ammo do you think they have left?"

"From what I saw? Not that much, Chief."

Moss shifts. He glances behind him, and looks at Seth again, then he twists forward to focus on Mike. "We keep baiting 'em, and we wait."

Fifteen minutes later, Moss and Mike note a marked decrease from the fifty-caliber guns as the steady popping from the AKs increases.

"If they had any rounds for the double-A, they would have used it," Mike observes.

Moss nods in agreement. "No doubt." Ax then notes the timbre of the battle—It's shifted. He eyes Mike.

"Yeah, I hear it," Mike confirms. "They're advancing; they're heading right for us." Then Mike eyes Moss more closely, and sees a look he's seen only one other time in his life. It sends a chill straight through him, but this time, he knows better than to stand in the guy's way. "I got you, Chief," he says.

Mike loads a fresh, ten-round clip into his G28 DMR, but when he turns back, Moss is already gone—Shit . . .

Mike moves into firing position. He stares through the rifle's telescopic sight, searches the area in front of him, and takes note of three armed men moving toward him on foot, but only three— You fuckers don't know you're being hunted . . .

Mike can't see Ax, but as he scans the thin patches of dry scrub that dot the desert in front of him, Mike suddenly realizes there's now only two men visible. He sweeps the scope back across his field of vision and picks up a brief movement. Mike adjusts the zoom and tracks it down as a light breeze plays with a scrap of checkered fabric. It's lying across the dirt. It's partially hidden by brush; then it moves again, but it's not the wind; someone's just dragged it out of sight.

Mike holds his fire and waits. The two armed men advancing toward his position continue to squeeze off sporadic bursts from their AKs. Mike can see they've become more relaxed as they steadily advance up the low hill. The lack of return fire has made them more sure of themselves. They're now about seventy meters away. Mike continues to watch, and he waits.

The technicals are positioned amongst thicker scrub at the bottom of the hill near a dry creek bed. Mike can only marginally make out the three pickups with his scope. He sees zero activity, and there's still no sign of the chief. Another blast of rounds peppers his position, but Mike continues to hold his fire. The two men shooting at him are now only around thirty meters away from where he sits—but Mike still waits.

A few more seconds go by, but they feel like minutes. Mike peers through his scope and continues to scan the brush at the bottom of the hill. He searches for any movement at all, any sort of activity, but he sees nothing.

The two men directly in front of him have begun to relax as they loosely carry their 1970s vintage Kalashnikov rifles. They're only spitting out a few rounds each, more for show than anything tactical. Mike even watches one of them casually stop and reload.

He scans the bottom of the hill again; he focuses on the technical with the clearest view, one of two mounted with a 12.7 x 108mm Soviet DShK. Mike is looking right at it when the Dushka's barrel suddenly shifts position. He looks harder; someone's just swung the gun one hundred eighty degrees—It's Ax.

Mike shifts away from his telescopic scope, and visually sights his targets. He fires off two quick rounds and watches the two men drop.

• • •

Cal lies flat on his stomach at the farthest edge of the upper aft deck and prepares to fire an H&K G28 DMR, the twin sister of the one Mike took with him. The dedicated marksman rifle rests squarely on its folding bipod as Cal leans into the telescopic sight and tries to blot out the pressure and his own uncertainty.

His target is four hundred meters away and bouncing like a jackrabbit. The vibration coming up through the deck of the ship is causing the crosshairs to dance like lines on an oscilloscope, and now that he's the guy in the hot seat, Cal holds a whole new level of respect for Mike's extraordinary ability.

Long-distance shooting is a perishable skill, and at this moment, Cal is silently thanking Mike for the extra time he took during their training sessions. But Mike's not here, it's just him pulling the trigger this time, and it's gotta work. Cal allows the distance between himself and his target to close as he softens his breathing. He settles inside the patterns of motion in front of him. Then he feels them as he allows his own instincts to take over.

From the rifle's ten-round clip, Cal gently squeezes off a single, 7.62 x 51mm round, and it's a miss. He squeezes off two more rounds in a steady, measured sequence—Nothing but air . . . fuck . . . breathe you stupid dick . . . Then he hears it—Pop! Pop! Pop!

He's out of time; the skiffs are in range, and the ship's taking fire—Do it you dumb fuck . . . Cal resets. He fires off another shot, then a fifth round leaves the muzzle of the G28 . . .

Razz is kneeling down on the deck next to Cal. He has his binoculars trained on the target, when he witnesses a puff of crimson momentarily envelope the gunner's head—Holy shit . . . Cal hit him right in the fucking throat . . .

The bullet that pierced the pirate's esophagus tumbled up through his neck and then exited behind one ear on the left side of his skull. The impact knocks the corpse to the bottom of the skiff, but not before he reflexively pulls the trigger on his shoulder-mounted RPG. The exhaust plume generated by the rocket-powered grenade cooks the inside of the skiff and ignites the boat's fuel tanks.

Cal, watching the action through his scope, experiences a moment of genuine elation at the sight of the skiff suddenly exploding into a blackened fireball. But the sensation evaporates as quickly as it arrived. Fearless is still taking fire from the five remaining skiffs—a lot of it.

Rich, Murray, Dan, and now Razz, unleash a storm of return fire. But Cal can't take his eyes off the smoke trail tracing a high, dark line across the clear sky above. The rocket propelled grenade streaks up at seven hundred feet per second until it reaches an altitude of one thousand meters, its internal fuse burns out, and the rocket's armored tank warhead detonates.

"What the hell just happened?"

Cal's attention snaps away from the blast as he looks straight at Murray. "The warhead missed us," Cal announces. "It detonated on its own; we got lucky."

Murray lowers his MP5. "Not the warhead, mate," he says before he points aft. "I mean them!"

Cal looks out at the pirates, and he can't believe what he's seeing. The five remaining skiffs have abruptly broken off their attack—They're retreating.

Chapter 13

Judgment

A high sun glints off Damascus steel as Alex Moss wipes his blades of blood. He steadily breathes in, and then out again, as he methodically cleans the twin kukris with the headscarf of one of his victims. As soon as his mind levels, he returns the blades to the sheaths strapped to his back. Placing his hands on his hips, he looks around at the gruesome carnage his unleashed rage just produced, and then sighs in disgust.

Nearby he sees the dismembered corpse of who, he's guessing, must have been Abshir's uncle. Then he spots the satphone still gripped inside the warlord's hand.

Moss walks over to where the man's severed arm rests in a moist patch of deep red sand. He bends down and gently dislodges the phone. He straightens, and then he reads the phone's LCD screen. He notes the recent calls; all went to the same number, and the last one was made only in the past few minutes.

Moss unfolds the phone's antennae, and then proceeds to initiate a call. He puts the phone to his ear and listens as it electronically beeps and clicks through its programmed protocols. The signal eventually triangulates the three nearest satellites orbiting overhead, searches for the correct connection, and then Moss hears it begin to ring.

The phone rings only three times before someone answers. Moss recognizes the voice; it's the one from the video, but he can't understand a word of the rapid Somali now bombarding him by satellite. He can just pick up the whine of an outboard engine in the background. Add to that the wind noise, and he's certain the pirate leader is speaking from a fast-moving a skiff, which means he's out at sea. Moss waits until Abshir stops talking.

"Abshir . . ."

Another high speed flourish of Somali follows.

"Abshir . . ." Moss repeats.

The connection goes silent for a couple of seconds before Moss hears the voice again, but this time, in English: "Who is this?"

Alex Moss now clearly recognizes the voice of the man who threatened him, attacked his ship, and who is the reason why he is currently standing in remote southern Somalia and surrounded by dead men.

"Abshir," Moss barks, "this is Captain Moss. Your uncle is dead . . . I killed him."

Moss waits a moment until he's certain Abshir heard him, then he ends the call.

He folds the phone's antennae back in place, powers down the unit in order to preserve its battery life, and then stuffs it inside a side pocket of his fatigues. He shifts back, and then sizes up the three armed pickups—Time to move out . . .

Mike exhales slowly. The first few moments after a battle's just ended are always the most stressful for him. In the thick of a fight, there's not much time to think, but the aftermath is different—thinking is all he does. Mike draws in another long breath before he gets to his feet and goes to check on Seth.

The team's medic took a hit right after the shooting started. Mike even heard the Crack! that is the audible sensation left by a bullet that has passed so close that the sound of it breaking the sound barrier can be heard. Any closer, and you won't hear a thing, because you're dead. The near miss flew past Mike and then ricocheted off a rock before it clipped Seth in his left leg. Moss and Mike each knew it was Seth who got hit; they heard the screaming, but they had their hands full, and neither had a chance to find out how bad it was.

Mike smiles at the sight of Seth's bandaged thigh as Andrea and Fabri help him to limp clear of their rock-strewn stronghold.

Seth tries to smile back. "I'm good," he says. "Hurts like hell, but it's just a deep graze is all. I got lucky." Then Seth pats the shoulders of the two Italians. "These two guys did a great job patching me up."

"Are you okay to travel?" Mike asks.

Seth nods. "Absolutely."

Moss turns his attention toward the two Germans, Jannik and Niklas being the first ones to arrive at the base of the bluff. "Either of you guys know anything about trucks?" Moss asks. "About engines?"

Jannik and Niklas glance at each other before Niklas clears his throat. "Yes, Mr. Moss, we are both students of advanced mechanical and hydraulic engineering. We understand the properties of the combustion engine extremely well."

"Good," Moss says. "Follow me."

Mike remains behind for a few more minutes in order to collect the remaining weapons and ammunition. He starts to leave, but then stops short when he catches sight of Lars and Elsa standing outside near the bodies of the two men he's just shot. Mike can see that Lars is trying to comfort his wife, but she's crying, and even though Mike doesn't understand the language, he knows Lars is trying to convince her to ignore the bodies and go with him.

"We can't just leave them," Elsa mumbles through her tears in Swedish. "Who does that?" She rubs her eyes and then looks sternly at her husband. "What kind of people does this make us? Who shoots men dead like this? Who leaves them like animals?"

Lars takes ahold of his wife's hand. "Elsa please, we have no time, we must escape this hell. God will forgive us."

"And what of the men who did this?" she says. "So many deaths, Lars, and for what? Is it worth it? Do you think God will forgive these men?"

"No . . ." Lars sighs, "I think not."

"We are a part of this, Lars, we are as guilty as they are."

"That is for God to decide," Lars answers. "Now please, we must go, please."

At that moment Mike walks up and stands in front of the elderly couple. He's dressed for combat, in full battle rattle, and he reeks of day-old sweat. He's hungry, thirsty, and he's exhausted. His G28 carbine is strung from one shoulder, Seth's MP5 sub machine gun hangs off the other, while his own MP5 is strapped across the front of his body armor.

He eyes the grieving Swedes inquisitively. "You know, folks," Mike says in a gruff tone, "everyone has a job in this world, and if we're fortunate, we get to do a job that really means something. Right now, my job is to get you people safely out of this godforsaken shit-hole so you can go back home again. Is that okay with you?"

Elsa looks away in embarrassment while Lars steps toward Mike, then he looks the old soldier in the eye. "Please forgive us sir, but we have no understanding when it comes to war."

Mike grimaces. "Unfortunately, I do. We need to leave right now, so let's go."

As Mike, Lars, and Elsa reach the bottom of the hill, Mike can't help but shake his head at the scene playing out in front of him. He walks over and then takes up a position next to Moss. "What the hell you got those two fairies doing?"

Moss smirks. "Well, first I had them evaluate the trucks and pick the two best ones."

"So they went for the two Toyotas; good call," Mike says. "Wish we had ammo for those Dushkas mounted in their beds."

"Yeah, me too," Moss agrees, before he shifts his weight, and gestures toward the third truck. "Next I had them disable the Ford, syphon out its gas, collect the extra jerry cans and salvage any useful gear."

Mike smiles. "So now you got 'em pulling apart a Sergei ZU-23, double-barreled antiaircraft gun?" Mike rolls his eye before staring back at Moss. "Chief, we really need to go. If, and I can't stress this enough, if we do have some headway, hear? We need to use it."

At that moment Niklas runs up to Moss. "I have them!" he announces. "I have the firing pins; without these, the gun is useless."

Moss looks down at the pair of tapered, machined rods lying inside the kid's open hand. "Good job; let me have those."

Niklas hands Moss the two firing pins.

Moss takes one of the slender steel rods, spins back, and then heaves it out into the rock-strewn desert, then he shifts and sends the other hurtling in the opposite direction. He looks back at Niklas. "Load up, we're moving out."

Moss is at the wheel of the first truck, while Mike drives the second. They first drive for over an hour across a loose sand track before they hit harder ground, and a road surface that resembles actual pavement. It's here that the two trucks hang a left and head southeast, in the direction of the Kenyan border.

Along a narrow, desolate stretch of road, the sun eventually slips out of sight and the cloudless sky turns a thick shade of fiery orange. Seth sits in the front passenger seat next to Mike. He bends forward and rummages through his pack, then pulls out a bottle of water. Seth then carefully opens a packet of electrolyte powder and pours it inside. He replaces the cap, shakes the mixture up, then hands the bottle to Mike. "Here, you need this. Drink it, drink all of it."

Mike glances at the bottle. "You gave me one of those a while back, remember?"

"Look, Mike, I know severe dehydration when I see it, okay? Humor me, drink it."

Taking the bottle from Seth, Mike tips it up and guzzles most of it down, then he wipes his mouth with the back of his hand. "Thanks." Mike then glances over at Seth: "Mind if I ask you something?"

"What do you wanna know?"

Mike pauses, then rolls his mouth into a tight line just before he opens it to speak: "Is it those crazy blades of his? I mean, is that why everyone calls him Ax?"

Seth reaches up and pinches the bridge of his nose. He groans a little, and then rubs his eyes. "Oh . . . Um . . . no Mike, not really."

Mike keeps his eyes on the road. "So what is it then?"

Seth exhales slowly, then he looks over at Mike as the old soldier continues to drive. "Well, actually, Ax is just short for Alex."

Mike smiles. "Come on Seth, there's more to it than that. Just about every special forces guy I know has heard of The Ax. The stories are crap of course, so why don't you tell me the real one?" Mike glances over at Seth. "You were there, right?"

Seth looks ahead at the tail lights of the truck Moss is driving. "Yeah, I was." Seth shifts in his seat, winces at the throbbing pain and the staples gnawing into his raw flesh. Then he sighs, tries to relax, but then he figures, Why not? He shifts position once more, and starts talking.

"We were dropped into what was left of COP Keating after Kamdesh, on a supposed clean up mission to take down a remaining Taliban cell. Our orders were to bring the cell's leader in alive. Well, anyway, we wound up getting into a totally fucked up firefight."

Seth takes a deep breath and looks out the open window at the last of the color streaked across the sky, then he stares back at Mike. "A couple of our guys got wounded, and I really had my hands full at that point. The mission was deteriorating fast, and our air cover turned out to be a no-show. Ax went ballistic. He just stood up and marched down the hill shooting like some kind of insane crazy person. He was off his hinges, and there was nothing any of us could do to stop him; he just went straight for the haji's holdout."

Mike grimaces at the thought. "Holy shit . . ."

"Yeah, it was fucked up," Seth confirms. "Ax was taking out the enemy left and right though . . . I don't know, maybe four? Six kills? Anyway, he took two chest hits to his body armor, and that alone should have knocked him back but it didn't. I guess it was force of gravity, I don't know, but it didn't slow him down, no sir. It was some crazy kind of shit. So, Ax makes it all the way down to their camp, and that's when the head haji comes out shooting."

Seth takes in another long breath and then exhales slowly . . ." Anyway, Ax clipped the guy in the shoulder, but then he ran out of ammo. There wasn't time to reload, but he happened to be standing right next to this woodpile. There was this axe someone left, it was right there, it was just stuck in a log like it was waiting for him. So Ax drops his weapon, he grabs this axe with both hands, he yanks it out of the log and he swings it before the haji gets a chance to return fire."

"So what happened?"

"He cleaved the guy's head right in two . . . right down the middle."

"Sweet Jesus . . ."

"Yeah, and Mohamed too . . . anyway, ever since then, he went from being just Ax, to everyone calling him The Ax."

At that moment Mike sees the brake lights flare on the Toyota in front of him. "Something's up."

Seth strains to see what's ahead. "Shit, it's some kind of road block."

Chapter 14

Detour

"Malcolm, again? Are you telling me you guys got my boat shot up a second time?"

Malcolm Rafferty shifts uneasily in his seat. His own deep sense of responsibility and duty to his crew, forces him to watch in silence as Marcus Waverley's round, red face barks at him from over a secure satellite feed.

Waverley's puffy scowl fills the laptop screen in front of him as Razz silently idles and dutifully takes the heat. His outward demeanor is calm, yet inside, he's thinking of how great it would feel if he told Marcus Waverley exactly where to stuff it. Then Waverley finally takes a breath, and Razz gets a chance to say something.

"We were unexpectedly attacked by heavily armed pirates a second time, Mr. Waverley, this is correct," Razz answers flatly. "We defended the ship to the best of our ability."

Waverley gasps at the news. "Look, Malcolm, I apologize. The board members have been really fuming over this whole thing, and I'm the one twisting in the wind here." Waverley folds his hands; his look of concern is genuine. "Did anyone get hurt? Are you guys all okay?"

"We're good, and thank you for asking," Razz says as he relaxes a bit. "I've stayed in contact with NATO. They've been sending me regular updates, along with the Seychellian coast guard. They told me that this pirate leader, his name is Abshir, the one I told you about, anyway, his gang has attacked three other vessels in the past few days."

"My god." Waverley frowns. "I don't understand; if NATO knows about this guy, then why don't they take the bastard out? I mean, isn't that the international law of the sea? Isn't that why they're out there on patrol?"

"It's not that easy, sir," Razz replies. "Abshir has a sophisticated network, he controls dozens of boats and a small army of men, and he's well financed." Razz leans in closer to the screen. "Mr. Waverley, this guy came at us today with six skiffs, and twenty-four men armed with automatic weapons." Razz pauses a moment. "They tried to hit us with an RPG."

Marcus Waverley's face goes pale. "Jesus H. Christ," he whispers as he briefly puts his hand to his mouth. "Malcolm, I don't believe it, I mean . . . what did you do?"

"We took the gunner out, sir," Razz replies. "It was my call. I ordered our sniper to shoot, and he did shoot. He was able to prevent the gunner from firing on Fearless, and as a result, the skiff the gunner was aboard was also destroyed."

"So that's when they broke off the attack?" Marcus asks.

"It was shortly after that," Razz answers flatly. "I've thought about this a lot; I can't say for certain what caused Abshir to retreat, but we were very fortunate he did."

* * *

The finality of dusk casts muted shadows across the mutilated human remains that lie across the ground in front of a grieving man. Diric Abdirashid Abshir stands motionless as he stares down at the bodies of his uncle, his cousin, and his youngest brother.

He turns to his closest associate. "The dogs who did this, they have been seen?"

The man standing next to him silently nods.

Abshir's eyes remain fixed on his dead. "Gather all that we have left to fight with."

• • •

Alex Moss moves his right hand down, unsnaps the holster strapped to his hip, and then releases the safety on the Sig Sauer P226 9mm pistol. He gradually slows the truck, while he holds his forward gaze on the menacing shapes that block the road two hundred meters in front of him.

"Who are they?" Fabri nervously asks.

Moss glances down at the MP5KN resting on the seat in between himself and Fabri. "In your military training," Moss asks, "did you ever use one of these?"

Fabri eyes the compact submachine gun. "Yes," he says, "I know it."

Moss sighs. "Right, listen up: I want you to cock it, but keep it in your lap, okay? You got that? Hold it in plain sight."

Fabri does as he is told. "Now what?"

"Now we relax," Moss answers. "These guys see small arms all the time, and trust me on this, it's better if they know we're armed. What gets them twitchy is if they think we're trying to hide something. We have civilians with us, and that'll put 'em at ease, but what they're really going to be interested in are these two fifty-cals we got bolted into the beds of these trucks."

"But who are they?" Fabri asks again.

As his view improves, Moss needs only a few more seconds to study the small contingent of uniformed troops and armored vehicles that block the road ahead. "My first guess would be AMISOM."

"What?"

"African Union Mission in Somalia," Moss replies. "They're more or less a peacekeeping force, and these guys look like troops from Burundi."

"More or less?" Fabri questions.

"Just keep that weapon handy and let me do the talking."

Moss gently slows to a stop as the armed, Burundian troops move in close and mingle curiously around the two trucks.

Mike's been following the chief's lead the whole time as he too gradually slows to a stop. He lets out a long sigh, shifts the truck into neutral, then leans back, and waits. He keeps the engine at idle, and both windows down. He says nothing as armed soldiers soon arrive and surround the truck.

Seth stares straight ahead, and silently watches as the soldiers pass back and forth through the shafts of the Toyota's headlights. He finds it strange that the troops appear oddly unconcerned with the two technicals they've just stopped, but he's not about to start a conversation on the subject.

Mike can see the faces of Lars, Elsa, and Niklas as they huddle together in the bed of the truck the chief is driving. They all look pretty spooked, but, thankfully, they're keeping still and staying quiet. He glances briefly over at Seth; he's taken up a relaxed pose as he casually rests his right elbow on the door frame while his left hand rests atop the MP5KN submachine gun lying across his lap.

Jannik fidgets nervously as he sits in the bed of the truck Mike is driving. He grabs Andrea by the arm. "What is happening?" he whispers.

"Shhh . . ." Andrea warns, "don't speak, and do nothing . . . please, for the love of god, just be quiet."

Mike has unholstered his Sig Sauer P226. He holds the gun in his right hand and looks straight ahead, ignoring the soldiers walking just beyond his open window, and focusing Instead, on an officer mingling amongst the troops. Then he sees the guy turn back. The officer walks over to the truck the chief's driving, bends down, and then starts talking to him through the open window.

"That guy's not with the Burundi military," Seth observes.

"Nope." Mike slides his sidearm back into its holster. "British special forces . . . just what we need." He lets out a long breath and then leans back again. "This should be interesting."

Moss looks up at the SAS officer standing outside his open window. "Good evening sir," Moss says. "We're moving these civilians across the Kenyan border to safety. If you could assist us in any way we would be extremely grateful."

The heavily armed and fully kitted-out British commando eyes Moss inquisitively. "So who are you guys anyway? Private contractors?"

"Something like that," Moss answers.

The officer glances over at the Soviet DShK fifty-caliber heavy machine gun, then he stares down at Moss. "Well . . ." he sighs, "I'm not going to ask how, or why, you're driving a pair of technicals across the Somali desert in the middle of the night. It's none of my business, and frankly, I don't care." He moves one hand to his hip, while he leans against the door frame with the other. "But you're currently mucking up my operation."

Moss cringes . . . Shit . . .

The SAS officer then steps away from the window and gestures in the direction Moss just came from. "There's a road that crosses this one approximately ten K's back in the opposite direction; turn right, and you'll be on your way again." The British SAS officer then leans in close to Moss and smiles politely. "Now be a good chap and bugger off."

Chapter 15

S.O.G.

"This isn't a road, it's a camel track . . ." Moss grumbles.

Fabri clinches a small LED flashlight between his teeth as the truck bounces over the rough terrain. He's got one of Mike's makeshift maps opened up and in his lap. He holds the laminated printout in place with one hand, while he grips the handle protruding from the truck's dash with the other.

"So which is it?" Moss asks again as he maneuvers the Toyota across a rutted washout. He downshifts the late 90s vintage, 4 x 4 Toyota pickup into a lower gear. The parched, dusty ground is loose and scarred from rain that fell months before. He then holds both hands on the wheel and decides to stick with a marginally navigable patch of ground nearest the tree line. He can see that the track ahead narrows, and is lined on both sides with densely tangled scrub.

Fabri pulls the light from his teeth. "This is the road; we should be in the right place." He glances at Moss. "But it's another twenty kilometers to Jilib."

Moss only lets out a groan in response. The truck's suspension squeaks, and other parts rattle while it bounces along at a crawling pace. He strains to see the road ahead when the headlights shine across a series of fresh gashes cut through the bush in front of him. He knows that these ruts weren't made by the weather.

"Someone recently came through here in a hurry," Moss says.

Fabri looks out at the dimly lit ground ahead. "Large trucks I think, much bigger than ours." He looks up ahead just as a group of odd-angled shapes come into view. "What is that?"

Then Moss sees it too. "Hold on!" he shouts. He jams on the brakes and shoves the gearshift into reverse. Moss then twists back, and hits the gas, while his passengers cling to each other inside the bed of the pickup.

Mike sees the Toyota's brake lights flare as the chief's truck suddenly stops, then lurches into rapid reverse. "Look out!" Mike shouts.

He shifts gears and tries to turn around. Mike shoves his foot to the floor; the engine whines and tires spin. He then careens off the road in reverse as the pickup Moss is driving rushes toward his.

Mike backs up into a dead-end gap in the brush, and is forced to brake hard. He skids to a stop just as a sudden rush of rapid shouting, and multiple rifle barrels, fill the truck's cab.

Seth lifts his hands up and into plain sight, while Mike slowly draws his back from the steering wheel and the gearshift. The grip of his 9mm pistol brushes against his right wrist, but he quickly allows the thought to evaporate, and instead, he raises his hands, too.

Moss lifts up both hands, and then stares into the cold, focused eyes of the man currently pointing an American-made, M4 carbine at his chest.

The blue patch with a single white star sewn to the left shoulder of the man's uniform tells Moss the guy's Somali military, but he's never known them to carry weapons like these. He quickly concludes that the man threatening to shoot him, isn't regular army at all, but a member of some sort of elite force. Moss knows there's just one problem with that theory—Somalia doesn't have an elite force.

The shouting continues until Moss hears someone loudly cut through the din and call out in English. Moss pauses to listen— The accent's American. He watches the eyes and the expression of the man pointing a gun at him and waits. A few more seconds go by before the same voice starts giving orders in Somali. Moss doesn't need to understand the language, because he can see the change. The soldier's hardened stare suddenly softens. He withdraws his weapon, and then steps aside as another man takes his place.

Moss has never seen this guy before, but one look tells him he's most likely CIA. The special ops commando in front of him meets the type—wiry, not too tall, under six foot in fact, with a stubbled beard and scrappy dark hair. The guy's well-armed, and dressed in full tactical. But his uniform is atypical desert camo, and totally generic, with nothing to indicate a country of origin.

The fact that Moss has run into this guy in a part of Somalia overrun by Al Shabaab, and the fact that he's giving orders to Somali military, tells Moss that the American currently standing outside his window is SOG, Special Operations Group, and a member of the Central Intelligence Agency's covert special forces.

The guy shoulders his carbine, then he leans in against the door frame, and locks eyes with Moss. "May I see your license and registration sir? Do you know why you've been pulled over?"

A grin spreads rapidly across the guy's face until he launches into a fit of self-amused laughter. He doubles over as he continues laughing, while Moss reacts with only a blank stare. The guy chuckles some more, then quickly recovers. He unfolds into an upright position and then stares again at Moss. "Fuck, that was funny . . ." he sighs. "Shit . . . geez, I've always wanted to do that . . ."

He takes a deep breath and then exhales loudly. "Oh man, that was good." He places his elbow against the door of the Toyota and leans in close to Moss. "Was it good for you too?" He reads the stern expression on Moss's face, sighs once more, then he straightens and extends his hand through the open window.

"Hi, the name's Josh."

Moss grasps the man's hand briefly but firmly, then lets go. "Alex Moss," he says.

Josh freezes momentarily. "Did you just say Alex Moss?" He takes a step back. "As in Alex The Ax?"

Moss sighs just as Fabri cuts in. "Mr. Moss? Who is this man? You know him?"

"No," Moss responds, "we've never met before." He swivels back to Josh. "We're trying to complete a rescue mission. We have to get these civilians across the border and into Kenya. If you can assist us, we would appreciate your help, if not, we'll be on our way."

Josh puts his hands on his hips and relaxes. "Yeah, well, that's the rub, right?" He folds his arms. "You and me need to talk— alone."

Moss turns to Fabri. "Go tell Mike and Seth what's going on, and help keep these people calm. I'll be right back." Fabri nods in response, then Moss gets out of the truck and follows Josh into the darkness.

An acrid stench hanging in the night air alerts Moss as he walks a few paces behind Josh. He keeps his hand close to his sidearm as he watches Josh unclip a handheld, and radio to a second party. Moss then shadows the guy's movement as Josh pauses, stops in his tracks, and then transmits a rapid stream of orders in fluent Somali. In that instant, a flood of intense light nearly blinds Moss. He shields his eyes for the next few seconds until they adjust, then he lowers his hands, and gapes at the scene that lies in front of him.

The still-smoldering wreckage of what was once a military convoy lays scattered across blackened ground. The sight is perhaps fifty meters beyond where the Special Operations Group operative now stands. The headlights of four, mine-resistant, armored personnel vehicles clearly illuminate the area.

The glaring light shines a path across the carnage, and in that moment, Moss realizes that what he's looking at is the remnants of a drone strike. He watches Josh clip his radio back to his belt and then stride forward without looking back. Moss pauses, and briefly observes, before he follows after Josh, and toward one of the MRAPs.

The lingering odors of spent munitions, melted tires, and charred human remains swirls around Moss the closer he gets. The stench lines his nostrils and clings to his clothing, while the sensation catapults his mind back to places he'd rather not be. Shattered remnants of, what a short time ago, were living, breathing men, lie scattered across the road in front of him. It's the sort of scene he's witnessed before—too many times to count.

Moss reckons this was a hit on Al Shabaab, and most likely carried out within the past twelve hours. The Somali troops have returned to their duties. They hastily move around the strike zone collecting human remains of all sizes. They busily zip them into plastic bags as if they were merely picking up trash.

Moss can't help but notice that the more intact bodies are haphazardly dressed. They wear old, left-over uniforms, and many of the men were only wearing cheap sandals. Their mismatched, out-of-date weapons are surplus at best. Moss notes all of the details, as he silently, and very carefully, steps over the bodies.

Ax then continues to observe the CIA operative's mannerisms and movements as he walks along behind him. He watches his interactions with the Somali troops, and notes that Josh appears more than at ease in his surroundings. Moss is figuring this guy was once a Green Beret, or Delta Force, a standard career path for paramilitary spooks.

Josh stops walking, spins back, and then stares right at him. In the harsh glow of the MRAP's headlights, Moss sees the man's face clearly for the first time, and what he sees lifts the hairs on the back of his neck. It's a look he's seen before—This guy's a killer and he likes it.

"You're fucking crazy to be out here, but you know that, right?" Josh quips.

Moss stares back at Josh. "We should get out of your way as soon as possible."

Josh smiles, and in an instant—as if on cue, his eyes soften, and his expression shifts to that of a likable guy. "Sure thing Ax, I just need to clear it with my colleagues; we'll get you guys back on the road ASAP."

Josh starts to walk off again, but then halts dead in his tracks and turns back and points at Moss. "You know you're damned lucky I saw you. My guys were ready to blow the shit out of your technicals."

Moss senses a tingling sensation in the tips of his fingers, but he doesn't react, and instead—he waits . . .

Josh draws his right hand back to his hip and then lightly rests it near the grip of a Colt M45. "But I'd spotted you guys, like, two klicks back," he boasts. "I had plenty of time to scope you guys out. Then I saw you driving, and, I'm like, what the fuck? You know?"

He smiles as he nervously fingers the grip of the M45. "I figured, this guy's gotta be special forces, maybe a contractor, but what the hell's he doing out here? I couldn't believe what I was seeing, man. I couldn't just order my guys to kill you on the spot; I had to find out who you were."

Josh draws his hand away from the pistol and then folds his arms in front of him. He stares at Moss. "And now that I'm seeing you up close? You're either a goddammed psycho, or one badass motherfucker."

Moss sighs. He places his hands on his hips and stares silently back at Josh.

"Yeah, sure, I get you," Josh says and flashes another smile. "Your rep is legit, I can tell. You know, I was in Afghanistan too. I mean, it was a few years after you were there, but, that story about you killing all those guys with an axe, is that true? Did that really happen?"

Moss frowns. "It's just a story."

Josh's expression flatlines. "Goddamn . . ." he says, before his smile quickly returns. "You guys could probably use some provisions, am I right?"

Moss's stern expression softens. "Yeah, actually, anything you can spare would be greatly appreciated . . . thanks."

Josh spins back and continues on toward the armored vehicles. "So what do think of my operation?" he says without looking back. "Pretty cool, huh?" He turns toward Moss again. "This is the Somali government's brand new special forces unit. They're calling it Danab, means Lightning, it's a great name: Lightning Force . . ." Josh briefly strikes an aggressive pose. "Yeah, l like it." He glances back at Moss. "You're looking at my baby."

With the smoldering remains of the drone strike behind him, Josh lifts his hands up as if he were a preacher giving a sermon and shouts, "Welcome to SOCAFRICA's Joint Combined Exchange Training, Project Alpha!"

Moss moves his right hand closer to his sidearm—This guy's a lunatic . . .

Josh allows his hands to drop to his sides before he locks eyes with Moss. "So what do you think?"

Moss stares back at Josh. "Think about what? I don't need to be hearing any of this."

"No, you don't," Josh sneers, "but here you are, man, right in the middle of my op."

Moss keeps his hand close to the grip of his P226. "I didn't see anything, Josh, nobody did, we need to get on our way."

Josh's stare turns icy cold. "So is it true?"

Moss pauses. "Is what true?"

Josh suddenly smiles again. "The story, man, the story! Is it true?"

Moss sighs, shifts his weight, then he looks directly at Josh. "I only killed one guy with the axe; I shot the rest."

"Shit!" Josh smacks his hands together. "Wow!" He grins back at Moss. "Hey, don't sweat it, I'll get you resupplied and on your way, okay?" Then Josh playfully punches Moss in the arm. "You just made my day, man, seriously. I mean that."

Chapter 16

Old Soldier's Club

The first glow of dawn fills an empty horizon. Moss gazes out from the passenger seat of the Toyota as it rumbles over a dusty, blood-orange-colored road. The view ahead is equally divided above and below by two, equally flat, and equally endless, plains. The sky is pale ocher, while the earth is cast in deep umber. As for the road itself, its only discernible features are the marks left by previous vehicles. Other than that, it's made of the same sand as everything else that lies on either side of it, while only a few, sparse acacia trees make up what one might call landscape.

He's halfway between sleep and that place that wants to be sleep, but isn't, because it can't be, because his mind and his body are too busy arguing over the fact. Fabri drives. Moss shifts to face the open window and takes in the last of the night's cool, desert air. He draws in another long, deep breath, and then allows it to slip away. The only pleasant aspect of an otherwise shitty situation.

He's got a pounding headache, his ears ring like an alarm clock that won't stop, and his right knee is giving him grief again. Then there are the blood stains on his clothing; they're not his, he can't wash, he can't change, and it's bothering the hell out of him.

At the top of the list, though, and not just underlined, but flashing up there like a Las Vegas neon sign, is the gaping hole in the mission. Specifically, the three hostages they weren't able to locate. Mike even went back for a third sweep of the village that night, but came up empty. His source, a close friend, and a senior officer still on active duty with JSOC, had been certain Abshir would keep everyone in the same place for at least the first few days. It was his normal pattern to do so, but not this time.

For Moss, the hole is a clear failure, and he knows it's all on him. It frustrates him more than any other aspect of the mission thus far, and there's no way to fill it. They no longer have access to Intelligence. Mike would never take the risk of potentially compromising his source, and Moss won't ask him to. Besides, they don't have the ability, or the resources, to backtrack.

Moss knows he should be looking forward, not back. He knows he shouldn't be thinking about the hostages he wasn't able to locate. His full attention needs to be focused on his men, and the six civilians whose lives now depend on his ability to lead, and to make the right choices. But at this particular moment, he realizes he's mostly thinking about just one person.

. . .

Malcolm Rafferty shivers as he lies procumbent across the soaking wet deck of his ship. Foul weather gear? No time. And now? Just minutes into the fight? He's totally drenched. The ship's rain-soaked side railing presses uncomfortably into his right hip as he wipes his eyes and then peers through the dual combat sights of a G36 carbine. He looks first through the telescopic sight, then switches, and instead, goes for the unmagnified, reflex red-dot.

He can grab only fleeting glimpses of the rapidly darting skiffs in between waves, weather, and exchanges of fire. The pirates use the ship's imposing prow for cover, despite the fact that she's underway, and, given the conditions, at her best speed. Five-meter wave heights haven't put them off either. Razz rubs away salty rain in frustration and tries to track the men driving the slender go-fast boats. They joust with the steep waves and relentlessly keep pace with Fearless as she cuts through a rough, following sea.

The pirates took full advantage of the sudden squall, and if asked, Razz would give his opponents credit—it was a bold move. He'll give them credit for tenacity, too, if not for brains. Abshir's men raced in just before dawn with five, freshly armed skiffs. They altered tactics, approached from opposite directions, and this time, they fully dispensed with the customary show of force and came in shooting.

Razz tracks one of three narrow craft crossing the bow just ahead of him. The figures inside are barely visible—shrouded in a thick gray haze of sheeting rain. He pulls the trigger, fires off three quick rounds—Another miss . . .

Rafferty drops his head to the deck as a volley of return fire cracks above him. He's positioned starboard, just forward of midship. Murray's port side, and out of sight. Razz knows he needs more men forward, but he knows Rich and Dan have their hands full on the stern, so as much as he needs to pull 'em forward—he can't risk it.

He wipes his hand across his face once more and groans in disgust. The weather's playing out to the pirate's advantage. Mere minutes after the watch crew first caught sight of the fast-approaching skiffs, winds began gusting over thirty knots, and shortly afterwards, the clouds opened up.

Razz grimaces; he resets, fires off three more rounds, and sends another three bullets flying into the sea. He moves to fire again, but then hears Cal's voice crackle over the radio: "I can't get a clear shot," Cal complains. "I've gotta move back."

Then Murray suddenly breaks in over the handheld: "They've got grappling hooks out mate; they're gonna board."

Rafferty reaches back, snaps his handheld off his belt, then radios up to the bridge crew. He called Pete up from the engine room the moment the shooting started, and now he's glad he did, because of all the men on board, he knows the ship's capabilities better than anyone. The two men have a brief exchange that ends with a final order from Razz: "Wait for my signal."

Razz pushes himself to the edge of the deck and then strains to see forward. He holds the radio close while waiting for his opportunity, then—"Now! Now! Now!"

As Murray hears Rafferty's voice shouting over his handheld radio, he flashes a quick look back at Cal: "Hold fast!"

The men on deck sense the sudden shift beneath them as Fearless yaws powerfully to starboard. Murray and Cal each grip the wet railing hard and brace against the sharp shift in motion that wants to pull them both overboard. They feel the ship's rising port side lift them upward, while Razz hangs on as her starboard bow dives deep into the cluster of small boats beneath her prow.

Pete cringes from the bridge as he plants his feet and holds the helm hard to starboard. The veteran seaman then winces with guilt as his dramatic course change sends a wave crashing across the bow just as Fearless hits her mark. The wall of white froth blocks the three men clinging to the forward deck from view as they are buried beneath it. The engineer then grimaces in horror when the impact capsizes two of the open boats in a shattering explosion of shouting men and screaming outboards.

"Holy shit . . ."

Pete glares back at the crewman standing beside him before his eyes rapidly return to the forward deck. His relief is clearly audible when Cal, Murray, and Razz reappear from beneath the gushing torrent of seawater. He then gasps in astonishment when Cal and Murray immediately reengage the remaining skiff.

A few seconds more and the bridge crew hears Cal's voice come in over the comm as he announces flatly, "Two kill shots port side."

Then Murray, "One more kill port side."

Razz blinks the seawater from his stinging eyes as he rolls away from the railing and on to his side. He rests for a moment against the cold, wet surface to catch his breath when he hears Rich call in, "Skiffs in retreat off the stern."

Then Razz hears his radio again, but this time it's Pete. "I just heard back from that Belgian-flagged NATO ship; they said they'll assist. They have our position; they're on their way."

Murray suddenly cuts in: "Isn't that a fucking relief mates? We're saved!"

Razz slowly pulls himself upright and then climbs to his feet. He shoulders his weapon just before he grabs the front of his shirt and then wrings it out. A half liter of ocean splashes to the deck at his feet. Then he pauses and looks around. The squall is already subsiding as the rain slacks and the wind drops. He's chilled to the bone, and thoroughly pissed off. He briefly contemplates the next mandatory damage report, winces at the thought, then stretches his aching back and heads below.

• • •

Jannik pulls his T-shirt off and wraps it around his head. The sun has only just risen, yet, the heat of the coming day has already arrived. The dust is another thing. He sits with his bare back against the grit-covered rear window of the pickup. He sits perched atop a slat of wood that seems to have been left there for the purpose. Andrea is leaning silently against the cab with his eyes closed, and on the opposite side of the large machine gun that they don't have any bullets for.

The scraped and dented bed of the pickup feels like a griddle ready for cooking. The lead truck is kicking up a cloud of orange dust, and the truck he's riding in is kicking up dust too. All of it seems to swirl back over the gap where the tailgate would normally be and then fly directly into his face. Jannik tugs at the fabric covering his nose and mouth and silently vows that he will never step foot in another desert ever again.

The young, German engineering student then attempts to distract from his discomfort by analyzing the manner in which the heavy machine gun has been modified and mounted inside the bed of the truck. He studies the heavy steel plates mounted on either side of the barrel. The gun shield is rudimentary, and should be larger, he reckons. They welded the gun's swivel mounts right to the truck's frame. It's improvised work, he reasons, but the welding is good.

Then Jannik evaluates the weapon itself. The gun's mechanics seem simple enough, a credit to Soviet efficiency. He then eyes the heavy machine gun's twin spade handles, the simple loading and cocking mechanism, the butterfly trigger, and tries to imagine what it would be like to fire it.

The idea of arming a small, civilian pickup truck intrigues him. It's a simple design, but effective. Of course, a technical is nothing new. Jannik knows his history, and he's certain it was World War II era German soldiers fighting in North Africa, who first seized upon the idea to mount a heavy machine gun on the front of a light vehicle.

Good ideas always last . . . he reasons. And most of them are German . . . Jannik peers down at the rushing blur of the road passing beneath the pickup, before he shifts back once more to eye the dust cloud billowing off behind it, and then he sees something. He reaches across the bed of the truck and grasps Andrea's arm. Andrea lifts his head from between his knees, and looks up as Jannik points.

At first Andrea strains to make out the distant shapes obscured by the dust cloud, but then it registers. He twists and then hurriedly knocks on the truck's rear window. Seth slides it open. "We have trucks behind us!" Andrea shouts. "They're coming up fast!"

Fabri doesn't want to wake Mr. Moss, but he knows he has to. He reaches over and gently pushes against the commando's shoulder. "Mr. Moss?" he says. "I am sorry to wake you but . . ."

Ax opens his eyes and sees Fabri. "What's happened?"

"The other truck is flashing its lights," Fabri reports.

Moss quickly straightens; he checks his side mirror. "Slow down." He looks back at Fabri. "Ease up and pull off to the side . . . stop here."

Mike watches from the driver's seat as Moss's truck begins to slow. He shadows their movement while he keeps an eye on the fast-moving convoy of heavy military transports and armored vehicles though the dingy side mirror. Mike pulls off the road just behind Fabri, and hits the brakes. He then sits tight as the military convoy rolls by in a torrent of dust. "I count eleven," he says.

"Yeah, me too," Seth agrees. As the last of the trucks passes by, Seth notes the type, the fact that they're all painted white, and flying the Kenyan flag. "My guess would be KDF."

"Sure wish we could thumb a ride," Mike responds. "They're sure in some kind of a hurry though," he says as he swivels back to Seth. "They never gave us a second look."

A little over an hour later, it's Moss who gets the second look. He's at the wheel when the convoy of white, military transports come into view once more. Moss eases up on the gas as the Toyota approaches the last truck in the convoy. The transports all appear to be parked at a standstill, and lined up along the side of the road. He downshifts the pickup, slows to a crawl and then stops some one hundred meters back.

Moss turns to Fabri. "Wait here; don't let anyone leave the truck."

"Are you sure?" Fabri questions. "Maybe we should just leave them be?"

"They're Kenyan Defense Force," Moss answers. "We need to get to Kenya. It's worth trying to talk to these guys."

Moss shifts back and then glances out at the convoy through the Toyota's dusty windshield. He sighs, then he pulls his pistol from its holster and places it on the dash. He leaves the rest of his weapons with Fabri, before he pushes the truck's creaking door open and then steps outside.

He's suddenly reminded of the pain in his right knee as he walks slowly toward the last vehicle in the convoy. He's careful to keep his hands held out from his sides, and in plain sight. Moss quickly draws the attention of a small band of KDF troops gathered outside near the rear. They were busily chatting away in Swahili, as they huddle together inside the meager patch of shade the truck casts across the scorching sand.

At the sight of an approaching foreign soldier, the armed troops rise to their feet. In seconds, they noisily surround Moss and then search him. Then one of them radios to his superior, and proudly announces in English that they've captured an American commando.

Thirty minutes later, Moss is still standing under guard, and in the beating sun with his hands clasped behind his head. He silently observes until eventually, he spots a group of uniformed men walking down the line of trucks toward him. Of even greater interest, however, is the senior British special forces officer who is walking amongst them.

Moss keeps his mouth shut and observes every detail, as the men approach, then surround him. The SAS officer then steps forward, and plants himself directly in front of Moss. He leans in close and stares intently at the prisoner. Moss silently notes that the graying officer's desert camo is smeared in axle grease, and his heavily weathered face is bright red. It's obvious he's not in the mood for idle conversation.

The officer spends a few seconds of his time evaluating the stranger in front of him before he spins back and barks out something in Swahili to the men gathered around him. Then his attention returns to the stranger who's just interrupted his bad day. "What the bloody hell are you doing here?" he demands.

Moss straightens but keeps his hands clasped behind his head. "Sir, I apologize for interrupting your mission. My colleagues and I are moving a group of former hostages to safety across the Kenyan border."

The SAS officer carefully eyes Moss. He shifts his weight as he glances past him to the technicals parked some distance down the road before his eyes return. "Independent contractors then?" he asks. "Well, I can't help you, so it's best if you be on your way." Then he eyes Moss again. "Oh, uh, you can lower your hands," he quips. "It's not likely that we're in any danger, are we?"

Moss lowers his hands to his sides as the British SAS officer turns to walk away. "Sir . . ." Moss calls out, "if I may ask."

The man halts in his tracks before looking back.

"Are you experiencing mechanical problems?" Moss asks.

An hour and a half later, the British officer is sharing his tea with Moss and Mike while the three men watch Jannik and Niklas complete repairs to one of the vehicles. The officer lifts a stainless steel cup to his lips, then lowers it, and answers Mike's question. "I was in Afghanistan for three years," he says, "Iraq for two, then Libya, Sudan, Syria, and now this." He looks back at Mike and Moss. "At this point, I'm just counting the days until retirement."

Moss smirks. "I am retired."

Then Mike chuckles. "I retired twice."

The clatter of a diesel engine kicking over abruptly ends the men's conversation. On cue the three old warriors stand simultaneously and observe as Jannik and Niklas direct the driver to shift the armored vehicle into gear and then move it forward. Niklas excitedly spins back toward Moss and flashes two thumbs up.

Moss then turns back to face the British officer. "Commander Cox," he says, "it's been a pleasure to meet you sir." He extends his hand.

"The pleasure is mine, Mr. Moss," Cox answers. "Best of luck to you both." He briefly grasps Moss's hand. "We should check on your wounded man, and the civilians, see what sort of progress my medics have made." Then he sighs. "I'd run you back across the border myself if it were possible, but I'm to rendezvous with a second contingent, and I'm dreadfully behind schedule."

Moss is standing beside one of the Toyotas when the last of the KDF convoy pulls out and then departs. He hears Mike's voice above the low rumble of Caterpillar, turbo diesel engines. He shifts back and sees Mike waving him over.

"Hey Chief," Mike says, "have a look at this."

Moss walks back to where Mike is standing near the tailgate of the pickup, then gazes down at the bed. "So where do you think those came from?" he quips.

Mike grins. "Let's have a look." He draws his field knife and slices across one of two large boxes stamped with the USAID logo. Mike flips open the box and peers inside. "Well now, that's a sight for sore eyes."

Moss gazes down at the box packed with .50 caliber ammunition belts. "Thank you, Commander Cox," he says, "thank you very much."

Chapter 17

Shhh . . .

A shallow shaft of late afternoon light streams through her small room's lone window. Trish has her legs crossed in front of her and her head down. She sits on the tiled floor in total silence, while inside her head, her mind is still screaming in denial at the terror of her reality.

The African sun bakes the outer walls of the multistory, masonry building like a bread oven. It is only the latest in a string of makeshift prisons she's been held in over the past two days. The floor is warm, and she can feel the day's intense heat radiating off the walls. But then there is the smell of the place. It's subtle but pervasive, and there seems to be only one explanation that can describe it—a faint odor of death.

Trish gently lifts her head and then leans back against the wall. Her entire body aches. She's dehydrated, hungry, and can hardly move her neck without experiencing shooting pain, but through her cotton headscarf, she can still feel the small folded pocket knife she'd wedged into her hair.

She sighs in disgust at the sensation. What a joke . . . they grabbed you and you couldn't stop them. They put their hands all over you, they hurt you, they now own you, and you can't stop them . . . you and your tactics . . . you've been utterly ridiculous . . . Then Trish stops herself—Jannik, Niklas, Andrea, and Fabri? They couldn't stop them either . . . and Angelo is dead . . . you've been taken hostage by maniacs with machine guns . . . honestly . . .

The room's lone window offers the first clear view she's seen in the past forty-eight hours. After being dragged ashore from the mothership, someone tied her hands, and she was then forcefully loaded, along with Shelly and Maggie, into the back of an SUV with dark tinted windows. Her head was then covered. She couldn't see, but she knows they drove for hours. Roads were rough at first, then gradually got better. It was late at night when they finally stopped for the first time.

She hasn't seen Maggie or Shelly since midday, which was before they arrived here, but she knows they must be close by—she's heard them. She's certain they're being held on the same floor as her, but the others? Trish stops herself again; she can't allow herself to think about where they might be or what may have happened to them.

She lifts her arms up in front of her face and briefly examines the multi-colored bruises that cover them both. She sighs in disgust once more, then lowers them back to her lap as her attention is drawn, yet again, to the window. It's open to the outside, but it's barred. She does know that her room, or more accurately, her cell, is on the top floor of a squat three-story building, with a shear drop to the alley below.

The moment she felt she was alone, Trish went to the window and looked out, and what she saw surprised her. A sea of rooftops, a mishmash of haphazard construction all colored in the same dingy tan, and spread out for what seemed like miles. She stood at the window and looked out until she spotted a lone figure walking just beneath her.

It was a woman; she was draped in traditional dress, and she was passing through the alley. Pushing her arms through the bars of the window, Trish waved and shouted for help, but the woman paused only momentarily to look up at her. The woman's face showed no expression; she simply pulled at her hijab as if to shield her eyes, and kept moving.

Shelly is crying again. Trish reckons she must be across the hall, and for the first time since they arrived, she can now clearly hear her sobbing. It's been a few hours since she last heard anything. It irritated her at first, all of the crying; it seemed useless. When they were first taken captive, it was obvious the pirates enjoyed seeing their prisoners suffer. Trish caught glimpses of them grinning at each other when the other two girls cried. The pirates laughed out loud, though, when the men did.

At the moment, however, she oddly takes comfort in the sounds of Shelly's soft weeping as it enters her room from beneath its bolted door. Trish continues to listen, and she's reminded of something her mother once said about looking after her when she was a toddler, about how a sudden outburst of crying never worried her—It's a loud thump followed by silence that stops your heart.

The city has fallen silent now that sunlight has dwindled into night. The last hints of dusk vanished a long time ago, or at least, it seems that way. She takes in another long breath as she makes an honest attempt to think clearly. Her room has no lights, no furnishings, only a hard floor and a plastic bucket, but thankfully, it's no longer quite as hot.

Trish climbs to her feet then walks to the window again. She presses her face against the whitewashed rebar embedded in the window's masonry frame and stares out. There are few lights. The alley below has fallen under near total darkness. She draws in the meager night breeze as she stares down at the deserted alley. She's looking at nothing in particular when something below, someone in the alley . . . moves.

With her attention focused, she tracks the movement. The rough texture of the rebar digs into her cheeks as she pushes against it harder in order to see further down. The pounding in her chest rises up through her throat as the dark shape moves briefly across her narrow field of view.

Then she sees a second armed commando, and her heart jumps—Is this real? Am I hallucinating?

She watches a second man take up a position behind the first, just as a soft audible cry leaves her lips. The men in the alley stop; they look up and then directly at her.

Shoving her arms through the bars again, she holds her hands out, and then waves them toward the men below. She spreads her fingers wide to be as visible as possible. She is staring down through the bars when one of the commandos looks back. He gestures for her to be silent.

Trish pulls her arms back inside and then steps back from the window. Her pulse is buzzing, and she feels dizzy. She paces the room then sits again in the same corner where she was before. She waits; she tries to breathe. A few more seconds go by, but she hears nothing.

Trish draws her knees into her chest then rocks back and forth inside the darkened room while an eternity of complete silence follows. She stares across at the empty wall in front of her.

Her initial excitement wanes, while a deep sadness floods into the void as she begins to question what she really saw—Was I hallucinating?

Maybe . . . yes . . . probably . . . My god you're mad; you've lost it completely . . .

Trish tries to comfort herself, but her anger won't allow it. She's furious that her mind would be so cruel as to play such an evil trick on her. Then she hears something. She ignores the sound at first—It's not real . . . She pulls her knees up closer and covers her ears. "Stop it!" she shouts.

But even with her ears covered, the sound only grows louder. Trish pulls her hands away, and realizes that she's shaking. The steady, percussive beats and shrill whine of what she recognizes to be from a helicopter rapidly fill the room. The floor vibrates under the increasing pressure. The sound builds until it reverberates through the walls behind her. She presses her hands to the tile to steady herself just as a series of heavy thumps hit the roof above her head.

She stares up at the ceiling. The roar of the chopper rapidly fades leaving behind the blows from boots on the roof above her. Her eyes then dart toward the door and toward the shouts that have erupted in the hallway outside. A burst of gunfire follows: it's loud, sudden, and brief. Then more gunfire, but different— softer, suppressed. In that moment the door to her darkened room is kicked open.

A light shines in her face. "Trisha Louise Peterson?" a man's voice calls out.

"Yes!" she cries out. "I'm Trisha!"

The man grabs her hand. "Australian SAS," he barks, "and you can thank your dad for this," he says as he stares at her face. "Are you injured?" he asks. "Can you run?"

"I'm alright," she answers. "Yes . . . I can run."

She reaches up behind her head and then tears away the scarf. Her blond hair comes undone and the small knife she'd kept so carefully hidden is instantly forgotten as it drops to the floor.

He pulls her to her feet. "Stay with me," he orders. "We're getting you out of here. You'll be safe, but you've gotta stay with me."

The soldier pockets his small light, then guides her out. She can feel the man's arm firmly under hers, lifting, pulling her along with each step forward. She stays close to his side in a blur of pain, adrenalin, and stunned disbelief. They first move into the hallway. She's wedged in tight amongst half a dozen other armed men in full tactical. They regroup for only a moment before she feels a hand on her back pushing her forward.

Someone shines a light toward the end of the hall, and in the sharp glare, she glimpses Maggie's agonized face, then Shelly's frightened red eyes, but only for a second as the group swiftly ushers the girls out of view. Another brief pause, and then the soldier's hand grips her again. She sees the top of the staircase, a downward flow of helmets; she reaches out with her free hand and braces against the back of the man just in front of her. The stairs fly away beneath her feet—one flight, a turn, then another, they turn again, a third flight, and in seconds they're outside.

The grip on her arm tightens. The roughness of the man's uniform brushes against her elbow. His gear bumps and scrapes against her side as the two of them rush forward through the alley together. It's still so dark, she can't see, then she feels the man's breath in her ear: "We gotta move," he says. "Run with me."

Night air brushes across her face as the soles of her trainers hit against the uneven ground. The tight grip on her arm lifts and jerks and pulls her forward with each step. She runs through a city that is nothing but a dull, dark tumbling blur. Her battered body skips and trips and fights to keep running. They reach the end of another alley, then a left, a long right, maybe right again, she can't tell anymore, because everyone's so close, and they're all moving so fast. The open spaces between the buildings grow. Their pace quickens.

She knows she's in a full sprint, but inside her shock it's as if she's watching herself do it. In between her gasping breaths, she catches a fragment of a radio call. Then she hears the noise—The helicopter. Her legs pump, her lungs burn, the grip on her arm hurts, but she pushes herself harder toward the roaring sound.

A strong gust of wind buffets her; sand bites at her face. She shuts her eyes, but then the voice in her ear shouts above the rotors: "Move! Now!"

The hand on her arm lets go just as two more soldiers grab her, rush her forward, and then shove her up and then inside the helicopter. The sound is deafening as the rest of the team crowd in on either side of her. She glimpses only fractions of dull shapes inside near-total darkness. She's wedged in between them, the edges of their combat gear push into her bare arms. She can smell their sweat. Her ribs vibrate as the helicopter's turboshaft engines scream up to full power. A rapid, rising rush pulls at her gut as the chopper lifts off. Trish closes her eyes as her tears flow . . . It's real . . . my god it's real . . .

• • •

Josh slowly exhales as he leans back against the armored hull of an MRAP. He looks on with detached boredom as the Somali special forces troops he's been training for the past five months clean up the last of the drone strike. The bombed-out hulks of two transport trucks and four technicals have now been nearly picked clean. Evidence that will be used to justify additional funding, training, and arming of the Somali provisional government's elite unit.

His troops have worked steady shifts for the past twenty-six hours to painstakingly remove all traces of the forty-seven Al Shabaab jihadis the strike took out. They've confiscated any and all ammunition, along with weapons, serviceable or otherwise, and recovered any document fragments or electronic devices that managed to survive the thermobaric reaction. Which wasn't much, in the wake of a nano-thermite-fueled inferno unleashed by Hellfire missiles launched from an MQ-9 Reaper.

It's the sort of work that makes Josh glad he's officially an observer. But this particular strike is special. It's the biggest success he's pulled off since the mission began, and, truth be known, he's ecstatic. He'll leave nothing to chance. His superiors have been demanding higher body counts, and as the last of the plastic bags filled with charred and dismembered human remains are packed for transport—remains the families of the dead combatants will never see and will not be allowed to recover—Josh congratulates himself. You guys want a real war? Well fuck, that's exactly what I'm gonna deliver right into you greedy sons of bitch's dirty hands . . .

Josh slips a small leather pouch from his pocket and retrieves a few more fresh khat leaves. He rapidly rolls them into a tidy bundle between his palms, then deftly pops it into his mouth. He pushes the bundle into position with his tongue then bites down hard. The action sends the leaves' bitter juices flowing into his saliva glands, which, in turn, sends the plant's natural amphetamine rocketing straight to his brain.

Josh leans his head back against the armored vehicle and enjoys the first rush as the drug takes effect. Then he hears someone calling to him. He closes his eyes and grimaces . . . Fuck . . . what is it this time? He opens his eyes only when the voice repeats. He recognizes it as coming from one of his officers, and he's speaking in Somali. Josh swivels toward the approaching man as he leans away from the vehicle and then straightens.

"Sir," the officer repeats again, "there is a man here to see you; he says he knows you."

Josh looks past the young officer to the slender dark figure lurking a few meters back. "He's okay," Josh responds. "You can leave us alone."

Diric Abdirashid Abshir eyes the soldiers passing close to him before he focuses on Josh. He walks over, and then stands directly in front of the CIA operative before he shifts to English. "I was told men traveled through here," he says. "Who were they?"

Josh sighs. He shifts his weight then places his hands on his hips. "You can't come barging into my operation like this, man, what the fuck?"

Abshir's eyes narrow. "I am here, so now you will speak to me."

Josh folds his arms in front of him. "Okay, Diric, but make it quick. I have work to do."

"You saw two of my uncle's trucks. Who were the men driving them? Where did they go?"

Josh cocks his head slightly to one side before his face loses all expression. "We had two trucks come through here, but it was last night; it was over twelve hours ago. I don't know whose trucks they were, Diric, and I don't know who those guys were."

Abshir's jaw tightens as he leans close into Josh's face. "Do not speak to me with your fish-eating mouth."

Josh takes a step back while his hand moves to his .45. "You need to get a grip, man, you need to back the fuck off before I drop you right here and now."

Abshir lowers his eyes and briefly lifts his palms toward Josh as he moves back a step. He waits a moment before his eyes return to Josh. "You and my uncle worked together; he helped you to locate your enemy, the Al Shabaab fighters, so now you will help me locate my enemy."

Josh glances down at his feet as he relaxes his stance. "Yeah, I worked with your uncle; he was a good informant, but as you can see, I've been reassigned."

"You and my uncle made a lot of money together," Abshir continues. "Now he is dead, and the men you saw driving his trucks are the ones who killed him. I am the new leader of my clan, so now I am the one who is offering you a deal."

Josh briefly scratches his chin. "What kind of a deal?"

Chapter 18

No Good Deed . . .

"Mike, we're lost; we need to use the plugger." Seth lowers his flashlight and folds away Mike's map, then he digs the brick-sized GPS unit out from his kit. Mike sighs. He grips the wheel more tightly as he leans forward and strains to see beyond the patch of blank desert sparsely lit by the Toyota's headlamps.

He glances up at the rear view; the Chief's still following close behind him. Mike shifts his attention back to what lies ahead, which isn't much, only more sand-filled nothingness. It looks exactly like all of the rest of the sand-filled nothingness they've been driving through for the past several hours. Mike frowns at the meager circle of light just beyond his bumper, and the orange-colored blur passing under it. "We can't be that far off; have another look at the map."

"I'm using the plugger," Seth answers flatly. "We've been saving the battery for a reason, and here it is." Seth powers up the unit then plugs in its remote antenna. He unfolds the antenna's cable, reaches up through the truck's open window, and slaps the magnetic disc onto the roof of the pickup. Seth watches the unit's LCD display while the military-grade, encrypted GPS triangulates the signals from the cluster of satellites currently orbiting over-head.

"It's not a good idea, Seth," Mike grumbles.

Seth ignores Mike's warning and continues to watch the screen before Mike suddenly reaches over and grabs the unit out of his hands.

"What the fuck, Mike?"

Mike flips the unit off with his thumb, then lets it drop back into Seth's lap. "It's a bad idea," Mike says without looking at Seth.

Seth groans in protest before he reaches up and then jerks the antenna back inside. "Jesus Mike, we're lost, you can't—"

Seth's argument is cut short as the pickup sharply swings side-ways when Mike jerks the wheel hard left. "Hold on!" Mike shouts as he swerves to avoid the massive vehicle careening in from the right.

"Shit!" Seth barks as the huge truck then roars in so close to his window that he can see the glow of the driver's night vision goggles. "Shit! Shit!" Seth lets go of the plugger and grabs for his MP5.

The Toyota's rear wheels let loose in the sand. It fishtails, Mike compensates but a second huge truck rockets in from the left to block his path. He hits the brakes and slides to a stop just short of the vehicle's side door, while a thick cloud of dust fills the shafts of the Toyota's headlamps.

Seth starts to push open his door, his MP5 cocked and ready, when someone outside suddenly kicks it shut and the muzzle of an M4 carbine appears in front of his face. Mike slowly lays his P226 on the dash in plain sight, then moves his hands back to the wheel.

"Out of the truck, both of you, right now."

Mike notes the accent and then sighs . . . Shit . . . South African . . . just what we need . . . The guy standing outside Mike's window opens the driver's side door.

"Get the fuck out," he orders again.

The guy motions with the tip of his M4, its flash guard only inches from Mike's face. Mike keeps his hands in sight as he pushes open the door with his left elbow and slides out.

He straightens, then studies the grizzled face of a man not unlike himself. "Who the hell are you guys?" Mike asks.

The guy sneers back at Mike. "We'll be the ones asking the questions. Who's in charge?"

Mike smiles at the guy. "Former South African Defense Force, am I right?"

The guy ignores Mike, and instead, shifts his stance just enough that he can see Moss approaching. Mike swivels back to see that Ax has two more guys holding carbines on him, as he slowly walks forward with his hands held up. Fabri's just behind him, and walking with his hands folded behind his head.

"You guys mind taking it easy?" Moss asks. "We're transporting civilians, and they've been through hell already."

"It's okay, Mitch."

Ax shifts his attention and sizes up his counterpart. A man of medium height and average build waves off his men's aggressive posture. "You guys take a breather," he says before shouldering his weapon and then walking up to Moss. Close enough to have a quiet conversation but not so close that he'd find himself having to look up at Ax's six-foot four-inch frame the whole time. "You're a tough man to track down, Mr. Moss."

Moss lowers his hands to his hips and stares straight back at the guy. "You seem to have a lot more information than I do, so why don't you tell me why we're having this conversation."

The guy smiles. "Right, okay then, how much you getting for these hostages?"

Moss glares back at the guy. "We liberated these people from a pirate compound a couple of days ago; we're moving them across the Kenyan border to safety."

The guy's pale gray eyes narrow into a pair of thin, crinkled slits, while his bushy gray eyebrows fold together into a single wiry clump. "Yeah, whatever, I don't give a crap, I just wanna know how much you're gonna get for 'em, and who's paying you."

Moss sighs. "We aren't being paid a dime for these people."

The guy grins back at Moss, The smile rapidly widens, then he starts laughing. "Shit!" He pauses to laugh some more, before he stops and stares into Moss's face. "You're serious?" He twists back toward his men. "Is he serious?"

They all start to chuckle. "I don't think so," one of them pipes up, then a second chimes in. "I'm not buying it."

The guy with the bushy eyebrows turns back to Moss, "I think you're full of shit." He pulls a .45 pistol from his vest, steps in closer to Moss, and then points it at the base of Moss's neck. "I'm tired of fucking around. We've been tracking you guys, and it won't be for nothing, so who's paying you?"

Moss's expression goes ice cold. "Nobody is paying us."

"Stop! Stop this now! Right now!"

The guy looks past Moss, and spots Lars. "Get back in the truck, old man," he says.

Lars stops and stares at the guy with the bushy eyebrows as he raises a slender finger and points. "I know who you are; you're Simon Schmeck."

"What of it?" Simon answers. "Get back in the truck before you get hurt."

The old Swede's expression hardens as he plants his feet and stands his ground. "No . . ." he says. Lars glances over at Moss, then stares back at Simon. "It's you and your men who are leaving."

Simon cocks his head to one side and smirks before he lowers his pistol and then holsters it. "Excuse me?" he says.

Moss shifts his focus to the elderly Swede. "Lars, please, get back in the truck. You shouldn't be here."

"No I won't," Lars responds. "Mr. Moss," he continues as he stares at Simon, "you don't know who these men are, but I do. They are South African mercenaries. They work for a private security company. They were in charge of security at the mining company I worked for." Lars then looks directly up at Moss. "These are dangerous men, Mr. Moss."

"We used to work for the security company," Simon corrects, "but not anymore."

Moss quickly scans the scene, then returns his attention back to Simon Schmeck, "These F350 armored personnel carriers, they still have the company's logo."

Simon smirks. "Part of our severance package."

"So your plan was to track us down, take these civilians and collect ransom?" Moss asks.

"Ransom?" Simon scoffs. "Who do you think we are? We're legitimate!" the man complains. "We aren't the fucking pirates! We're here for the cash reward!" Simon looks down at the ground while he shakes his head. Then he focuses back on Moss. "We're businessmen, same as anyone else, but we just happen to be in the war business."

Simon rubs his hand across his balding, gray head before he locks eyes with Moss. "I've been fighting Africa's wars for thirty years, Mr. Moss. There's hardly a scrap of this continent I haven't left my tracks in. I've fought for, and against, countries that don't even exist anymore."

Simon pauses, He lifts his hands to his waist as he steps in closer to Moss's face. "Wars are like weeds in Africa; as soon as one dies out, you can bet more will sprout up. Somalia's tapped out, so we're moving on. Nigeria's where the real action is." He looks over at Mike. "We could use a guy like you. The Nigerian government's recruiting contractors to take out Jamā'at Ahl as-Sunnah, and I'm talking serious cash—millions, mate . . . I can cut you in, so what do you say?"

Simon doesn't wait for an answer from Mike, but instead, he gestures toward the three, 385 horsepower, four-door, armored Ford F350s. The new trucks sport matching, desert tan paint, and are the ultimate technical. Custom built in the States, each one is mounted with an armored gun box and a heavy machine gun turret. "We've got air-conditioned comfort in these beauties," Simon adds. "You can all come along with us; we'll get everybody safely across the Kenyan border, and all you need to do in exchange is hand over your contact."

Moss frowns. "There is no contact, Simon, there is no money. We're only trying to do the right thing here; we just want to help these people."

"That's bullshit and you know it!" Simon jerks his pistol from its holster just as Lars lunges for his arm.

"Stop!" Lars screams. "He's telling the truth!"

Moss tries to reach for Lars but the shot from Simon's .45 has already gone off. The elderly Swede briefly utters something in his native language, staggers back, then slumps to the ground.

Simon ignores the unarmed man he's just shot while his narrow eyes rapidly shift around. Then he steps back, lifts his hand high above his head, and twirls his finger. "Load up, fellas, we're out of here."

Dropping down beside Lars, Moss pulls his flashlight from his vest and shines it on the wound. "Seth!"

Seth already has his med kit out, He pushes past the departing South African mercs to get to Lars, then he gets a look at him—Jesus . . .

Jannik and Niklas approach. The two young Germans are on either side of a weeping Elsa, while Mike stands silently beside Fabri and Andrea. Moss helps Seth roll Lars on to his back, and as they do, Elsa cries out at the sight of the hemorrhaging chest wound.

Seth rips open a blood clotting patch and places it over the gaping hole left by the .45. He looks up at Moss. "Don't put too much pressure on this." Seth then leans in and examines Lars' eyes with a small light. He feels for a pulse—He's got nothing . . . Seth knows Lars is already gone, but he continues to work anyway—because Elsa is watching.

Mike hears the three armored truck's turbo-diesel engines roar to life behind him. The old DEVGRU warrior then pivots toward the sound. He stands in the darkness and looks on as the three huge trucks' running lights all suddenly blink on. The armored F350s then pull out, one by one, in a glowing red halo of dust.

Mike watches them leave, while part of him, a pretty good-sized chunk actually, would like nothing better than to swing one of the fully loaded fifty-cals in their direction and open her up. Mike grits his teeth at the thought; twenty years ago he would've done it already. But back then, he did a lot of selfish, crazy shit. Mike sighs in disgust as he observes the cluster of lights rumble off into the blackness of a Somali desert night before he shifts back toward Moss. Ax has noticed Mike; he was watching too, but he doesn't speak, he just stares back at his ace sniper. The Chief doesn't have to say a word. Mike already knows what's next, he knows the Chief won't leave a man behind, not even a dead one.

Chapter 19

Wrong Time Wrong Place

Malcolm Rafferty stands at the shoulder of his helmsman while he calmly directs a constellation of simultaneous activity as Fearless arrives in the bustling industrial port of Antwerp KEMBA. The urban sprawl of Mombasa lies just beyond the three-hundred-and-eighteen-foot-long science vessel's bow. Early morning smog cloaks Kenya's second largest city in a veil of musty yellow. Rafferty looks down from the bridge and observes his crewmen busily securing lines on the foredeck. Then he hears Murray call in from the stern—"All secure aft."

Razz scans through his list of the final checks before he orders Pete to shut down the engines. He relieves his helmsman, then reaches for the ship's log. Stepping over to the polished mahogany chart table at the center of the bridge, Razz opens the logbook and begins recording the day's entry.

"So when do we leave?"

Razz lays his pen down, looks up at Murray, but says nothing.

"We're going after them," Murray says. "We have to; they should've made it across the border by now."

Razz closes the log book, straightens, then looks Murray in the eye: "We'll be needing transportation," he says.

Murray flashes a brief grin. "Already have it sorted; should be showing up any time now."

A thin, cautious smile appears on Rafferty's face. "Gear and weapons?" he asks.

"Got that all sorted as well."

Razz folds his arms in front of him then leans back against the chart table. "So who's coming with us?"

"Cal."

Razz nods in approval: "Good choice."

• • •

Moss rests his arms across the wheel of the Toyota while he stares out at a seemingly endless, open desert in front of him. "Have we crossed the border yet?" he asks.

Seth has his eye on the plugger's LCD screen. "Just a couple more klicks, Chief, almost there."

Moss glances up at the rear view mirror. Mike's not following too close behind, but it's not because of the lead truck's speed. Ax is taking it slow. It's because he's got four passengers stuffed into his truck, while Mike and Fabri only have one lying in the bed of theirs.

Moss squints against the glare while the scorched horizon ahead shimmers and dances in the furnace-like heat. They left the road behind hours ago, but you'd never know it. The two trucks steadily trace their way across a featureless sea of rusty sand stretching as far as the eye can see in all directions. A scene topped off by a stark, cloudless sky, Africa's ever-blistering sun, and somewhere out there, although completely invisible, an international border.

Once upon a time, some European cartographers stood in a room together and calculated an imaginary line across a desert thousands of miles away from where they were. And, unlike most places, where a mountain range, a valley, a river, or some other geographic feature aided in the decision as to exactly where such an imaginary line would be located, here they didn't have much to go on. So at some point, somebody, somewhere, took a ruler and just drew a straight line across a sheet of paper.

Like the rest of Africa, and the Middle East for that matter, the historic boundaries between indigenous, ethnic populations were never a consideration when rich Europeans divvied up the spoils of their conquests. The lines were drawn, the continent was sliced up, until eventually, the lines got some Western bureaucrat's seal of approval and became official borders.

"Here it is, Chief." Seth holds the plugger up close to his face and watches the steadily shifting degrees of longitude and latitude flash across the GPS unit's LCD screen. "Coming up in three . . . two . . . one . . ." Seth looks over at Moss and smiles. "Welcome to Kenya."

Moss allows himself a slight grin at the news. "Okay Seth, power up the satphone."

• • •

Left turn, then turn right onto freeway . . . Murray grimaces from behind the wheel at the mass of rush hour traffic stacked up in front of him. "At this rate, we'll lose half a day just getting out of the city."

In two hundred meters, make a Left turn, then turn right onto freeway . . .

Murray glances down at the Land Rover's sat-nav screen. "Yes dear, I heard you the first time."

Cal leans forward from the rear seat. "I checked the map and the handheld. I don't see a faster route; we might as well do as she says."

Razz suddenly holds up his hand. "Hey guys, we just got a text on the satphone."

"Hoo-rah!" Murray shouts before he slaps the steering wheel. "It's about damned time!"

Cal lets loose with a loud whistle as he claps his hands. "Fuck yeah!"

Murray then reaches across the center console and fist-bumps a grinning Razz.

Razz looks back at the satphone's display, then glances toward the back seat. "Cal, write these numbers down and plug 'em into your GPS."

Cal pulls a pen out from the pocket of his desert tan T-shirt. "You got it, fire away."

• • •

Mike lifts the last jerry can as high as possible just to be sure every drop of remaining gas drains into the tank of the Toyota.

"Is that it?" asks Moss.

Mike lowers the empty can. "Yep, that's the last of it."

Moss wearily rests his hands on his hips as he gazes ahead and down the empty desert track that supposedly leads to civilization. "It'll be enough," he says. Moss shifts back toward Mike. "'We only have twenty-eight klicks to go before we reach the rendezvous point."

Mike wipes the sweat from his brow with the back of his hand. "Dadaab . . . have you ever seen it?"

Moss searches Mike's weathered face. "No, but the United Nations operates a relief facility there. It's the closest thing to assistance we're gonna get for these people; we don't have much choice."

Mike screws the top back onto the empty fuel can then hands it over to Jannik. "Well, I've been there and—" Mike then cuts off the rest of his own sentence. He glances over at the people gathered near the back of the truck, and for the first time, he sees a hopefulness he doesn't want to risk snuffing out. His eyes rapidly return to Moss. "Yeah, you're right, Chief, Dadaab's our best bet. We better get going."

It's late in the day when the ragged outer edges of Dadaab, the world's largest refugee camp, become visible through the veil of a shimmering desert furnace. Opened in 1992, the camp now hosts a mostly Somali population of nearly 350,000, officially registered refugees, but in reality, the camp has swelled into a makeshift metropolis of over half a million inhabitants.

As Mike drives, Moss looks out at the passing clusters of crude, dome-shaped dwellings divided into tidy grids by European architects. The dwellings mostly consist of United Nations-issued, temporary structures, of which many have been here for decades. Whole generations have been born and raised inside Dadaab.

The landscape is dotted with thousands upon thousands of UN-issued, white plastic tarps intended to reflect away the intense desert heat. They rise above the flat plane of orange sand like tiny dome-shaped islands. At first only handfuls appeared at the camp's farthest fringes, but then the clusters grew in number until counting them would be a meaningless activity.

The two technicals, carrying three exhausted special operations forces veterans, five liberated Europeans, and one rapidly ripening corpse, roll in through the camp's crowded central road, a dusty track lined with a tight assortment of equally drab and dusty prefab structures. The two vehicles' forward motion steadily slows the closer they get to the center of the camp until Mike is forced to inch the pickup along through swarms of bustling refugees. They eventually reach the downtown of the ramshackle city pieced together from surplus hand-me-downs and scrap.

Seth rests his arm on the doorframe and studies the empty faces drifting by his window. Many of the refugees simply ignore the two passing trucks, while others stare suspiciously back with a collective, wordless expression that can be summed up with one statement—You don't belong here . . .

It's the same sort of look Seth remembers from his time in Afghanistan, and especially in Iraq. He felt as out of place then, as he does now, but just like back then, he has a job to do, a mission to complete, and the people looking back at him aren't a part of it.

Fabri strains to look out through the truck's grimy windshield. "Is that the flag?" He glances over at Seth before he shifts back, and stares once more at the road ahead. "What do you think?"

Seth leans out the window in order to gain a clear view before he drops back inside the cab of the Toyota. "Yeah, that's it." He sees the truck Mike's driving pull over in front of an unpainted, single-story cinder block building. The light blue flag of the United Nations hangs loose and lifeless from a pole mounted atop the building's corrugated metal roof.

Fabri steers the truck in next to Mike, hits the brakes, and then cuts the engine just as Moss steps over and leans in from the outside. "Seth and Mike are gonna wait with the trucks. I'll walk everyone inside, see if I can get some help."

Seth stares up at Moss. "Sure thing, Chief."

Jannik, Niklas, and Andrea help Elsa climb down from the bed of the pickup. Fabri watches silently from the driver's seat as they all walk slowly by Seth's window. He then shrugs with indifference as he pops open his driver's side door. Seth watches Fabri get out and then trail after Moss and the others.

The covered porch of the building is lined on either side with benches packed full of people waiting. Moss walks past the benches and through the open door. Inside he finds a single large room stuffed with yet more benches, and all of them stacked to capacity with people waiting. Along the base of the room's outer walls, people sit clustered tightly together on the floor, while a few others stand, but all their eyes seem to be drawn intently to the strangers who have just entered.

Moss strides to the back of the room, and to where a slender, balding man in his late thirties with light brown hair sits behind a large table. The man is quietly speaking in Somali with a woman holding a sleeping infant when he catches sight of Moss.

His eyes narrow and his lips tighten as he observes the stinking soldier who has just interrupted him. He looks back at the woman seated beside him and politely excuses himself. She briefly glances up at Moss, then turns away as if to shield her baby, while the UN worker shifts forward in his chair, and then gently folds his hands together on the table.

"And who might you be?" the man asks in perfect English.

Ax clears his throat. "Alex Moss," he answers, "and excuse me for interrupting you sir, but my men and I liberated these people three days ago. They were hostages being held by pirates. We've traveled a long way to get here, and we could use your help."

"My help?" The man's tone is incredulous. He unfolds his hands, then turns his palms upwards. "Do you see all of these people here?" he asks, before he folds his hands again and then leans in slightly toward Moss. "All of the people that you see here need my help, Mr. Moss, and they've been waiting here for a long time."

Moss sighs as he raises his hands to his hips. "I apologize, sir, but we have an emergency situation going on. Is there someone else we can speak to? Is there another facility you can direct me to?"

The man shakes his head in bewilderment, then he stares back up at Moss. "You people think you're more important than everyone else in this camp? Do you think that possibly, these people sitting, and waiting patiently all around you here, that perhaps they also struggled to escape conflict?"

The man leans back in his chair. "I am currently the only person left still manning this facility, sir. Every other relief organization has pulled out for lack of security. Médecins Sans Frontières was forced to close their hospital. They've since relocated back to Nairobi. I have no paid staff, I have no superior on site. There is no law here. I remain only because these people have no one else. This United Nations outpost is the only facility with the authority to process refugee requests for asylum."

Moss bends forward and then rests his hands on the edge of the table. He leans in to the face of the beleaguered aid worker.

"We aren't here to request asylum, sir; I'm just trying to get these people home."

The man's expression suddenly softens. "If this is truly the case, Mr. Moss, then I must inform you that you have arrived in the wrong place."

Chapter 20

Heads Up

The unpaved road that snakes past the front porch of the United Nations' outpost is thick with a heavy flow of pedestrian traffic. A steady stream of people move past Mike and Seth with the sort of silent mindfulness one applies to the mean-looking dog in the neighbor's yard. Then, of course, there is the decomposing body lying in the back of Mike's truck, which doesn't improve his image one bit. For the most part though, people don't seem to be paying much attention at all to the pair of armed commandos dressed in full battle tactical, leaning against two armed technicals.

Under the circumstances, Mike figures there's nothing all that surprising about the locals lack of reaction. In fact, one could say it's even typical, in a part of the world where armed military are a common sight, and the open-air market is just as likely to have a vendor with a collection of fully automatic machine guns neatly laid out on a blanket, as a woman selling melons.

Mike leans back against the door of the Toyota while he watches people pass by, and he contemplates the reasons why he gave up smoking. At the moment, he can't find intelligent meaning in any of them. Mike methodically scans the crowd, shifting his field of view from left to right and then back again while he sifts through the sea of faces, and processes what he sees.

He searches for signal, for anything out of place, while a long afternoon sun beats down on the back of his neck and bakes his body armor. It's an unpleasant and oppressively harsh situation, and there's any number of places he'd rather be, but he's on a job, and the job's gotta get done. If somebody really wanted to know his opinion though, he'd have to say that given a choice between an ass-freezing combat zone, and a roasting cooker—he'll take the cooker every time.

Why? Because he's learned through decades of hard-won experience that his personal comfort isn't worth a rat's turd in a battle. War sucks, no matter what type of weather you happen to be fighting in, but what sucks the most about it is getting killed, and one thing's for certain, he shoots better when he's good and warm.

Mike scans across the flowing river of passersby once more before he glances over toward Seth. He catches Seth's attention just as one enterprising soul stops and offers to sell the veteran combat medic a bottle of water. Mike watches Seth turn the guy down. As much as Mike could use a drink, given the choice between dehydration, and a high likelihood of contracting hepatitis-E, Mike's gonna stick with dehydrated.

Mike shifts his weight. He's got his right hand lightly resting on the grip of his P226, while his MP5 hangs loose off his left shoulder—out of habit more than anything else. He continues to observe the gaunt faces of the refugees that steadily flow past him. He's guessing there must be thousands on their way to who knows where, and that's the unfortunate truth of it, because they're all stuck in a hell hole of a place that's in the middle of a godforsaken wasteland. To be honest, as much as he'd like to feel sympathy for these people, he doesn't, because he lost that part of himself a long time ago.

He peers through the crowd and briefly locks eyes with Seth again. Seth looks in pain, and uncomfortable, as he leans against the side of the second truck with his MP5 strapped across his chest, and his arms folded over it as if he were resting them on the edge of a table. His eyes never stop moving though, which lets Mike know, that in spite his injury, Seth's on high alert, just as he is.

The old soldier sighs as he shifts away from Seth, and then redirects his attention toward the open door of the UN outpost, which lies only a few meters away from where he's currently standing. He's actually staring at the opening, in fact, when his instinct picks up something strange. It's a noise, and it's of the sort that strikes him as being somehow out of place.

Mike pauses as he focuses his attention on the odd, tinkling sound. It's almost mechanical, something like a high-pitched clatter, and steadily rising in volume—even above the low-grade din of the crowd moving past him. He turns toward it, and then fine tunes his attention . . .

It's metal against metal, and it's coming from just above his head. Mike shifts his gaze toward the noise just as a small object clears the edge of the corrugated roof above him. His eyes catch sight of a flash of sunlight glinting off the object's surface as it swiftly falls, and then he sees it again when it hits the ground near his feet with a harmless light thump . . .

Mike stares down at the shiny, fresh 7.62×39mm cartridge as it glints in the sand near the tip of his combat boot . . . Shit . . .

"Heads up Seth!" Mike shouts as he draws his pistol and then raises it up toward the roofline. He locks on to a pair of armed targets, he aims, fires—one shot, one down. He moves his arm slightly for a second shot, fires again—Two down. Mike spins back toward Seth just as the thick crowd of refugees that surround the two men erupts into a shrieking, screaming stampede.

As the two shots fired outside are heard indoors, Moss spins toward the two Italians and the pair of Germans. "Stay here," he orders. "Get down on the floor, stay down, and stay inside." Moss draws his sidearm and is pushing his way in the direction of the room's single door when he hears Fabri call out to him. He pauses to look back at the Italian Army veteran. "I need you to stay here," he shouts. "Stay—here," he repeats before he turns away, and then folds into the room's panicked crowd.

The overcrowded UN outpost is in full panic as Moss fights to get outside. Everyone who was waiting is now on their feet, and, just like Moss, rushing the single exit. As he pushes toward the door, Moss hears a second exchange of gunfire coming from the street, and this time, it's the telltale trill of a compact, 9mm submachine gun. The sound reverberates through the building while he shoves people out of his way and makes for the opening leading outside.

Seth crouches behind the front bumper of the second truck, and beneath the storm of lead being traded between Mike, and a second group of combatants on the roof across the street. He listens to the rapid exchange of fire. He knows Mike's switched to his MP5, he knows there are more than two shooters on the rooftop opposite Mike's position, and he knows Mike's 30-round clip is almost dry. But he's pinned down, and there's nothing he can do about it until something changes.

Searching for Ax, Seth rechecks the door of the UN outpost, but he sees only the desperate faces of people trying to escape the firefight. They pour out through the narrow gap by the dozen before stumbling onto the building's front porch. Once there, they realize pretty quick they've made a terrible mistake, but it's too late, and they can't turn back.

Seth picks up the face of a young woman. She's running right for him, as they each, briefly, lock eyes. He quickly motions for her to get down on the ground, but in that instant she's knocked flat on her back. Seth saw the blood when she took the headshot. His pulse spikes as his eyes rapidly pass from her empty shoe, to the dying twitch in the toes of her left foot . . . Fuck me . . .

Seth risks a peek before he pushes through the intense pain in his thigh and forces himself onto his feet. His aim is a blur as he joins Mike, and opens up on the roofline across the street. A few seconds later, Seth's finger is still firmly on the trigger of his MP5 when he senses a hand suddenly grip his shoulder, while a familiar, gruff voice barks into his ear. "Seth, you got 'em," Mike says. "Enough now, you got 'em."

Mike pats the medic's shoulder before he turns back toward the outpost and spots the Chief emerge from the shrieking throng still fighting to escape. He clears the doorway while hundreds of panicked bystanders around Mike and Seth continue to flee in all directions. Mike locks eyes with Moss, but he merely shrugs in a moment of disgust, a moment that is shared equally between them. Then Mike turns back to the task at hand as he jerks the spent clip from his MP5, and then shoves in a fresh one.

Pushing his way over to the pair of Toyotas, Moss shifts his attention to Seth. "Are you okay?" Moss asks.

Seth groans at the raw wound in his leg as he leans back against the pickup. He nods a silent response back at Moss before he winces against his pain. He breathes in deep and then shifts his gaze to the rooftop, to where the bodies of the three men he just killed lie at odd angles across the corrugated metal sheeting. Seth stares at their corpses for a brief moment, but the icy cold chill the sudden revelation gives him doesn't feel good at all.

Ax is watching Seth when he notices the fresh blood seeping through the leg of his trousers. "We need to patch you up," Moss says. "Where's your med kit?"

Seth glances down at his bleeding leg. "Shit, I ripped the goddammed staples."

"I'll get the kit," Mike says.

But Seth suddenly holds up his hand. "No, don't."

"And why the fuck not?" Mike growls.

Seth points. "There's no time: look."

Moss shields his eyes against the glare as he looks toward the far end of the street, across the dust-shrouded mob of heads and the two fully loaded technicals heading their way. "Shit." Moss swivels back to Lars's corpse lying in the bed of the Toyota before he shifts toward Mike. "Help me get his body out of here," he orders.

Mike's inside the bed of the truck when he catches a glimpse of someone reaching past him to help. Mike looks up to find Fabri's sober face staring back at him, but before Mike can even open his mouth, he hears the Chief.

"I told you to stay inside."

Fabri grabs the old man's body by the ankles while Mike quickly lifts from inside the bed of the truck. "You're not Rambo," Fabri says without looking up. He helps Mike drag the body from the bed of the pickup. "You need all the help you can get."

Moss lets out a growl as he leans in to help with the corpse. The three men swiftly move the body over to the empty covered porch of the UN outpost. They unceremoniously drop it near the doorway before they race back to the two trucks.

Moss returns to find that Seth's managed to wedge himself in behind one of the heavy machine guns. He already has the loaded fifty-cal cocked and ready and pointed in the direction of the approaching technicals when he calls out to Moss, "You're driving," Seth says, but Moss isn't listening, and instead, the chief's stopped dead in his tracks.

Seth painfully forces himself to twist back, and then look in the opposite direction, and toward the other end of the street to what Moss is staring at. Seth does a double take before it fully registers that what he's looking at is an American-made, armored vehicle. It's flanked by two more technicals, and the whole stinking monstrosity is roaring right at 'em. A shutter of dread jabs Seth right through the gut. "Oh fuck no . . ." he moans. "That can't be what I think it is."

"It's an MRAP," Mike announces flatly as he adjusts himself behind the second fifty-caliber machine gun. "Fabri!" He shouts. "Get us the fuck outta here!"

Fabri is already regretting his moment of valor as he nervously climbs in behind the wheel of the Toyota. He fumbles to buckle a ragged seatbelt then get the engine started. "Si, si, sto guidando . . . sto guidando," he rapidly repeats. The Italian then eyes the truck's nearly empty fuel gage. "Mama mia . . ."

Moss climbs inside the second truck and fires up the engine. "Stay with me!" he shouts across at Fabri. Moss then shoves the truck into reverse, and spins it around, before he backs up close to the now deserted porch of the UN outpost. He revs the engine before slamming the vintage Toyota into gear and mashing the pedal to the floor.

Fabri is still getting turned in the right direction when he sees Moss steer his truck, with Seth braced inside the bed, straight up the steps of the pre-fab structure across the street. Without hesitation, Moss then plows the Toyota pickup right through its front entrance.

"We're taking fire!" Mike barks back at Fabri before he lets loose with a volley of fifty-caliber rounds. "Get us out of here!"

Fabri's pounding heartbeat lumps up into his throat as he grips the wheel and shoves his foot to the floor. The vintage truck's engine lets out a high-pitched whine, while the rear tires spin and it lunges forward. He's unable to breathe as he peers ahead through the truck's dingy windshield as the smashed-out facade of the pre-fab structure races toward him.

The front wheels hit the building's four rows of wood plank steps and bounce so violently that the steering wheel is nearly wrenched free from Fabri's hands. Mike rides inside the truck's bucking rear bed, clinging to the welded machine gun mount. The truck's body twists and lurches as if in an effort to toss Mike out. Fabri briefly closes his eyes the moment the truck tops the steps and then skids through the gaping hole Moss left for him.

Once inside, Mike twists forward then pushes himself upright and above the cab. Just enough to see what lies ahead. The vibrating clatter of the wood floor passing rapidly beneath the truck's wheels rattles up through the bed and then pounds into his knees. Mike sizes up the exit as Fabri races the truck through the center of the empty, darkened structure. The bright, glaring opening at the other end looks high off the ground, maybe too high. "Ah shit," Mike complains, before he ducks back down and then braces for impact.

A blinding flash stings Fabri's eyes when the truck reaches the opening and the desert sun reappears on the other side. Fabri holds his foot to the floor as the truck flies out through the building's shredded back wall.

The seatbelt pulls at his waist during the fraction of time the truck is airborne before the front wheels drop nearly two meters and hammer into the ground. The impact plunges the Toyota's front bumper into the desert sending a wave of sand up over the hood and then showering across Mike. The truck then continues forward while the old DEVGRU warrior tenaciously hangs on.

The impact sends Fabri's face into the steering wheel like a hard punch to the nose but he doesn't let up on the gas for one second. The Italian army veteran then drives headlong toward the cloud of dust already cutting a path across the desert in front of him. He knows it's Moss, and no matter what, he's not gonna loose him.

• • •

"Still no answer?" Murray glances briefly over at Razz before his eyes return to the congested road ahead. He currently has the Land Rover clocking at 120 kph as he speeds along Kenya's B8 motorway toward Dadaab. He'd like to go even faster, but at the moment, the pace of surrounding traffic is holding him back.

Razz lays the satphone back up on the dash. "They've got their phone turned off; must be saving the battery." Razz leaves the remote antenna plugged in just in case. The cable connecting the phone to the magnetic disc clamped to the roof of the Land Rover runs up through Razz's window, which is cracked open just enough to allow for it, but not so much that the air conditioning can easily escape.

Razz looks back at Cal. "You spent some time here, didn't you?"

Cal grimaces as some pretty ugly memories suddenly flood back into his brain, specifically, the time Al Qaida blew up the U.S. Embassy in Nairobi, and his team was the first one on site. "Sure, but it was quite a few years ago," Cal answers.

"What about Dadaab? Were you ever out there?"

Cal rests his left elbow on the back of Murray's seat and leans forward toward Razz. "We drove a convoy through there once; it's just a big refugee camp . . ." Cal pauses a moment. "Actually, it's a group of camps all clustered together. Even back then it was more like a city; by now it must be huge."

"Is it dangerous?" Razz asks.

Cal rolls his lips tightly together as his right hand rubs across his chin. "Hmm, well, it's a rough place for sure. Our intel showed Al Shabaab uses it as a base, but I think the guys'll be fine. There's a lot of relief organizations operating out of there, so it can't be too bad."

Chapter 21

Boom

Jannik slowly stands up from the dull, gray painted plywood floor of the UN outpost and then looks around. He finds the entire building deserted with the exception of himself, Niklas, Andrea, and Elsa.

Elsa's the first to notice Jannik's movement. She observes for a moment before she reaches over and gently touches her hand to Niklas' arm. "What is he doing?" she asks in English.

Niklas focuses his attention on his partner as the young student walks to the center of the room, stops and then looks up at the ceiling. "What the hell do you think you're doing?" Niklas demands in German. "Sit back down and wait as you were told."

Jannik ignores Niklas, and when Niklas protests again, Jannik simply holds up his hand. "Be silent for once, will you?"

Niklas sighs in disgust. "You're going to get us all killed," he says.

"Just listen . . ."

Niklas frowns, then he waits a moment. "I don't hear anything."

Jannik crinkles his nose as he rests his hands on his hips and continues to stare up at the unfinished wood rafters.

"You've got some stupid idea in your head," Andrea says in English. He climbs to his feet, then steps over to where Jannik is standing. He moves in close until he's directly in front of him, then Andrea lifts his hand and waves a finger in Jannik's face. "I can see it cooking there behind those pretty blue eyes of yours."

Jannik says nothing as he simply turns his back toward Andrea and proceeds to stride off in the direction of the door. Andrea watches Jannik leave before lifting both hands in exasperation. "What?" he calls out. "Did I hurt one of your precious little feelings?"

At that moment Jannik simply holds up his right hand again. He raises it high above his head as he continues to walk, and with his middle finger prominently pointed back in Andrea's direction.

Andrea chuckles at the rude gesture. "This I understand." He spins back just as Niklas brushes past him.

"What?" the Italian demands.

Andrea turns and then tracks Niklas as he heads for the door. "Now you too. Niklas?" Andrea scoffs. "I thought you were the smart one."

"You're not helping," Niklas growls.

Andrea shrugs before he turns back to find that Elsa has quietly seated herself on one of the empty benches. Then Andrea notices the anger in her face, and he knows it's not for Jannik. He shrugs again. "What?"

Niklas strides over to where Jannik is standing near the open doorway. "Tell me what you are doing," he demands in German.

Jannik shifts back toward Niklas. "They've left us here, don't you understand?" he says. "We're on our own now."

Niklas takes in a long breath as he contemplates what Jannik's just said. "No," he answers, "they wouldn't do that."

"How do you know this? Can you say for certain?"

Niklas pauses a moment. "No but—"

"My point exactly."

Niklas frowns. "So what do you think we should do then?" he asks. "Hitchhike to Nairobi?"

"Don't be ridiculous," Jannik quips. "We have several options. We just need to use our heads, but we will need protection."

"Protection?" Niklas scoffs. "You mean guns?" He leans in and then eyes his partner more closely. "And where are we to magically find these weapons?" he questions. "And also, of course, the correct ammunition?"

After hearing Niklas's words, a tight grin briefly crosses Jannik's face. He lifts his hand and then points a finger straight up.

Niklas glances upwards toward the roof before he stares again at his partner. "You believe they are still up there?" he asks.

Jannik folds his arms in front of him. "There is only one way to find out."

Niklas briefly evaluates the determination in his partner's face. Then he sighs, steps over to the open doorway and peers out. He looks to the right, then stares left, before he rocks back inside to face Jannik. "The street is deserted," he announces. "There is no one out here."

"Let me see," Jannik says. He steps outside, and quickly catches sight of the body of Lars lying near the outside wall. It's only slightly to the right of the doorway. The day-old corpse is just a few feet away. It lies fully exposed, stiffened and prone, and on one side, facing the building. Jannik quickly covers his nose before he steps back inside. "There is one person out there," he tells Niklas.

Jannik silently watches as Niklas first nods in agreement, then swiftly turns away. Walking back over to where Elsa is seated, he kneels down directly in front of the elderly woman, then Jannik overhears his partner speak to her. His voice is soft, sensitive, respectful. Then Jannik watches as Niklas reaches in and gently grasps her hand, before he stands again, and returns to where Jannik is standing.

"I believe the best way to access the roof will be from the rear of the building," Niklas announces, "so let's go."

The two Germans exit the building to the left and then make their way cautiously through a narrow alleyway that lies between the closely built structures. Once they reach the rear corner of the building, Jannik leans forward. He briefly peeks out and around, then quickly shifts back.

Niklas reads the fear on Jannik's face. "What is it?" he asks, before he pushes past him in order to see for himself.

Jannik grimaces as he watches Niklas disappear around the corner. He takes in a deep breath . . . This was a stupid idea . . .

Niklas steps in close, and then stares down at a granular patch of fresh blood forming in the sand beneath the edge of the corrugated metal roof. He then looks up at the dead man partially hanging from its edge. The Somali man's body is suspended by chance only a couple of feet above his head.

The man's right arm, with its opened, empty hand, extends outward into the air and beyond the metal sheeting as if he had been reaching for something. An AK-47 dangles down from a strap stretched across the dead man's shoulders. The machine gun drapes within easy reach in fact, and practically right in front of

Niklas's face. He eyes the weapon before he excitedly spins back to find Jannik standing behind him. "This was a good idea," Niklas says.

Niklas then steps back in order to better see the roof in its entirety. He studies it a moment before he looks toward Jannik again. "Help me up, will you?" He steps forward and then, reaching up with both hands, he grips the edge of the corrugated metal. "Give me a boost."

Jannik glances up briefly at the roof before he reluctantly steps in and then shoulders Niklas up onto the corrugated metal sheeting. Niklas first manages to swing his right leg up and then over the edge as Jannik continues to push from below. With awkward coordination, Niklas eventually rolls himself onto the roof's hot metal surface.

He steadies himself, then maneuvers into a kneeling position before he cautiously goes to work relieving the dead man of his weapon and ammunition belt. Niklas lowers the gun first, then the ammunition belt. Jannik takes the AK from Niklas. It's heavier than he thought it would be. Next he grabs the ammunition belt. Jannik then lays both the gun, and its ammunition, on the ground, but when he looks back toward the roofline, Niklas has already vanished from view.

"What are you doing?" Jannik calls out.

Niklas briefly reappears. "There is another body near the top; I can see his gun. I'm going to get it."

Jannik frowns up at Niklas. "But—"

Niklas ignores Jannik's protest as he quickly turns away to focus on the task of inching his way up the sloping corrugated roof. The thin, overlapping edges of sheet metal bite into the tips of his fingers while his shoes scrape against its hot surface. He can clearly see the body of a second man sprawled out just above him. At the most, he estimates, it can only be four meters away.

As he draws in closer, Niklas feels pity for the dead Somali. He's dressed poorly in a pair of ragged trousers and a grimy T-shirt. A shirt now soaked in his own blood. Niklas is careful to stay clear of the thin trickle that slowly makes its way past him and down one of the corrugated sheeting's many channels.

He crawls up the roof a bit further until he's close enough that he could now easily touch the corpse. It's at this moment that Niklas suddenly realizes something. The annoying sound that he's been listening to is actually his own heart pounding inside his chest.

Niklas gulps hard, while his ears pulse with the throbbing beat. His hands shake as he reaches in and then hurriedly unbuckles the dead man's ammunition belt. The man's eyes are frozen upward in a wide-open stare, as if his final question had a surprising answer.

He pulls the belt free, and then swings it over his shoulder. He finds the small effort has left him gasping as if he'd just finished a sprint. Niklas shifts back on his heels, takes a deep breath, then moves in again. He starts to remove the AK-47, but quickly finds the task more difficult than he expected.

Niklas pulls hard at the strap wrapped beneath the body. The sudden force partially lifts the corpse, which sends the head slumping forward. It's at this moment that Niklas realizes the dead man's head is now resting against his left shoulder. He works frantically to wrestle the gun from its dead owner, and nearly gives up in a panic, before he finally yanks the rifle free, while the dead man's head drops back to strike the metal surface with a thud.

Niklas struggles to regain his breath as he slings the liberated AK across his back. Then he steadies the fully loaded ammo belt over his left shoulder. He's only just begun his return when the sudden, percussive beat of rapid weapons fire echoes above Dadaab.

He drops down and then flattens himself against the hot surface. He tries to breathe, and he listens. A few moments pass before he realizes the gunfire isn't close by at all, but some distance away. Niklas pushes himself back upright until he can just see above the roof's peak. He scans the bleak landscape until his eyes stop at the rising dust left by two pickups. He's certain they're the same two trucks he's been riding in for the past three days.

The Toyotas look to be more than a kilometer away, and they're not alone; other vehicles are chasing them—Jannik is right . . . we are on our own . . .

The rumble of high-powered gunfire rolls in toward Niklas from across the desert. He shades his eyes against the glare and tracks the trail of dust rising from the vehicles in pursuit. He quickly surmises that the trucks chasing Moss are faster, they have more men, and more guns.

Niklas rises to his knees for a better view of the spectacle. He's focused on the sounds of the distant gun battle when he overhears a fragment of conversation. He quickly looks around, but finds no one nearby. He waits, listens, then picks up another brief exchange from the same animated voices.

Niklas nervously swivels back and forth before his attention is drawn to the rooftop directly across the street. A prickly tingle walks up the back of his neck. The voices are from a pair of armed men, and each is wearing a black head scarf. Niklas dips down so as not to be seen. He then observes as the two men stand side by side, and converse between themselves near the peak of the roof-top. It's obvious to Niklas that they are each as mesmerized by the dramatic chase across the desert as he is.

He watches as one of them points at something off in the distance, and in the direction of the chase before he sees the other retrieve a small, handheld radio from his pocket and then lift it to speak. Niklas can only pick up snippets of the faint sounds as the man suddenly begins to talk very fast into the radio, while the second appears to gesture excitedly.

The echoes of the running gun battle still rattle through the deserted streets of the refugee camp. Niklas continues to watch as the radio exchange goes on for a few more seconds. He lies motionless across the roof's scorching metal surface and looks on as the man holding the radio ends the exchange. Then Niklas sees the man reach for his companion and hug him. They laugh together, then return to stripping the three bodies lying at their feet of weapons and ammunition.

• • •

Mike jams his right foot against the sidewall of the jolting, jerking bed of the beat-up, Toyota pickup. He grips the twin, vertical spade handles of the Soviet DShk 12.7 x 108mm fifty-caliber machine gun that's mounted to a welded tripod in front of him. He sights his target through a cloud of billowing dust. His thumbs press down equally on the butterfly trigger between the spades and the old weapon dutifully pounds out the lead.

The road is crap, and Fabri's driving like he's only being chased by the Arma dei Carabinieri. Next to Mike's desert tan combat boot, a live, slithering viper made of 5.45-inch-long cartridges clank steadily up from the bed of the lurching Toyota. The rounds feed into the left side of the gun, while bullets fly from the barrel, and the belt-links disintegrate into bits that eject out the right. Mike grimaces at his still advancing target while smoldering hot shell casings bounce and clatter around his feet.

The spades jerk inside his hands as the barrel pulses on recoil with each round that leaves the chamber. Then he hits pay-dirt. It's one of the technicals. He catches only a quick glimpse as the front windshield blows out in a shower of powered glass. Mike shelters from a burst of return fire before he lets loose again. His rounds cut through the truck's front grill. The hood separates from its hinges and tumbles back over the cab, while the truck's engine implodes in a cloud of white smoke and water vapor—One down . . .

PING! PING PING! Mike shields from the incoming rounds—Whoever welded on this guard plate made it too fucking small . . . He eyes the bulges forming in front of his face as bullets strike the heavy steel plate that's keeping him alive—If they had armor-piercing rounds I'd be dead already . . . He fires off another short burst before he ducks back down behind the guard plate.

Return fire bangs against steel and shatters into his ears. From the sound alone Mike knows he's taking hits from the armored vehicle. From the last glimpse he got it's about two hundred meters behind him, but it's coming up fast. Mike presses down on the trigger again and sees his rounds pelt across the front of the MRAP . . . How'd they get their hands on a fucking MRAP?

"Mike! Mike! Shit!"

Mike spins back toward the open sliding rear window of the Toyota's cab. "Drive Fabri! Drive!" he bellows.

"No benzina!" Fabri shrieks. "The gas! She's finito!"

"Drive until it's dry!" Mike shouts.

He spins back, waits, then strafes the MRAP a second time. His rounds pepper the armored vehicle as the windshield lights up with a row of bright white circles from high-caliber impacts. He ducks back down behind the steel guard just as the Toyota's engine starts to sputter—Fuck me . . .

Mike waits out a few more seconds of return fire before he raises back up behind the Dushka. He's about to press the trigger when the window behind him explodes. He drops back down, shields his eyes from a shower of glass, before his hands return to the spades, and his thumbs press down on the trigger.

Fabri's desperate hold on the wheel has turned his knuckles white. He can't breathe. His vision is a blur. The percussion from the impact rattles inside his head, while fragments of glass dance across the hood in front of him. Dust from the truck just ahead now blows directly into his face through the opening.

He frantically stomps the gas pedal to the floor, but the truck's engine only sputters and coughs in response. It's losing speed fast. Fabri cries out for the engine to keep going, he begs, pleads, he stomps his foot to the floor again and again, but the engine only croaks out a final gasp.

Moss checks his mirrors; Mike's Toyota is rapidly losing ground. "No, no, no, Seth!"

Seth looks for an opening, then fires on the MRAP with little effect. He can't see Mike. He can see Fabri though, and he's spooked as all hell.

Moss lifts his foot off the gas and slows to stay with Mike and Fabri

Seth knows Mike's got no chance, and his aren't looking any better. The last of the staples that once held his thigh together have torn away from his flesh. He hears another volley of rounds hit the steel plate keeping Mike alive. He drops down as more rounds strike his. Seth then raises up, points the heavy machine gun at the armored vehicle, and presses down on the trigger. In that split second, the MRAP goes airborne.

Inside a moment that seems to last forever, Fabri's grip on the wheel is violently wrenched away. His vision then goes from a blur to black as the truck he's driving is tossed like a toy. The force of the blast lifts the back of the Toyota and ejects Mike from the bed. The pickup torques then rolls two complete turns before coming to rest on one side.

Mike lies flat on his back in the hot sand and coughs. His head feels like someone just hit him with a hammer. He forces an effort to get up, but his body refuses to cooperate. Lifting one hand, he holds it up in front of his face, but sees both of them—Not good . . . In between his two right hands, Mike can just make out a fast-rising column of thick black smoke. Intense heat from the flames radiates out from the blast site in steady waves. He can't see the inferno, but he'd bet even money as to what just happened— Someone just triggered an IED on the MRAP . . .

Chapter 22

Tick Tock

Moss slams the brakes and skids to a stop while thick, choking dust rolls in through the open windows and fills the Toyota's cab. Ax reaches for the MP5 wedged between the truck's cracked vinyl seats with his right hand. He pops the door with his left, then kicks it open.

He launches from the cab of the truck while his eyes dart across the scene in front of him. He searches through the rolling shrouds of heavy smoke and dust for the second technical. The Toyota is about fifty meters away, on its left side, and with the bed facing toward him. Mike lies face up on the ground. He's only a few meters left of the truck, and he's moving—Good sign . . .

A hundred meters further on from where Mike hit the ground lies a burning hulk that was, just moments ago, a mine-resistant, armored personnel vehicle. It's now completely engulfed in a raging fire and surrounded by a solid wall of flame that bakes into Moss's face. The inferno rises up directly in front of him like an angry, hellish beast the size of a two-story house.

Moss glances back in Seth's direction. "I got you," Seth calls out.

Moss lifts his MP5 and lays down a round of suppressive fire before Seth closely follows with a punishing blast from the fifty-cal. Above the roar of the inferno, Moss can hear Fabri screaming. Lowering the MP5, he looks again at the overturned truck, and picks him out. He can see Fabri moving inside the truck's cab—Another good sign . . .

Moss quickly advances across the stretch of open ground between himself and the overturned truck. He then crouches down behind the truck's rear bumper. He waits, and listens, before he makes a move toward Mike.

Moss is just about to head in Mike's direction when three running targets suddenly come into his view. It takes Moss one, perhaps two seconds to track, aim, and then fire on the three men. All three are armed, and all three are in the process of fleeing the flames like Olympic sprinters.

One goes down immediately after the first three-shot burst. Moss fires again, but the second and third sprinters make cover behind a line of heavy brush. Moss fires off a final burst in their direction—to keep 'em running. Then he shifts his attention back to Mike.

His right index finger lightly touches the trigger of the MP5. He scans for additional targets while he holds his position. He watches Mike, and he waits. Then he hears Fabri scream again. Moss swivels toward the smashed-out cab of the truck and locks eyes with the slim Italian.

Fabri nods back toward Moss before he turns away and then scrambles out through the truck's blown-out windshield. He crawls on his belly toward Moss, and he's dragging Mike's G28

DMR behind him. The traumatized man then lifts his head to speak but Moss only motions for him to stay down. Fabri nods in acknowledgement before he quickly scrambles some more, wriggling over the ground like a crippled lizard until he reaches Moss.

"Are you injured?" Moss asks.

"No . . . I don't think so," Fabri stammers.

Moss points up at the heavy machine gun still attached to the tripod welded into the bed of the pickup. "I need you to remove this ammunition belt and take it back to Seth. Can you do it?"

Fabri glances up at the Dushka. The gun came to rest at an odd, oblique angle with its barrel pointed toward the sky, and its ammunition belt dangling down into the sand like the tail end of a cobra. He then stares back at Moss before he answers in a breathless voice: "Yes . . . yes, I can do it."

"Get to work," Moss orders.

Moss shifts his attention back to Mike just as a death blossom of indiscriminate, automatic weapons fire erupts from behind the flames. Rather than return fire immediately, Moss listens. He rapidly processes the few seconds of information into a clearer picture of who he's up against.

The numbers of rounds fired, the crossed trajectory, and the mixed caliber, convey much more than sound alone. Mainly that the other technicals in the convoy that chased them out from the center of the camp could still be operational. And that, by his estimate, anywhere from six to ten combatants survived the IED attack in fighting condition.

From the smell Moss reckons a number of them went up with the MRAP. And by the heat intensity, the fire won't be dying down any time soon. Based on his experience, the IED bore all the hallmarks of Jihadi, budget-priced overkill; a helluva lot of na-palm, and enough explosives to destroy an MRAP. The likely source being an artillery shell packed with extra PE4, and the most likely culprits being Al Shabaab.

The whole package was then buried and triggered by remote, because if they had used a pressure plate, Moss knows he'd be dead already. His truck was the first one to cross over, so his would have been the one to set it off. This bit of information is the most disturbing to him. Not only because he nearly bought it, but because it means that whoever triggered the IED is likely still close by. It's the same sort of shit he encountered in Iraq, and far too many times.

A few more seconds go by before the blossom of panic fire dies down. Moss swivels back to where Mike still lies flat on his back and he makes his move.

"Can you walk?" Moss asks.

Mike winces up at him. "Yeah."

Kneeling down beside Mike, Moss rolls the old soldier onto his side before he reaches around his chest with both arms and then lifts him up. Mike coughs, lets out a low groan, then finds his footing. He presses his boots into the ground as he pushes his vintage frame upward. Moss pauses, and Mike takes a breath. Mike winces some more against the intense pain before he finally un-folds himself into a standing position.

With timed precision, Seth strafes the blast site with another round of suppressive fire. The brief report means only one thing to Moss—Time to move . . . The two men say nothing to each other; there's no need. Their next action is automatic—turn back toward the cover of the overturned truck, and get there fast.

• • •

Niklas inches his way back down the sloping metal roof. The rough edges of the overlapping metal tug and pluck and scratch at his bare legs. He's frustrated that his T-shirt has rolled up around his armpits, and that his belly is now fully exposed to the sizzling hot metal sheeting.

His hands are occupied. He holds onto the rifle's strap with his right, while the ammunition belt dangles from his left. He can't let go of either, so he can't stop, or make any adjustments. He's fully committed.

He braces against the pull of gravity with his elbows, as he methodically walks them backwards. First with the right, then the left, a pause in between, then he repeats the painful maneuver.

Niklas allows himself a brief grin the moment he senses that his feet have reached out beyond the roof's edge. He stops and twists around, until he catches sight of Jannik's outstretched hands. He then slowly lowers the AK, followed by the ammunition belt.

"I heard an explosion," Jannik says as he grabs for the dangling machine gun. He then takes the ammunition belt from Niklas. "What happened?"

Niklas swings his legs down from the roof, then lowers himself to the ground. He wrestles his rumpled T-shirt back down over his waist. He brushes off his clothes, and then quickly checks himself for injuries before he breathlessly answers his partner. "This is a dangerous place," he says, "perhaps even more dangerous than Somalia."

"But the explosion?" Jannik asks again. "What was it? Did you see what happened?"

Niklas takes another deep breath. "Yes, I saw it." He retrieves one of the AKs from Jannik and then slings it across his chest. "You were right, Jannik; we are on our own."

• • •

Moss has one arm around Mike as he lowers him down, and then into a seated position behind the rear bumper of the overturned pickup. "How bad are you injured?" Moss asks.

Mike smiles up at the chief. "I can still shoot." He chuckles at his condition, then winces again as he grabs for his side. "Fuck . . ." Mike leans forward and braces against the sharp pain. "I may have cracked a rib or two."

"Shit . . ." Moss responds.

Mike sucks in some air, then he straightens before he stares back at Moss. "I'm good to go, Chief."

The raging fire still roars above sporadic pops and cracks, and the now less frequent, scattered weapons discharges. The battle, for the moment at least, has ebbed. The acrid stench of burning tires now fills the air, while its oily residue coats the backs of the two men's parched throats.

Moss takes note. Round one is over, but the column of thick, black smoke rising straight up into the clear, Kenyan sky will be visible for miles in all directions. There's no telling who may be drawn in to investigate, or who else may already be watching.

Moss and Mike each know the battle's lull can mean any number of things. The enemy has run low, or perhaps even run out, of ammo. The enemy is reloading, or, if they're lucky, retreating in order to regroup. Either way, the two veterans know the lull will be brief. It's precious time Moss also knows he must use wisely, because he'll never get it back.

Moss shifts away from Mike and then uses up two, perhaps three seconds off the ticking clock to rapidly evaluate available options before he makes his next move. The brief stretch of open ground that lies between where he and Mike now sit, and where they need to be, is doable. Next he locates Fabri, and finds he's already made cover near Seth. Moss glances up at the now empty fifty-cal strutting out from the overturned truck's bed—Good job . . . time to go . . .

Moss shoves his left arm under Mike's right shoulder, then grabs ahold of his belt with his right hand. Moss pulls Mike back up, and then onto his feet, and the two men run.

Gripping the Dushka's twin, vertical spade handles, Seth presses both thumbs down onto the butterfly trigger and then blankets the blast site behind Moss and Mike with a hail of suppressive fire.

Moss can feel Mike's ragged breaths. Each one timed with each uneven step, and each one a signal to Moss that Mike's in real trouble. Seth observes the two men struggle as they approach his position. He grimaces at Mike's condition before he sends another round of suppressive fire though the wall of flame. He keeps it up until he sees Moss and Mike finally make cover and then move behind him. "We gotta get the fuck out a here!" Seth shouts. "Load up!"

"You heard him!" Moss bellows at Fabri. "Load up!"

Moss pops the passenger side door and then pushes Mike inside. All while he keeps close count on the ticking clock in his head . . . Thirty seconds gone . . . Fabri climbs into the back with Seth . . . thirty-five seconds . . . Moss sprints to the opposite side of the truck and then folds his six-four frame in behind the wheel . . . forty seconds . . . He reaches for the keys still dangling from the

ignition and then turns the crank. The engine sputters, and then .
. . nothing . . .

Chapter 23

Oscar Mike

Diric Abdirashid Abshir clinches his jaw tight as if he still had khat, which he doesn't. He paces in rapid circles behind the last truck in his convoy, which also happens to be the last one still drivable. He pauses just long enough to point his weapon at the flames and then fire off three more rounds. Three more rounds spent on an enemy that he cannot see. The last three rounds from his last clip, and as the third bullet explodes out from the over-heated barrel of his AKSU-74, Abshir's red eyes twitch, his body quivers, and he screams.

Even with the clip emptied, Abshir's finger still reflexively pulses against the trigger of his AK. But each successive, dead click that follows only ratchets up his rage. Abshir lets out another long, shrieking scream at the blinding wall of flame in front of him, before he finally lowers his empty weapon.

He spins back, barks out a rapid and malicious stream of ex-pletives at his three remaining men. He then pulls the empty clip from his weapon, tosses the hunk of metal to the ground, then goes in search of another one that may still be loaded.

The odor of burning flesh clings to his clothes and collects inside the sweat that streaks down his face—the flesh of men Abshir had known for his entire life. The roadside bomb killed five, while four more men of his men now lay dead from the gun battle that followed.

He walks amongst their bodies as he attempts to subdue his anger long enough to focus his mind. He must regroup, and the place to do it is inside the camp. He will end his fight there, he is certain of this, just as he is certain the camp is where his enemy will be hiding.

He has allies inside Dadaab, men from his own clan, men he knows he can count on. Abshir suddenly stops, his eyes dart across the remnants of his convoy until he spots what he is looking for. He marches over to where a man lies facedown and then kicks the body over. Wrestling a rifle free from the dead man's grasp, Abshir lifts the weapon, pulls the clip, and grins.

. . .

Moss rotates his wrist as he clamps down on the Toyota's ignition. The engine briefly struggles to turn over before sputtering out a final cough. Moss pumps the gas pedal, he checks the gages and then attempts to start the dry engine a third, and then a fourth time . . . sixty-five seconds . . .

"We have to go on foot, Chief," Mike mutters . . . "We gotta go right now."

Moss tries one last time, but Mike's already grabbed up his gear. Mike grimaces from the pain as he pushes his door open and then slowly climbs out. Moss draws his right hand away from the dangling keys before he slips the strap of his MP5 around his neck . . . seventy-five seconds . . .

Moss drags a spare ammo pouch out from under his seat. He clips it to his vest before he twists back, and then extends a thickly muscled arm down and behind the passenger seat. His fingers quickly grope then grasp the nylon back harness attached to the twin sheaths that hold his Kukri blades. He yanks the pack free, then gets out of the truck . . . ninety seconds . . .

Seth and Fabri have already disengaged the ammunition belt, about twenty rounds worth, from the fifty-cal. Seth slings the ammo belt over his shoulder before he lowers himself down off the tailgate with Fabri's help.

"Can you walk on your own?" Fabri asks.

"Sure," Seth answers. "Get my med kit, will ya?"

Catching up to Mike, Moss grabs for his left arm in an attempt to assist, but Mike only pulls it away. "I'm okay, Chief," he grumbles. "I'll make it."

Moss allows himself to use up a few more seconds off his mental clock in order to size up the surroundings. The flat, desert landscape is a patchwork of low-lying thickets of dry brush, mostly consisting of thorny acacia trees. He estimates a straight walk back to the refugee camp would need to cover no more than three kilometers. Not much distance at all, but what lies between his team, and the camp, is another matter entirely. Then there's Razz; his brief message was clear—On our way . . . Moss has been meaning to send Razz an update on their position, but unfortunately, he's had his hands full.

Moss swivels back, then catches sight of Seth. "Can you walk?" Moss asks his medic. At which point Seth lets out a chuckle.

"Everyone keeps asking me that." He smiles at Moss. "I'll be fine, Chief. As soon as we make cover, I'm gonna open up the kit, take care of Mike, and patch myself up—"

"Save it will ya?" Mike growls. "I'm fine, and I'll be a whole lot better once we take out the rest of these goat-fuckers and complete the goddammed mission."

Seth takes a breath. "Sure Mike, I hear ya, but first we need to make cover, right?"

"Right," Moss answers.

• • •

Razz squints against the glare as he looks out from the driver's seat of the Land Rover. He sizes up an ever-widening sea of parched, rust-colored sand, and bone-dry scrub. He doesn't like what he sees—not one bit. He'd much rather be back onboard ship. He's always hated deserts. Especially after his stint inside the Iraqi sand box. He hated it then, and he hates it now. But unlike the vehicles they used in Iraq, at least this one has air conditioning, and a cup holder with a cold drink inside of it.

Late afternoon sun beats down hard on the speeding Land Rover and the asphalt road the vehicle is currently traveling on, but that's the last thing that's bothering Razz. The first thing is the fact that, since this morning, there's been no update from Ax—no news at all. Not since the brief text they received containing the team's location, and that was over six hours ago.

There could be any number of reasons why he hasn't received an update. The phone's battery may have quit, or the unit's been damaged in some way. If either of those things are the reason Ax hasn't sent an update then Razz is fine with moving ahead on ice cold information. They agreed before the mission even began that communication would be limited, which means, even if the satphone is working, it's probably switched off.

But then there's the other possible reason there's been no news. It's the one Razz would rather not think on too closely, because it means Ax has his hands full. After almost ten years of knowing the guy, Razz can say one thing for certain: when Ax has his hands full inside a hostile situation, the last thing anyone should do is get in his way—or surprise him . . .

. . .

"What the hell are you two idiots doing with those AK-47s?" Andrea snipes at his first sight of the two young Germans.

"See?" Jannik chides Niklas. "I told you the guns were Russian."

Niklas only frowns in response before Elsa abruptly stands, and then approaches the pair. "This is a terrible idea," she says before she approaches, and then stands directly in front of them. "Jannik, Niklas, please, you must put those guns back where you found them. No good will come from having them; they are instruments of death."

"We need protection, Elsa," Niklas responds. "We are on our own now; the commandos have left us here; they won't be back."

Elsa listens to Niklas, then she calmly steps forward. She moves in close, so close that her face is only inches from his. "What you see in front of you is an old woman," she says, "and I got this way by using my head. Lars and I have spent over twenty years together in Africa. We've lived in six different countries, and never once have either of us felt the need to own a gun."

"And yet you were captured by pirates," Niklas chides, "and held prisoner for eighteen months." Niklas folds his arms in front of him. "We don't want that happening to us."

Elsa's expression hardens. "Young man," she begins, "I hate to break this news to you, but this has already happened to you both." Elsa raises a slender finger and points it at Niklas. "Lars and I never asked to be rescued by those men." She lowers her finger and then steps back. "We were quite certain, because of our age, we were certain the pirates would release us once they knew they would receive no ransom money for us."

She folds her arms and stares back at the two young men. "There were six of us captured that day. The others were subordinates of my husband. They were all employees of the same company. Everyone except me. Lars had just finished leading a two-week field project, and he was excited about the data. He'd been with the same company for twenty-five years, but when the corporate office got the news that we had all been taken hostage? Well, let us just say—they ran the numbers."

"How can you know this?" Jannik asks. "What happened to the others?"

Elsa smirks. "Ha! They were all released! It happened quickly. At the time, Lars and I, well, we didn't know what to think." The old woman folds her arms in against her body more tightly as if she were shivering. "The only reason we discovered the truth was because the pirates told us what happened; one of them even apologized!"

"It was your husband's pension, his benefits, yes?" Andrea interjects. "Twenty-five years is a long time—a lot of money."

Elsa's eyebrows go up briefly before her expression darkens. "It's always about the money." Then her gray-blue eyes focus on the two German students. "Lars was thinking of me; he always hated violence, but that night, when those men suddenly appeared at our door? We have four grandchildren. He saw the opportunity, and I can't say I didn't agree. I did. But now?" Her voice trails off. "I've lost my husband." Her eyes well up with tears as she stares up at the two young men. "Please, Jannik, Niklas, please, don't make the same mistake; you love each other, right? Get rid of those guns . . . please."

· · ·

Abshir raises his freshly loaded weapon and listens. He hears nothing other than the crackle of the raging fire in front of him. To waste more ammunition would be foolish, but to step beyond the edges of the fire, and into the open, is a risk he is still not yet willing to take. So, he waits. Abshir crouches behind his last remaining technical with the last of his men. He checks his watch . . . Two minutes . . . three minutes . . . Abshir stares at the plastic Casio digital strapped to his wrist . . . four minutes . . . nothing . . . He groans in disgust before he stands up.

"What are you doing?" one of his men asks. "They have your uncle's guns."

"I am a man," Abshir answers. "I will kill the dogs who murdered my uncle."

"Do you want your uncle's guns to kill you?"

Abshir responds to the man's comment by simply walking away.

"Diric!" the man calls out, but Abshir is already striding away from the technical and toward the outer edge of the fire. He has his AKSU-47 raised tight against his shoulder, while his finger lightly touches the trigger. The wind has shifted, sending the heavy

208

smoke billowing around him. It fully envelops him. He breathes it in, allowing the smoke to fill his lungs as he marches through the opaque haze.

• • •

Moss pushes his way deeper into the thick, thorny brush. Progress is slow. One foot in front of the other, in pace with his wounded men. He's behind Mike, Seth, and Fabri, with Fabri in the lead, Seth next in line, and Mike's battered, off-kilter frame lumbering along just in front of him. Moss keeps watch over his injured men, while still keeping an eye out for more trouble. His right hand rests against the freshly reloaded MP5 hanging in front of his body armor. He lifts his left arm and checks his watch . . . four minutes . . .

Moss takes a few more steps, then he pauses, and looks back in the direction of the burning MRAP. They've barely covered a hundred meters. Moss knows it isn't nearly enough; in fact, it's nothing. He peers back through the broken tangle of acacia, and that's when he sees him.

A lone, slender figure emerges from the smoke, then marches toward the overturned pickup. Moss observes as the man strides up to the wrecked Toyota—like he owns it. Moss tracks the man's movement, studies his gait, his features, and as he does, his left hand rolls into a tight fist, while his right finger twitches ever so slightly against the trigger of his MP5—I know who this guy is . . .

"What do think, Chief?"

Moss twists back to find Mike standing right behind him. "Abshir," Moss snorts. Then Moss turns back toward the solitary figure and continues to observe as Abshir approaches the over-turned pickup and looks inside.

"This guy's on a mission, Chief."

"I agree."

"I say we take this guy out while we have the chance." Mike unslings the G28 DMR and checks the clip.

But Moss isn't looking at Mike; he's still staring out through the brush. He hears Mike cock his weapon, and that's when Moss quickly raises his hand: "Wait."

Mike flashes a look of exasperation. "What the hell for?"

Moss shifts and stares back at his perturbed sniper, then he points: "Over there." His voice then drops to a whisper. "Look at that."

Seth and Fabri are now standing beside Mike as Moss points off to the right. The three men follow the chief's finger to a spot farther up the road, and to a point less than a Klick ahead of the blown-out MPAP. The view is obscured, but not so much that they can't pick out what caught the Chief's eye.

Mike searches past the broken brush until he catches sight of a fast-rising dust cloud. He recognizes it immediately as the exact sort of thing vehicles traveling at high speed along a dry desert road would leave behind. Mike lets out a low, audible groan as he shoulders the carbine. He looks back at Moss. "You're right, Chief," he says, "we better keep moving."

Chapter 24

The Holdup

Adrenaline from the battle pumps through Abshir's veins. The chemical burns inside of him. A toxic cocktail shaken together with his raging anger and amphetamine withdrawal. Abshir drops to his knees and then peers into the shattered cab of his uncle's truck. He sets his weapon aside before he leans in through the opening where the front windshield used to be.

He speaks feverishly and nonsensically to no one but himself as he ransacks the smashed-up truck. His hands pass quickly over spent shell casings and brush aside empty plastic water bottles and food wrappers. He finds no fresh shells, no weapons, and no blood. Abshir pushes himself back outside. He stands, and then he screams again.

He snatches up the AK lying near his feet, and then walks to the rear of the truck and over to his uncle's fifty-caliber machine gun.

"Diric!"

Abshir shifts away from the gun and then toward the man shouting at him. He doesn't respond. He only turns back to the heavy machine gun and continues his inspection.

"Diric!" the man calls out again. "We must leave now!"

Abshir turns to stare back at the man. "Look around you," he says. "No one is here."

"Not here, Diric," the man says as he points toward the rapidly approaching vehicles and the rising cloud of dust, "there!"

• • •

Jannik picks up his pace in an attempt to keep time with Niklas. "What is the plan?" he asks.

"The plan?" Niklas answers without looking back or slowing down. "This was your idea, remember?" He grips the strap of the AK-47 as if it were the rucksack he carries to school, and he keeps moving.

Jannik drops back a step as the two young men pass through a series of narrow alleys just off the main drag. "A vehicle," he suddenly blurts. "We find transportation, and this time, something all of us can sit inside."

"Of course!" Niklas pauses and leans his head back as he lets out a brief cackle before continuing on. "It's a great plan you have!" he quips. "And what shall we steal?" He stops suddenly and then spins back into Jannik's face. "An Audi?" Niklas offers sarcastically, "with four-wheel drive and air conditioning?"

Jannik's expression sours. "How do you expect all of us to get out of here without transportation?" he says. "We take whatever we can find, of course, and yes, we will steal it, but in a place like this? Who cares?" Jannik braces for the angry response he's certain will come flying from his lover's mouth.

Niklas stares back at Jannik, then he sighs and his face suddenly softens. "I am afraid . . ." He lowers his head. "Elsa was right, this was all a stupid idea." Niklas lifts his face and looks back at Jannik. His eyes are red and wet, his left hand squeezes the strap of the machine gun hanging off his shoulder, while his thumb nervously rubs across its nylon webbing. "I don't want to lose you—I can't."

Jannik grabs ahold of Niklas and hugs him tightly, then he steps back. "You are not going to lose me. Now come on, let's go; we can do this."

• • •

Cal hits the wipers of the Land Rover again, and the action sends washer fluid squirting up onto the filthy glass in front of him. He looks on with irritation as the blades only manage to create smeared streaks of orange mud across the windshield. The effort results in only a minor improvement to his forward visibility. "This sucks." Cal leans forward and tries to peer out between the smears, then he hits the wipers again.

"Leave it, mate." Murray looks back down at the LCD screen of their handheld GPS. "We should be coming up on the outskirts of the camp."

"Well if we are, I sure as hell can't see it," Cal responds.

"I can." Razz swivels away from his backseat window. "We're here."

"Right then." Murray powers down his dust-caked window. He peers out as Cal navigates the Land Rover along a narrow sand track. A scar of a road that runs in a bone-straight line, through a bone-flat landscape made of bone-dry ground.

The road is lined with a hand-built, puzzle-like network of thick, dry brush fencing woven together from thorny acacia branches. The fencing surrounds row upon row of white, UN emergency shelters and other makeshift structures.

Murray looks out at the bleak habitation that half a million war refugees call home. Then he settles back into his seat. "Place looks deserted," he says. "I don't see anybody."

"Just keep driving," Razz orders. "There's a UN relief station in the center of town; head for that."

"You got it," Cal answers.

Cal drives on. He sticks with the main road, which gradually grows a bit wider and more deeply rutted the further along he goes, until the camp's central row of prefab, corrugated buildings comes into view. "This must be the big city," he quips.

• • •

Jannik unshoulders his weapon, then he leans forward and peeks out from behind the corner of a metal building. He stares down the deserted sand street at an approaching vehicle.

"What is it?" Niklas pushes past Jannik and looks for himself. "Scheisse, I don't believe it!"

Jannik then steps back and flashes a broad grin at his partner. "Ha! You wanted four-wheel drive? And air-conditioning, right?"

• • •

Cal gently presses his foot against the brake pedal and slows the Land Rover to a stop. "Who the hell are these guys?"

Murray squints out through the smeared windshield. "Well, one thing's for certain, those AKs they're holding look to be loaded." Murray subtly shifts his right hand to his P226 and then unsnaps its holster. "What do think, Razz?"

"Nobody move," Razz answers. "Look at 'em; they have no idea what they're doing. Just wait, sit tight; let them approach us."

"You sure about that?" Cal adds.

"Yeah," Razz says, "real sure." Razz eyes the two armed men. Both are white, clean cut, and young. And even with his crappy view, it's all the signal he needs. "I think I know who these guys are."

"I hope you're right," Cal quips, "'cause here they come." Cal lifts and then rests both hands on the wheel and in plain view, as one of the men approaches his side of the Land Rover. The guy has his AK tucked up under his armpit as if he were carrying a long piece of pipe.

The butt of the rifle sticks out behind him. Cal figures it's about the worst way to hold a loaded AK-47. Especially if you plan to hit what you're shooting at. Cal can also see that the kid's got his finger on the trigger, and that's the part he doesn't like one bit. But he takes Rafferty's advice, and he sits tight. The guy walks up to the driver's side window and then taps against it with the flash guard at the tip of the AK's barrel.

Cal rolls his eyes. "Ah geez, okay . . ." He slowly lifts his hands off the steering wheel. He holds them both up in plain view, and he makes eye contact through the glass. Then he nods in compliance.

The guy holding the AK nods back, then he taps on the glass again.

Cal holds eye contact as he eases one hand down to the center console, toggles the switch, and the window powers down with a high-pitched hum.

"Heben Sie Ihre Hände!" the guy shouts, "Schnell! Raus aus dem Fahrzeug! Raus!"

Cal holds up both hands, and he doesn't twitch a muscle doing it. His face shows no emotion. He just stares straight back at this freaked-out kid screaming at him in German and pointing an AK-47 in his face. He'd like to kill him, but Razz was right, and now Cal's pretty sure he also knows who this kid is. "You speak English?" Cal says.

Niklas realizes his body is trembling, and it angers him that he's so nervous. He wasn't expecting it; he thought he would have better control. His heart now pounds into his ears so hard that it hurts. He tries to breathe, but it's as if he's being choked. Then he hears the soldier sitting inside the vehicle in front of him speak to him in English—American English . . .

Cal holds eye contact—This kid's terrified . . . "Hey, uh, it's okay," Cal assures the boy, "we're friends." He keeps his hands in plain view and remains perfectly still. "We're with Alex Moss, do you know him? Alex Moss?"

• • •

Fabri is attempting to keep step just beyond the reach of the acacia's thorn-covered branches when he hears Seth's voice behind him.

"More to your right; we're getting off course."

The Italian sighs as he briefly lifts his hands up in front of his face—both are bleeding. Fabri twists back just as Seth looks up at him from the plugger. "But these trees," Fabri complains, "they are covered in thorns." Fabri quickly reads the indifference on Seth's face. He senses a pang of shame from his complaint. He sighs, then turns back without saying anything further, and heads toward the right as instructed. It's a track that leads straight into the worst of the thorns. Fabri begins to pick his way through the thick clump of Acacia before he suddenly stops short. "Mama mia!" he shrieks.

Seth halts in his tracks. His eyes dart away from the plugger's LCD screen, while his right hand moves to the P226 strapped to his hip. "What is it?" He then looks past Fabri toward the patch of orange sand Fabri's shaking hand is currently pointing at. "Ah shit," Seth complains, "I hate those things . . ."

"What is it?" Mike asks.

Seth gazes down at the three-inch long, golden-hued scorpion crawling over the sand only a couple of feet in front of Fabri. He raises an eyebrow. "A goddammed death stalker."

Mike glances down at the scorpion. "I hate those things." He swings his carbine off his shoulder, and in a single fluid motion, he flips it around and then jams the butt of the rifle into the sand. He grinds it in a bit and then pulls it away to reveal the crushed remains of the poisonous arachnid.

Mike kicks what's left of the scorpion out of the way, then he straightens, and looks Fabri in the eye. "Whatever you come across out here, son, snakes, scorpions, even a goddammed lion, it's nothing compared to those bastards back there gunning for us," he says and leans in toward Fabri. "You hear me?"

"What's the hold up?"

Mike pivots back. "Just a little vermin control, Chief, nothin' serious."

Moss glances down at the squashed scorpion and grimaces at the needless delay. "We need to keep moving. Once it gets dark, we'll be seeing a lot more where that thing came from."

The three men each silently face forward and then continue on through the bush, in a direction that will lead them back to the camp. Moss hangs back a moment. He stands in place as he observes the Italian, a man whose basic military training was ten years ago. Moss next evaluates Seth's condition as he limps behind Fabri. His eyes then move to Mike, who trails them both, and in Ax's opinion, he's doing a piss-poor job of acting like he's not seriously injured.

Moss then glances down at his watch . . . It's time . . . He reaches into his vest pocket and pulls out the satphone. He powers up the unit and then waits for it to initialize. The signal locks on to three satellites passing overhead and over four hundred miles up. Moss then taps out a second text message to Razz: N a sht sandwch B redy O M

Chapter 25

Easy, Mate

Niklas relaxes his grip on the vintage Kalashnikov slung under his arm. Then he allows the four-kilo assault rifle to rest against his side. Niklas draws in a long breath, but his pulse is still racing, and his head hurts. He can still feel the buzz of adrenalin—and the fear that came with it. He hears the American's voice again.

"You know him, right?"

"Yes," Niklas responds in English, "we know Mr. Moss."

Cal smiles. "We're here to help, kid, so you mind putting that thing away?" Cal cuts the engine and then pops open the driver's side door.

Niklas lowers the AK, and then he swings the assault rifle across his back as if it were a common garden tool.

Murray and Razz each push open their doors and then step outside of the SUV. As the three special forces veterans rise to their full height, Niklas stares up at them. The sight of the experienced soldiers, dressed in DCU and body armor, leaves Niklas feeling as small as he has ever felt. A wave of embarrassment suddenly washes over him. "Thank you for helping us," he says.

"No worries, mate," Murray responds cheerfully. He approaches Jannik. "Mind if I have a look at that rifle?"

Jannik nods in agreement before he starts to swing the AK off his shoulder, but Murray already has ahold of it. "There, there now, easy mate . . ." Murray gently relieves Jannik of the AK. Then he flashes a look of concern over at Cal. Cal now has the rifle Niklas was carrying. Murray's eyes narrow while his lips roll back into a terse line as he inspects the old Kalashnikov. "She's cocked and loaded," he reports. Murray removes the clip, then he ejects a round from the chamber. He turns the weapon in his hands. "Set on full auto."

"This one too," Cal adds flatly as he shoulders the disarmed AK.

"Right then . . ." Murray walks to the rear of the Land Rover, where he then opens the hatch. "No more guns for you two pups." He lays the rifle, the lone cartridge, the ammunition belt, and the clip inside before he's joined by Cal who hands him the rest.

Razz eyes the two young Germans standing in front of him. He raises his hands to his hips, then shifts his weight as he lets out a sigh. "So what are you guys doing out here by yourselves anyway? Where's Mr. Moss? Where's the men who were with him?"

"We don't know," Jannik answers.

"They brought us here," Niklas adds, "but there was a shootout."

"A shootout?" Razz's voice ticks up an octave as his relaxed posture stiffens. "With who?" He briefly locks eyes with Murray and Cal before his focus returns to the young German. He steps in closer to Niklas then stares down at the kid. "With who?" he repeats.

"We don't know," Niklas stammers. "We didn't see what happened, we only heard it."

"Shit, Razz," Cal says before spinning back toward the Land Rover. "Guys, shit, the satphone . . ."

. . .

Moss stuffs the satellite phone back inside his vest but remains still for a few more seconds. Without a thought, and as if on autopilot, he unslings his MP5. It's lightly balanced between his hands as if the weapon weighed nothing at all, as if it was just another piece of him. He scans right, left, then he turns back and searches the low scrub forest behind him . . . Still clear . . .

He spins back, then catches up to Mike. Moss then keeps pace behind Mike's uneven gait, close enough that he can step in if Mike stumbles, but knowing that he won't. He watches him, and he listens to Mike's raspy breaths . . . That's it . . . one foot in front of the other . . . you can do it.

Moss walks on while he tries to ignore his own pain. His head is pounding, his ears ring, and then there's his sore feet. They're hot and swollen inside his boots. Each sending up sharp jolts of pain with each successive step. As does his aching knee. The familiar shopping list of pain gnaws at his resolve, and pulls his mind back to places he thought he long ago left behind.

"Hey Chief."

The sound of Seth's voice breaks Moss free of the memory. He looks past Mike toward Seth. "How far?" he asks.

Seth holds the plugger up in front of his face. "One point five klicks in," he says and lowers the GPS unit. "Should be far enough, right?"

"Yeah," Moss answers, "unpack your med kit."

Cal fishes the satphone out from the Land Rover's glove box. He holds it up and allows the unit's antennae to grab ahold of a passing signal and then lock on. "We gotta text," he says.

"Read it," Razz orders.

Cal waits a few more seconds until the message downloads onto the phone's small LCD screen. "Uh . . . wow . . ."

Razz reaches over and takes the phone from Cal's hand. He looks at the LCD: "In a shit sandwich be ready oscar mike . . ." Razz lowers the phone. "Fuck."

"They're on the move, so we better get going," Cal says

Razz stuffs the unit inside his vest as he heads for the driver's side door. "We're too exposed; we gotta get out of here right now." Razz swivels back toward Niklas and Jannik, "You two, get in—move!"

• • •

The elderly man stares into Abshir's eyes. "Diric Abdirashid Abshir, salaam álaykum," he says softly as he grasps Abshir's right hand inside his own. "Welcome to my home; what is mine is yours."

Abshir gently shakes the old man's hand: "Salaam álaykum, Uncle." Abshir then takes a seat opposite the old man and alongside his remaining men. The group sits cross-legged at the center of a heavily worn carpet. The old man's wife soon arrives with a serving tray of small cups and a pot of shaah, a traditional spiced Somali tea.

Abshir and the old man spend the next several minutes calmly discussing many things while his men sip their tea and listen in silence. Eventually the conversation arrives at the point Abshir is most anxious to address.

"So you will need weapons, and men then?" the old man inquires. "Weapons and ammunition I can provide." The old man calmly lifts his teacup to his lips. "But men?" he adds cautiously. "Men will be in short supply. Many of our able young fighters have joined with the Al Shabaab."

"How many men can you give me?" Abshir asks.

"Not many, I'm afraid," the old man responds. "At most? I can only guarantee ten."

The old man's words bring a brief smile to the pirate's face. "Your offer is most generous, Uncle. I accept."

. . .

Murray sits up front with Razz at the wheel. He unfolds a satellite image of the camp that he downloaded off the web before they left the ship. Murray first studies the image in front of him, then he looks outside and back at the image. He orients himself, while Razz drives in the opposite direction along the same road they came in on.

Razz drives until they're clear of the settlement and then he hits the brakes. He twists back and locks eyes with Niklas. "I need to know everything you can remember; don't leave anything out. I need every detail."

Niklas leans forward toward Razz. "It's like we said, there was a shootout." He checks his watch. "It happened almost two hours ago," he says before looking back at Razz, "but that's not what you need to know."

Razz stares back at Niklas. "What do you mean? What do I need to know?"

"The second shootout," Niklas continues, "it wasn't here in the camp; it was out in the desert. That's where Mr. Moss is."

"The second shootout?" The sharp edge in Razz's tone is fully exposed. "Where? I need to know exactly; you saw this happening?" he questions. "Where?"

"Uh . . . I was on the roof and . . ."

"Where?" Razz shouts.

"Easy, mate . . ." Murray places his hand on Razz's shoulder, "give the kid a chance."

Razz sighs. "Yeah, okay, you were on the roof, and?"

"I saw them drive out into the desert," Niklas responds. "The men from the first fight were chasing them; they were all shooting." Niklas pauses to orient himself; he closes his eyes. "They were heading north, away from the camp."

"And there was an explosion!" Jannik suddenly blurts.

"That's right," Niklas adds.

Razz cuts the engine and then gets out with Murray and Cal following right behind him. Razz looks toward the north and searches the sky; then he sees it: a distant stain of black smoke. "There," he points, "they're over there."

Chapter 26

Heading South

There are more rules in place to govern the global trade in bananas than in AK-47s. By far the cheapest to be found in the world, AK-47s, that is, are to be found in Africa. The ubiquitous Kalashnikov is a form of currency in Africa. A fact recognized by The World Bank, which issued an economic assessment on the subject. "Even during times of conflict," the group reported, "Africa's notoriously porous borders guarantee that supply never dries up while prices remain low."

It's what is commonly known as the Africa discount. With millions upon millions of AK-like derivatives, cheap knock-offs, and even, occasionally, the real thing, circulating constantly across the African continent like euros traveling across Europe. During the 1990s, prices were so negligible that an AK-47 could be bought in Angola for only twelve US dollars. In Mozambique with a sack of corn, and in Uganda, with a single live chicken.

For Diric Abdirashid Abshir, the price is merely the confirmation of his family name. He follows closely behind the old man, a man that he has, in fact, only just met. A man who is not his uncle by blood relation, but as an elder member of his clan, the title is obligatory.

The five men walk from the old man's humble home and across his family's cobbled compound, until they reach what appears to be nothing more than a pile of brush. To an observer it would look like a mere pile of firewood, or perhaps a store of the thorny acacia branches used to create the rows of fencing that separate the family's allotted ground from that of their neighbors.

The low sun has begun to tint the sky orange. Abshir and his men stand with their backs to the stark light. Their shadows stretch out in front of them like inky cutouts laid across the rust-colored sand. Abshir watches closely as the old man casually bends down, lifts the corner of a tarp and then shakes it free of sand.

He rolls his bony hands around its edge before he tugs at the corner and the tarp begins to slide over the ground behind him. The old man silently continues his task until he pulls the tarp away to reveal a collection of rough timber, fitted inside a narrow frame. Not much, only a few pieces in fact.

The old man releases the tarp and then hurries to remove the meter-length boards until the mouth of a hole is revealed. Without hesitation he nimbly slips down inside. He first drops down low enough that only the top of his keffiyeh remains visible. He then pauses a moment before he disappears from view altogether. A few seconds go by before the butt end of an AK-47 appears, followed by another, and as Abshir's men quickly grab the weapons, still more appear.

One by one, the pile at Abshir's feet grows larger, and along with the guns, more fully loaded ammunition belts, and more clips. The old man's face then finally reappears. He looks up at Abshir with a broad, toothy smile. "Yes?" he asks. "This is enough?"

Abshir nods his approval. "Yes Uncle, it will be enough."

• • •

Even at a distance of two hundred meters, the sight of the blown-out, and still smoldering, armored vehicle, and the scattered, abandoned technicals, hits Malcom Rafferty like a sucker punch to the gut. The blackened hulk at the center of a blast site, the landscape, all of it propels him straight back to the sandbox with a single, jarring jolt. He wasn't prepared for this, and now he's angry with himself for not being prepared for it.

Razz slows the Land Rover to a crawl. "See anybody?" he asks Murray.

Murray straightens in the passenger seat while he peers through a set of binoculars and attempts to sight the wreck through the smeared windshield. "Not through this crap," he complains. "Hold up, right here'll do."

Razz brakes and then eases to a stop. He moves the gearshift into neutral, but leaves the engine running. The knot in his gut lingers as he draws his P226 from its holster and then opens his door. In that moment, he hears Cal in the back seat bark at the two Germans to stay put. Razz then glances up and catches a glimpse of Cal in the rear view mirror. Cal's DCU, the MP5 front and center over his body armor, and the carbine resting against his shoulder—it's suddenly all too close. Razz quickly looks away and then gets out, but the knot only tightens.

The three veterans exit the Land Rover with their eyes wide open and all seven senses on high alert. They stick close to the vehicle, only stepping far enough from cover to get a full three-sixty.

A thin greasy haze laced with the odor of burnt tires hangs in the air and in the backs of their throats. Cal has the G28 DMR up and in firing position, the composite stock pressed against the right side of his face, his sniper's eye on the scope, and his finger on the trigger. He sweeps the crosshairs over his field of view—ninety degrees, another ninety degrees, and then another, until he covers the full circle. Then he makes a second pass.

Cal reaches up and adjusts the zoom on the scope as he searches deeper into the tangled, parched bush for any sort of movement—anything out of place. Then he makes a third pass. "I got all clear," he announces calmly.

"Me too," Murray adds as he completes his own scan using the mark-two eyeballs. He relaxes his grip on his MP5 before he swings it aside and then lifts the binoculars to his eyes again. With an unobstructed view, he trains the lenses on the wreckage. He studies it, parses through the dozens of clues, then he lowers the binoculars and looks back at Razz. "This's been here for an hour at least."

Razz lets out a sigh as he holsters the P226. Then he raises his hands to his hips and stares across the two-hundred-meter divide between his position and the blast site. "One mother of an IED," he mutters softly.

He shifts back and then looks down the road they came in on with a freshly updated eye. He then turns back toward Murray and Cal. "We can't risk getting any closer than this," he says. "We don't know what else could be buried out there." Then Razz looks down hesitantly at his own feet, "or anywhere . . ." He takes in another deep breath and then lets it go—If we rolled over another one we'd be dead by now . . .

"Jesus, this was one hell of a fight . . ." Cal lowers his scope. "Shake and bake." He glances Murray's way. "You're the demolitions guy; what do you think?"

Murray squints through the lenses. "I agree." He spends a few more seconds passing the binoculars over the human remains—bodies that appear to have been picked clean of weapons and ammo. He then shifts to the other damaged vehicles, then back to the blast pattern before allowing the lenses to dangle from his neck.

"That heap of twisted metal over there was a category I MRAP," he announces. "It weighed fifteen tons, and there's hardly anything left, which means the baddies had heaps of explosives planted and heaps of napalm to go with it." He looks back at Cal. "That would be my expert opinion."

Cal smirks. "Thanks . . . thanks for that."

The knot continues to gnaw at his gut as Razz listens to Murray and Cal continue to speculate over which hybrid species of IED would be required to take out a mine-resistant armored personnel vehicle. But at the moment, he's much more interested in the dense line of scrub that lies just beyond the blast zone. It's where he would have gone if he'd found himself on foot. And, judging by the number of destroyed and abandoned vehicles at the scene, he figures that's exactly where Ax and the guys are right now—on foot.

• • •

Once he realized the thick wall of dense, thorny brush in front of him was actually a hand-built fence, Fabri sighed in relief—Finalmente . . . He turns back and then searches for the others before he spots Seth's pale outline moving toward him in the gray twilight. "We have arri-ved," he calls out.

Seth hears Fabri and smirks at the accent—We have arri-ved . . . that's damned funny . . . He limps up to the fence and then stares at the slim Italian with a sober expression. "So which way?" Seth asks.

"What do you mean?"

"You're on point," Seth answers, "so which way?"

Fabri looks at the fence again. He swivels right, then left, before he shifts back in Seth's direction. "We go right, to the south," he says.

"You sure about that?" Seth chides.

"He's sure," Mike interrupts. He walks up to Fabri. "Don't pay attention to this guy; he's wounded, he's in pain, and he'll dump it wherever he can."

"Keep it down."

The three men all shift back toward Moss. "Sorry, Chief . . ." Mike whispers.

Moss steps in close to Fabri. "You think we should head south?"

"Yes," Fabri answers.

"You're right," says Moss. "Lead the way."

. . .

Abshir checks his watch—21:00 . . . He then steps in front of the ten men his uncle promised him. They are poor quality, and not nearly as young as the old man had led him to believe. But Abshir consoles himself with the knowledge that Dadaab is their home—they all know it well. More importantly, they know where the Al Shabaab are.

Abshir walks down the line of wiry, gaunt men standing shoulder to shoulder. "You will each receive a share of the profit," he explains, "and if you do not survive, your family will be paid your share." Abshir stops in front of one of the men. "I was told you have information?"

The man nods.

"What did you see?" Abshir asks.

The man lifts his eyes to meet Abshir's. "I saw three American soldiers; they came by the main road, they came by car from the south. I saw two more men with guns join them, and then they all left together."

Abshir nods in approval. "Thank you." He then takes two more steps before he stops in front of another man. "And you? What did you see?"

The man's spine stiffens. "I went to where the explosion happened, and I saw three soldiers; they were driving. They looked very rich, they had a lot of guns, they seemed to be looking for something, and then they left."

Abshir nods again before he walks to the end of the lineup. "And you?"

A man in his forties with a graying beard stares back at Abshir. He quietly studies Abshir's face a moment before he opens his mouth to speak. "I have seen the man you are looking for," he answers flatly.

Abshir's expression suddenly hardens. "Where?"

"He travels on foot with three others," the man explains. "They have guns; I saw them near my family's home; they were walking south."

Abshir reaches up and pats the man on the shoulder. "Thank you."

"I know more. . ." the man quickly adds.

Abshir pulls his hand away, then focuses on the man's eyes. "Tell me."

"I know where your property is," the man answers. "I can take you to them."

Chapter 27

No Such Luck

Andrea lies face up along the length of a wood bench inside the deserted UN outpost. The sun went down hours ago, but the heat from the previous day lingers. He can still feel it radiating off the naked sheets of corrugated metal tacked to the bare rafters above his head. He's managed to stretch himself out. One arm is folded up behind his head, and his feet are crossed one over the other. He's exhausted, but he can't seem to sleep. It's as if his body has forgotten how.

He twists his head just enough to catch a glimpse of Elsa. He can just make her out across the room. She's curled up on another bench, and she looks so small to him, more like a child than an old woman. He shifts back, forces his eyes shut, and lets his mind drift.

A crazy story a friend once told him lifts itself from his distant memory. The guy bragged that he'd once spent three days at a private party in Ibiza. Seventy-two hours straight of celebrity hosted drugs, dancing, drinking, and nonstop DJs cranking out EDM. The kicker was that when the guy finally did try to crash, he said he couldn't, he was too whigged out, so he just went back to the party.

At the time Andrea thought the guy's story was total bullshit. But now, after more than three sleepless days and nights of pure hell, with every muscle in his body screaming at him, and his mind trapped in a state of perpetual overdrive, he figures the guy was probably telling the truth.

Andrea shifts position, while the feeble bench beneath him lets out a loud creak in response. He winces at the sound. He stops moving in the hope that he hasn't disturbed Elsa, but then he hears the sound again. He freezes, waits . . . There it is . . .

He lifts his head just as the sharp glare of a flashlight hits his face. Andrea shields his eyes while he moves quickly to sit upright. "Mr. Moss?" Andrea calls out. "We've been waiting . . ." He lowers his hands and tries to see.

A slender silhouette moves beyond the light beam and then into view. "I also have been waiting."

• • •

Through the greenish glow of night vision, Malcolm Rafferty grips the wheel of the Land Rover while he follows the outline of the road in front of him. He drives at parking-lot speed along a sliver of sand plagued by numerous washouts. Razz grimaces at the road's condition, then he hears Murray's twangy Australian again.

"We're coming up on it now," Murray says.

"How many more meters?" Razz asks.

"Less than a hundred," Murray responds.

Razz downshifts, then adds just enough power to cross over a loose, dry swale. The four-wheel drive effortlessly rolls up and then over the far side, while Murray keeps his eyes on the small LCD screen.

"This is it . . ." Murray says. He switches off the GPS just as Cal leans in from the backseat.

"Let me out here."

Razz removes his NVGs. He switches them off, and then lays the unit on the dash. He taps the brakes just as Murray and Cal each pop their doors and then get out. Razz shifts the Land Rover into neutral, then he leans forward and folds his arms over the wheel. He stares out at the scene unfolding in front of him. Murray is the first to flash a small light in Moss's direction, then Cal clicks his on. Rafferty lets out a long frustrated sigh when he finally gets a good look at them . . . Jesus Ax . . . you are such an ass . . .

He reaches for his door handle, pauses, then eyes the two Germans through the rear-view mirror. "Hey you guys—" Razz says.

"We know," Niklas groans in response, "stay in the vehicle."

Razz steps outside and closes the door. He then walks to meet the four figures moving slowly toward him. The men lumber at an uneven pace, and with the sort of broken gait that lets Razz in on the whole story before any of them even has to open his mouth.

Ax has one arm around Mike. He holds him up while the guy struggles toward the Land Rover as if it were the finish line of a marathon. A fourth man shoulders Seth along until Razz sees Cal quickly step in to relieve him.

Murray reaches in opposite Moss and then he lifts Mike up. "Easy, mate," Murray says, "we got you, you're gonna be all right." He looks over at Moss. "It's okay, Chief." Moss is reluctant to let go until Murray gently pushes him off. "I got 'em," Murray assures him. "It's all right mate, I got 'em . . ."

Moss stops in his tracks and then folds forward just as Razz steps in and grabs ahold of him. "Yeah buddy, I know the feeling . . ."

Razz pulls Moss back upright and then steadies him. "Let's get you some water," he says as he helps Moss reach the waiting Land Rover. Razz quickly discovers that Niklas and Jannik, with typical German efficiency, have already lowered the tailgate and retrieved the appropriate supplies.

"You two don't follow orders very well do you?" Razz complains, before he allows a brief smile to show. "Thanks." He grabs a two-liter water bottle, cracks it open, then hands it to Moss. "Here, this'll get you goin' again."

Moss takes the bottle from his friend, tips it up, and then drains it nearly dry before he allows the last bit to splash across his grimy face. He rubs a thick, wet smear of desert grit from his forehead with the sleeve of his sweat-stained shirt, then he looks back at Razz. "We have to move . . ."

"Sure, Ax," Razz answers, "as soon as we can."

Moss opens a second bottle, he draws down nearly half of in one gulp. He leans back against the tailgate. "Abshir . . ." he croaks. "We gotta go."

Razz swivels back toward Moss. "What's that, Ax?"

Moss grabs Razz by the arm. "Abshir . . . he's here, in force. We gotta go."

• • •

Elsa sits on a woven mat and pensively observes her new surroundings. She looks on, and listens, as a pair of women cook curried rice and chatter amongst themselves in animated Somali.

Elsa isn't tied or restrained, but she knows full well that she is a captive.

As a diversion, Elsa discreetly follows the women's conversation. They share complaints, mostly about their husbands, before the topic shifts to Dadaab gossip. She continues to listen as she studies the walls of the home. The entire house has been constructed from stems of stripped acacia woven with thatch, and layered between sheets of white plastic stamped with the UNHCR logo. It's a rudimentary structure, she surmises, but it is a home. It would be easy enough to escape from if she had a mind to— But what would be the point? To be recaptured? Or worse . . . to be shot?

One of the women spoons steaming rice porridge into a plastic bowl, then she tears an edge from a large loaf of flatbread and then lays it in the soup. She turns toward Elsa and hands the bowl to her. Elsa gently takes the bowl, smiles, and then politely thanks her in Somali. The woman cocks her head in surprise, then responds in her native tongue: "You speak Somali?" she asks.

"Yes," Elsa replies, "I know it well; peace be with you."

The woman's face suddenly drops to a blank stare for the next few seconds before her companion leans in close and then whispers, "How can she know our language?"

Elsa smiles again, then she looks up at the two surprised women. "I learned, the same as you."

* * *

Razz slowly eases the Land Rover up a narrow side alley that lies approximately three blocks from the UN outpost. He shuts down the engine, flips up his NVGs, then shifts his attention back to Moss. "Murray and I are gonna go check this out."

"That sounds good to me," Mike growls from the backseat.

Moss grimaces at the suggestion before letting out a graveled response: "I'm coming with you . . ."

"The hell you are," Razz barks. "Look, Ax . . ." Razz pauses, takes a breath. "Look, this isn't over. If you're right, then we're gonna need you on your feet. Are you reading me here?"

Moss sighs. "Yeah . . . I read you."

"Good." Razz glances back at Murray who only gives a silent nod in response. "Okay," he continues, "this shouldn't take long."

"So I guess I just pulled sentry duty then, huh?" Cal says as he steps outside with Razz and Murray. The lean, sandy-haired sniper lowers his NVGs into place and adjusts the MP5 slung from his right shoulder before he looks back at Razz. "No sweat, I'm on it."

Razz flips his own NVGs back down into position. He flashes a quick thumbs up back at Cal. "Be back in a few."

In the near-total darkness of the alleyway, Murray orients himself using a small compass. He then lifts his hand up and eyes a small and hastily sketched map of the surrounding area. It's nothing more than a note-sized piece of paper. But, processed through the photocathode at the front of his NVGs, the scant image is then multiplied exponentially via an electronic sensor, and instantaneously splashed in front of his eyes through twin phosphor screens that render it nearly perfectly. Murray references the series of squares representing nearby buildings and a line of arrows pointing the way to the UN outpost. It's primitive, but it's enough, and unlike the plugger, it's not giving off any light.

Murray stuffs the paper back inside his vest before he motions to Rafferty. Razz nods in response, and the two men move out.

They reach the rear wall of the UN outpost where they hold up, watch, and wait. In the stillness of pre-dawn, Malcom Rafferty is the first to pick up the smell. Soon though, Murray's own nose registers the distinct odor—dank, like a road kill carcass, but with a hint of sweetness thrown in like that of cheap perfume. The reaction of both men is instinctive, a visceral sensation that this smell isn't a common decaying animal at all, but a human corpse.

Ax had mentioned a run-in with South African mercs. The unfortunate result, he'd warned, was the body on the building's front porch. Knowing this in advance, Razz and Murray came prepared. But Ax didn't give much in the way of details, and Razz wasn't inclined to ask too many questions. He was hoping the first hostage he recovered would not be the dead one, but no such luck.

Razz pulls at the desert tan fabric of his face mask as he stares down at the withered corpse. Then he shifts back toward Murray to find he's already opened his pack and retrieved the body bag. The two men quickly load the body inside and then zip the bag closed. The job sucks, there's no other way to put it, but for Razz and Murray, at least the guy getting bagged isn't Mike, Seth, or Ax.

Chapter 28

Until the Job Is Done

"Not there?" Moss responds.

"The place was deserted," Razz repeats. He flips his NVGs out of the way before he bends down to grasp one end of the body bag. He flashes a quick glance up at Cal and then Murray. "Ready?"

"Yep," Murray answers.

"On three," says Cal.

The three men heave the loaded body bag up onto the Land Rover's roof rack. Razz takes a step back, sighs, then shifts to face Moss. "Look, Ax—"

"I'm not leaving those people behind," Moss interrupts before he stares back at Razz. "There's three women still out there somewhere, hostages that we weren't able to locate. I don't know what's happened to them or what will happen to them, and it eats at me enough that I would turn back right now if I thought there was any sort of chance of finding them, but I know it's impossible at this point, so don't ask me to leave anyone else behind, because it's not going to happen—it can't, Razz; I won't do it."

Razz brings his hands to his hips while his lips roll together tightly into a pained grimace. He glances at the ground before he shifts his weight and then gazes out at the first hints of dawn. He measures his next words before he stares back at Moss. "You've been through hell," he begins. "You've done all you could, more than anyone I know." He pauses and then takes a breath. "Ax, I'm telling you this as a friend; it's time to end this before anyone else gets hurt."

Razz can see Moss's answer written across his face. He grimaces again as his best friend in the world, a man for whom he holds tremendous respect, a man who stood at his side in battle, and later at his wedding, releases the one glaring character flaw he's always known would be what eventually gets him killed.

Moss folds his arms in front him while his jaw visibly tightens. "I'm not leaving those people. If you guys want out, I totally understand, but I am not giving up, not after what we went through. I won't do it."

The passenger side window behind the driver's seat of the Land Rover goes first. The glass explodes like a flash-bang grenade. There is no warning, and no time to react. The impact sprays shards of safety glass in a powdery haze that momentarily envelops the four men standing nearby.

The second shot, a split second behind the first, takes out the driver's side window. By now, Moss, Murray, Cal, and Razz have already returned fire. The two shots Moss gets off with his P226 take out one of two rooftop shooters. Murray's MP5 does the rest.

Mike takes the wheel, and he's screaming like all hell. Everyone piles in just as he slams the Land Rover into gear, mashes his foot to the floor, and bores out from the alley in a cloud of dust. "Goddammit!" Mike shouts again as he wheels the Land Rover back out onto open ground. "God fucking damn it!"

"Did anyone get hit?" Moss shouts. "Seth!"

"We got one wounded," Seth calls out as he twists, then stretches across the back seat in order to grab his med kit. On one of the twin bench seats of the Land Rover's rear compartment, Niklas cradles his unconscious partner in his arms.

Murray shines a small light while Seth briefly assesses the bullet hole in the kid's left shoulder. "Get his shirt off," Seth orders just as he rips open a clotting patch. Blood pumps freely from the finger-sized hole. Seth presses the patch into the wound. "Hold this here," he instructs. Niklas places his hand over the patch and pushes down, then Seth locks eyes with Niklas. "Hold this in place; keep it there."

Seth then reaches past Niklas. He sweeps his hand across the back of Jannik's shoulder, then expands his search—No exit wound . . .

"Mike!" Razz shouts. "We gotta find cover!" He glances back at the German kid, and he can tell right off that it's bad, but he's sure as hell not gonna say it.

Mike drives out from the center of the camp and makes for Dadaab's outer perimeter. Heading for the seemingly endless sea of makeshift homes, Mike steers deeper inside the ceaseless, handmade patchwork of thorny acacia. He locates a random side street, slows, and then turns in. Inside the fiery glow of an African desert sunrise, Mike picks out the slim silhouettes of a few curious villagers. As soon as they catch sight of the racing vehicle, however, they all flee. Mike watches them run . . . Not good . . . they know we've been made . . .

"Stop here," Moss orders.

Mike hits the brakes, then slows to a stop. He shifts into neutral before he leans forward into the steering wheel and lets out an agonized groan. "Jesus that shit always hurts like hell," he complains. "God dammit."

Razz looks back again at the two Germans. The level of emotion shocks him. He's seen it before, on the face of a fellow SEAL in Iraq. The guy's closest buddy was in the process of dying in his arms. For the first time Razz realizes what that look had actually meant. He turns away, and then faces Moss. "We need to keep going."

"I'm not leaving until the job is done," Moss growls.

"Ax, this is crazy, we can still get out of here." Razz looks over at Seth, who finds he can only shrug in response. Then he shifts to Mike. "We've got wounded," Razz says. "This kid could die, all right?" As the words leave his mouth, Razz sees Moss clip his MP5 to his vest before he reaches down in front of him and lifts up one of the carbines. "Ax . . . come on . . . don't do this."

Moss opens the door, steps out, then walks off without looking back. Mike already has his gear in order as he too prepares to leave.

"Oh come on Mike!" Razz pleads.

As he stands outside the vehicle, Mike shoulders his G28, then he bends down and looks Razz in the eye. "There's no anger here," he says calmly. "It's just what needs to be done, you get what I'm saying?"

Razz nods. "Yeah Mike, but you gotta understand my position in this. I'll do everything I can for Ax, and you too, but I also have twenty crew, and a two-hundred-million-dollar vessel that I'm responsible for. So do you get what I'm trying to say?"

"Yes I do," Mikes assures him. "You're doing what you have to, and so are we." Mike pivots away from the Land Rover and then tails after Moss.

Cal watches with a stunned expression as Mike and Ax disappear behind a wall of tangled acacia branches. "What the fuck do we do now?"

Opening his door, Razz gets out, and then moves back in behind the wheel.

Cal watches Rafferty's movements, then he asks again. "Razz, hey man, this is nuts, what're you doing?"

"I'm driving, that's what I'm doing. I'm getting us out of here."

Chapter 29

Overruled

The rapidly rising sun has already begun to warm Andrea's back. He sits upright in the sand with his legs crossed in front of him. He sits alone, and in silence, while he discreetly observes his armed captors. The two men have turned away, and they're talking again. So he works a bit more at the nylon cord that binds his wrists behind him.

He's sailed the East African coast long enough to have gathered some knowledge of these pirates. In particular, he has heard of their leader. He's familiar with their habits, and their tactics. As a general rule they treat their captives well, at least, by their standard of living that is. The one thing he's already decided, the event he will not allow to take place under any circumstances, is to be spirited back across the Somalian border.

Andrea knows this is why his hands are tied—he's a risk. It's an unusual move actually. They don't normally do this. Just as they don't, as a rule, indiscriminately kill captives, but he knows of exceptions—like Angelo . . . He squirms a bit in the sand while he picks away at the thin rope. He can feel the knot—he reads it with his fingertips. He's a sailor, he knows every knot there is, and even working blind, he can tell with certainty that this one is shit.

Andrea works at the knot some more before he's forced to stop. The two men guarding him turn his way, before their attention is distracted, and they both suddenly look in the opposite direction. Andrea overhears a flourish of rapid Somali, and then he sees him. Abshir walks into view. He speaks to the two guards, before he turns and stares right at Andrea.

Andrea freezes. His initial instinct is to look away, but instead, he simply holds Abshir's gaze. Abshir folds his arms. He briefly studies his Italian captive, then he approaches.

"Where are the others?" he demands in English. "You will tell me where they are."

Andrea stares up into the pirate's infuriated expression with indifference. "I wouldn't know," he says.

Abshir leans in close to Andrea's face. Andrea can see that the pirate's eyes, blood streaked, and inflamed, have been rubbed raw from khat withdrawal. They blaze only inches from his face. Abshir stares for a few more seconds before he bears his teeth. He sucks in a gulp of air before he lets loose a high-pitched shriek.

Abshir pulls back, raises his left fist as if it were a club and then hammers it into the side of Andrea's head. The impact knocks the Italian on to his back just as Abshir follows with a sharp kick to his ribs. "Where are they!" he screams.

An involuntary, agonized groan escapes from Andrea's open mouth. "They left yesterday," he croaks, "I don't know where."

Abshir stares down at his captive. "I will return," he says. "I will ask again, and you will answer."

Andrea curls himself into a ball while his head throbs, and his ribs ache. He lies on his side, with half of his face pasted to the ground and sand grit between his teeth. He lies still and groans, while his eyes track Abshir. He watches the gang leader until he disappears from view, then his eyes flit back to the two guards. The two armed men look back at him; they each laugh, while they flash rude hand gestures in his direction.

He closes his eyes for a few minutes, just long enough to allow the rifling pain coursing through his body to slack off a bit. When Andrea reopens his eyes, he finds the two guards have once more turned their backs to him. He fumbles through the twisted layers of cord for the knot, and then picks up where he left off.

• • •

"According to the plugger we gotta head west to hit the main road."

"That's gonna be difficult." Razz stares out at the tight cluster of shelters and the thick acacia fence blocking his path. "This place is like some kind of rat's maze."

Cal squints again at the LCD screen. "Okay then, double back, total distance will be three hundred and twenty-two meters." He looks up from the screen. "I spotted another opening when we came in here; I tagged it just in case."

Razz spins the Land Rover around and then turns back. He retraces his path until he locates the opening Cal was talking about. "Here, right?"

Cal looks up. "Yep, that's it; hit a left."

As Razz slows for the turn, he swivels to look in the direction of the opening just as a flash of motion fills his view. He's got no time to react as the blur rapidly sharpens into that of a crazed man's face—"Shit!"

Cal already has his P226 up and ready to fire past Razz when he hears Fabri screaming behind him—"No! No! Don't shoot!"

Razz hits the brakes just as the desperate man's hands thrust through the shattered window and grab ahold of him. "Aiutami!" he cries out. "Aiutami per favore!"

Andrea digs his hands in under the shoulder of Rafferty's tactical vest and locks on. "Please!" he shouts in English. "God please help me!"

. . .

"So what's our plan?" Mike asks as he tracks three paces behind Moss. The two men follow close alongside a line of acacia brush that points toward the center of the camp.

Moss pauses to look back at Mike. "We're improvising."

"Yeah," Mike answers, "that's what I figured."

Moss's mouth forms a thin, tight line above his stubble-covered chin. He stares back at Mike's heavily lined face, age made all the more visible by four days' worth of desert grime. "I wanna wrap this up as quickly as possible."

"Good plan," Mike says.

The two men cover half a klick, but then lose more than three hundred meters of progress when their path is unexpectedly cut short and they're forced to double back. They soon find that footpaths lead to family compounds, which lead to more footpaths, more rows of brush fence, and more interior roads choked off by ever-expanding settlement. The sun is higher and the day much hotter by the time the two old warriors decide to take a brief break.

"Here." Moss pulls a water bottle out from his pack and hands it to Mike.

"Save it," Mike answers flatly. "I'll have some when the job's done."

Moss tips up the bottle and drinks, then he replaces the cap and shoves the half-finished bottle back inside his pack. They stand side by side in a patch of sparse shade created by a lone live acacia tree. A minute or two passes, then Moss hears it first. He listens, then locks eyes with Mike, and Mike nods—He hears it too . . .

It's the growing voices of women approaching, and they're speaking in Somali. They seem to be heading in Moss and Mike's direction, and getting closer. The two veterans continue to listen. The women are now only a few meters away, and just beyond the point where Moss and Mike both stand. The women seem to be engrossed in a lively conversation, three women in total, and all busily chattering away as women so often like to do.

Moss continues to listen as he reads Mike's reaction, and yeah, based on the signal he's getting, Mike's also pretty sure that Elsa's voice is mixed in amongst the other two. A bit slower, more clipped, and with an accent, but still speaking Somali right along with the others.

Mike's eyebrows suddenly arch upwards at the shared revelation. He listens some more just to be certain, then he sees their opportunity. Mike signals for Moss to look behind him. Ax spins back, he sizes up the possibility for himself, then swivels toward Mike and nods in agreement. Mike takes up point position and the pair move out. Mike lifts his MP5, cocks it, and then raises it into firing position. He moves down the line of brush until the voices are parallel to his position.

Mike then heads for a break in the brush, a narrow gap left in the fence so as to accommodate a foot path. It's an opening the two men had walked past only minutes before. It's no more than three meters from where the women all now stand on the other side. Mike passes through the gap first. Moss is right behind him, his P226 in his hand, and ready.

One of the women lets go of her laundry basket and bolts at the first sight of Mike and his submachine gun. Mike watches her turn tail and sprint for the house. He briefly points his weapon in her direction, but he can see she's unarmed. He's never been the sort to shoot a fleeing woman in the back, and he's not about to start now. The second woman lets out a scream before she suddenly collapses to the ground. But Elsa only stands and stares silently at Mike's weathered face.

"You ready to get out of here ma'am?" Mike asks.

Elsa hurriedly nods, then she reaches for the old soldier's outstretched hand.

· · ·

Cal looks back at Razz. "Well, yeah, of course I agree with you, but that's not the point."

Razz shifts uneasily in the driver's seat before he twists back just enough that he can see Seth behind him.

Seth sizes up the expression on Malcolm Rafferty's face before he briefly lifts both hands in mock surrender. "You really want my opinion this time?" Seth asks. "Because last time I got overruled, remember?"

Razz silently holds Seth's gaze for a few more seconds. "What about the kid?"

Seth takes in a breath. "Yeah, he needs a hospital for sure, but so do I, man." Seth then leans in closer to Razz and drops his voice. "Look, his vitals are good, considering. We got the bleeding under control; I jabbed him with morphine. Near as I can tell he's stable."

Razz stares back at his medic for few more seconds. "Okay . . . we're goin' back."

Chapter 30

Man Down

Moss grips the P226 in his right hand while he guides Elsa with his left. He's got her moving at a pretty good pace, and the tough old bird is doing a good job of it too as she jogs easily off his left shoulder. He's got her positioned between himself and a thick wall of brush fence.

Mike's three paces ahead of him and moving at a rate Moss knows can't last. Mike holds the G28 DMR in front of him. Moss can see the end of the carbine's desert tan, composite stock swaying just beyond Mike's right elbow. Swaying in a way that lets Moss know the painful effort behind each step. Mike's head shifts steadily from side to side as he half-jogs along, his full attention focused on what may lie ahead.

Moss is trying to do the same—to stay focused, but right now his mind is racing as he sizes up their options—None of them good . . .

He pivots for another look behind him, then turns back. He evaluates the terrain in front of him—None of it's good . . .

In all directions lay patches of open waste ground, surrounded by endless clusters of white plastic-covered refugee housing and a labyrinth of brush fence. It's a landscape that doesn't offer much in the way of cover for his side, but holds numerous opportunities for the enemy. He grits his jaw as he grips Elsa's arm more tightly, and then he picks up the pace.

Crack! Thump!

The sound catches Moss's attention, but the round passed so close to Mike that fragments of splintered acacia peppered the old SEAL's grizzled face. In the brief moment it takes Moss to let go of Elsa's arm, Mike already has his weapon pointed toward the bullet's source. He locks onto a target, then returns fire.

Mike's target is a man just visible above a row of brush fifty meters out, and thirty degrees right of his position.

Moss witnesses the entirety of the exchange in the form of a brief vignette. A scene that unfolds in a matter of seconds. His eyes first dart across to the shooter. He can see him try to get another shot off as he fumbles desperately with his weapon before one of Mike's 7.62 x 51mm rounds strikes pay-dirt. It all ends abruptly when Mike's target is suddenly minus the top of his skull.

Moss grimaces at the sight before he sees Mike swivel back his direction and flash a broad grin. Moss can read the surge of energy on Mike's face loud and clear—there's nothing like the feeling of killing a man who's trying to kill you. It's the most important signal Moss has seen all day—Mike's back.

Mike lowers the G28, then shifts his weight. He switches to the MP5, then lays down a thick follow up of fully automatic suppressive fire. Mike lowers the MP5 before he focuses back on Moss. "We gotta move."

• • •

"Shit!" Cal shouts. "That was live fire! Did you just hear that?"

"I heard it!" Rafferty barks back as he spins the wheel. He skids the Land Rover in the opposite direction before he mashes back down on the gas. He shifts gears, then accelerates in the direction of the exchange, and the unmistakable high-pitched trill he knows came from an MP5.

"We're a huge target out here guys," Seth calls out.

"Yeah, don't get your panties in a wad," Razz barks. "I'm workin' on it." He taps the brakes as he slides into another turn. Out of the turn, Razz hits the gas. The Land Rover heaves up dust behind it as he accelerates down another narrow track. Razz rapidly scans the rows of makeshift refugee huts that now whip past his window—Enough of this shit . . . time to improvise . . . "Hang on!" Razz shouts.

"Oh shit!" Cal calls out as Razz jerks the wheel, swerves off the road, and then steers directly into a high row of thick brush fence. The safari vehicle's bull-bars burst through the heavy wall of acacia. The impact leaves a tangled clump of the thorny branches clinging to the glass and obscuring his view, but Razz isn't letting up.

A woman tending to an outdoor cooking fire shrieks in terror. She leaps out of the way just as the vehicle that has suddenly crashed through her family's compound races past her, then crashes through the wall on the far side.

Two men walking down a rutted road are forced to lunge for cover as the fence in front of them is suddenly flattened. Razz down shifts, then hits the gas again. The Land Rover bounces over the ruts in the road before it hurtles straight through the fence on the other side.

. . .

Moss squeezes the trigger of his MP5. He fires another three-round burst at a dingy, plastic-covered hut just off his two o'clock and at approximately thirty meters from where he stands. A chaser of suppressive fire to follow up Mike's lethal dispatch of another of Abshir's men—his third kill of the day.

Moss breathes in and relaxes his trigger finger before he softens his hold on the compact submachine gun. He shifts his weight then glances down again at Elsa. She's crouched on the ground just behind him, and near the base of an acacia tree. Her slight frame is folded into an even smaller package, with her knees at her chest and her hands over her ears.

Mike spins back in Moss's direction. "We gotta keep moving."

Moss nods in response, then he reaches for Elsa's arm.

The two former SEALs move along the fence line with Elsa in tow. The stacked row of brush ends abruptly at the intersection of a pair of rough, rust-colored roads. The two dried-out and rutted tracks form a crooked cross, with four uneven points, that then snake deeper into Dadaab's seemingly endless labyrinth of thorn-infested brush fence. The rows of acacia are everywhere; it's an irritation, but it's also served as the only reliable cover they've had.

Moss grinds through the details of the past hour as he sifts through the resulting data for a signal. He squints upwards and notes the late morning sun, then he locks eyes with Mike,

"Abshir's scattered his men all over this place," he says. "They could be anywhere."

"I agree," Mike croaks back. "He's probably offered a bonus to the first one to take us out."

"Yeah . . ." Moss answers before he pauses, then flashes a slight grin back at Mike.

Mike's eyebrows arch up slightly. "So none of these bastards wanna share, do they?"

"Nope."

Mike's smile briefly reappears, but this time it spreads across half his face. "Well, shit . . . I guess we just keep picking 'em off as we go then."

Moss clips his MP5 to the front of his vest, then shifts the G36k forward, and into firing position. "I think we should keep working our way southwest."

"You got it, Chief," Mike says and shifts back toward the intersection. He takes a couple more steps forward, then stops just short of open ground. He risks a peek, before he rocks back, and then locks eyes with Moss. Mike lifts his left hand and flashes two fingers.

Moss nods—and then he waits . . .

Mike turns back toward the corner. He checks his weapon, raises it, then snugs it up to the right side of his face. His left hand supports the weapon while his right index finger lightly touches the trigger. He leans into the weapon's sights, quietly breathes out, then steps clear of the fence.

Elsa watches Mike vanish from view, then she turns away, and cowers in silence. She presses her hands over her ears, but then she hears it—POP! The single discharge shudders through her before—POP!

Moss watches as Mike lowers his weapon. He's still standing out in the road, and looking in the direction of contact. Mike raises his left hand, he signals—All clear.

"We gotta move." Elsa raises her face toward Moss and nods obediently before she gets to her feet and follows behind him.

Moss steps clear of the thick wall of intertwined branches and out into the open, with the carbine raised and ready to fire. He briefly scans the empty road to the west in front of him, then he pivots right, and looks up the deserted road that runs north. He shifts again, and then scans left.

He notes the two bodies. Two men, both armed, and both near the left side of the southbound road. They were only fifteen meters back from the corner he's just stepped away from. The two men now lay sprawled across the ground, with one still holding on to his AK, while the other man's rifle lies beside him.

Ax shifts his focus back to Mike. The old sniper nods silently in response, then signals for them to move out. Mike then turns away from Moss. He heads out to cross the intersecting roads at a brisk walk. He still holds his weapon high, and ready to fire. He advances in the direction of the opposite corner, where another line of brush fence picks up, and the next stretch of rough road continues south.

Moss eyes Mike's lumbering gait as the guy forces his body to march forward. Then Ax shifts away and checks that Elsa is still behind him—CRACK! THUMP! THUMP! THUMP!

Moss spins back toward the point of contact and opens fire with his G36K. He sends off two three-round bursts in a measured sequence, then he waits, and squeezes off two more. He shifts back to where Mike was, but he's no longer there. A numbing dizziness swims through Moss's head when he looks down. Mike's flat on his back, and he's not moving.

Moss spins back toward Elsa: "RUN!"

Moss rapidly shifts away from the old woman. He points the carbine back up the north bound road, then opens up with a fully automatic hail of lead. Moss grips the trigger hard until the last round leaves the chamber. He pulls the spent, thirty-round clip, lets it drop, then retrieves a fresh one. He reloads, then continues to advance toward the point of contact.

CRACK! THUMP!

Moss returns fire with a short burst while he marches steadily toward his attacker. He takes an angle that puts him near the fence on the opposite side of the road. He moves in close alongside the prickly wall of dry brush, before he picks up his pace.

CRACK! CRACK! CRACK! THUMP! THUMP! THUMP!

Splinters of wood pepper the left side of his face. Moss returns fire, then hammers out another curtain of suppressive fire before he crosses the west-bound road and then advances north.

CRACK! CRACK! THUMP! THUMP!

He sees him. The guy's only about thirty meters ahead of him, and hiding behind another line of brush fence that picks up at the next corner. Moss shifts his angle again. He squeezes off another short burst at his target, then he continues to advance toward him, as he continues to watch and wait.

Moss is looking in the right direction when the guy pokes his head out to take another shot at him. Moss isn't thinking at this point; his training is doing it for him. He returns fire.

The moment he realizes he's just killed a man passes quickly. It's followed by the next moment, which is one of profound relief. Moss breathes in as the man's body lands face down in the street. He lightens his grip on his weapon and takes in another breath. He waits a few more seconds, then he turns back, and heads to where he left Mike.

Chapter 31

Time and Place

Moss rubs his fingertips across each of the two rounds embedded in Mike's chest plate and grimaces. He can hear Mike mumble something. The guy's trying to speak, but Moss knows Mike's in no condition to do much of anything—he's been benched. Moss reaches for Mike's G28, and slings it across his back, then he hears Mike's graveled voice—

"Go shoot the bastards, will ya?"

Moss stares down. "First I gotta move you out of the road," he says, as he shifts, then positions himself behind Mike's head. He bends down, slips his hands under Mike's shoulders and then lifts him up.

"Fuck that shit . . ." Mike grumbles.

"Save it," Moss says as he leans back hard and then drags Mike out of the street. Moss moves his injured teammate over near the brush fence on the opposite side. He lowers Mike to the ground before he moves in close and then looks Mike in the eye: "Stay here."

"The hell I will . . ." Mike growls.

Moss frowns. "Stay here, dammit."

Moss straightens, but as he does, every joint in his body screams at him in protest. He winces at the pain as he pushes himself back to his feet. The pain, he knows, will only get worse, but then a sound grabs his attention—Engine noise . . .

He pauses, listens . . . It's civilian, it's moving at high speed, and it's heading his way. Moss steps to the corner for a quick glance—Shit . . . He steps back, checks the ten-round clip on Mike's G28 . . . Still loaded . . .

Moss lifts the powerful assault weapon into firing position before he steps clear of the fence. He stares through the telescopic sight and aims for the windshield of the light Ford pickup. Packed on board is a contingent of shouting, screaming, angry armed men, all brandishing AKs. The truck suddenly accelerates as it bears down him at high speed from a fast-closing distance of one hundred meters.

Moss opens fire—three steady rounds in sequence. A surge of energy pumps through his body as the glass lights up in response before it explodes into a cloud of shimmering white fragments. The truck suddenly lurches left and skids across the sandy road before it crashes through a nearby fence and then vanishes from view.

Moss advances along the fence line toward the breach left by the disabled technical—CRACK! CRACK! THUMP! THUMP!

Moss aims and returns fire, then he ducks down, and pushes himself in tight against the thorny brush. He waits out a second volley of return fire, before he rises up from his crouched position and advances a few more steps—CRACK! THUMP! THUMP!

He never heard the second round but the sledgehammer-like hit to his chest knocks him back off his feet. Moss hits the ground like a sack of bricks.

He opens his eyes, moves his hands in the sand, and realizes he's lying flat on his back. He blinks as he struggles to orient himself through a fog of pure pain while he fights to breathe. He reaches up and feels for the hit. His fingers rub across the torn hole nearly dead center of his body armor. He finds the slug—It didn't penetrate . . .

Moss rolls over on his side, coughs, then he sucks in a raspy breath. He forces himself through a wave of intense pain in order to push himself back upright. He leans back into the stacked wall of thorny brush behind him as he continues to gasp for air.

Moss rests the G28 across his lap, then moves his hand to the MP5. He unclips it from the side of his vest. He brings it around in front of him and then he cocks it. He raises the small submachine gun, and then points it in the direction of the armed men striding toward him—four in all, but one stands out.

Moss has his finger on the trigger, but then he hears it, the high-pitched howl of an internal combustion engine at full throttle, and in that precise moment, an oversized blur blots out his field of view.

Malcolm Rafferty grips the wheel as he holds his foot hard to the floor. He steers a dead straight line while he aims the bull bars at the group of armed thugs directly in front of him.

"Now-now-now! That's it! You got 'em!" Cal shouts.

Abshir and his men spin toward the rushing vehicle just as Razz plows it right into them.

Rafferty slams the brakes and skids to a stop, but Cal already has his MP5 pointed out through his open window. He opens fire on the men scattered across the ground in front of him. Rafferty shoves the gearshift into neutral, pops his door open, and then steps out onto the road. He draws his P226 as he walks over to the one guy he recognizes. Rafferty focuses his full attention as he points his pistol down at Abshir.

Diric Abdirashid Abshir gasps for air as he lies on his back and stares up at the man pointing a pistol in this face. "You call us pirates," he croaks, "but we are the protectors, we are the guardians of our country. It is you who are the criminals."

Rafferty frowns in disgust. "You attacked the wrong ship, motherfucker, and you know what? Now you're dead." He pumps two rounds into Abshir's chest, then follows with a third to his skull.

Rafferty calmly holsters his weapon as he lets out a sigh of relief. He turns back and then briefly eyes the smashed fence and the overturned truck. He shifts his weight, raises his hands to his hips, and then he searches the empty street in front of him. He spots Mike first. The guy looks like day-old shit warmed over, but at least he's on his feet.

He can also see that Mike's not alone; an elderly woman is helping him. Then Razz shifts again, and that's when he catches sight of Ax. He's sitting upright on the ground with his back against a brush fence and his legs splayed out in front of him. Razz lowers his hands, and then he walks over.

Moss manages a weak smile as Razz approaches.

Malcolm Rafferty stares down at his best friend. He lets out a long sigh that ends with a groan of irritation. Then Razz leans in and offers his hand. "So are we finished here?" he asks. "Can we go home now?"

Chapter 32

Face to Face

Three weeks later, Alex Moss sits alone at a quiet cafe table overlooking the Victoria & Alfred waterfront of Cape Town, South Africa. He takes a sip of his coffee and gazes out at the morning light sparkling off the water inside the harbor. He's still enjoying the peaceful moment when the laptop sitting open in front of him begins softly beeping. Moss glances down at the screen, then he reaches for his headphones.

"Alex! How are you?"

Ax stares back at his former boss, Marcus Waverley. "I'm fine, sir, thank you for asking."

Over the secure video connection routed from the foundation's own servers, Moss notes that Marcus is speaking to him from his home office, and not headquarters in Long Beach. He's dressed casually in a pastel polo, rather than his usual tailored Italian suit.

Marcus flashes a broad grin that briefly exposes his perfectly capped and sparkling white teeth. "Well," he says, "it's been quite a week here, Alex. I've been up to my neck in meetings over this thing. I've been on the hot seat with the foundation's directors, the Kenyan government, the Seychellian Coast Guard, hell, even the U.S. State Department."

"I'm sorry to hear that, sir," Moss says.

Marcus leans in closer to the camera as his suntanned face goes sour and his well-groomed eyebrows fold in on each other. "You should be; that stunt you pulled could have caused an international incident."

Moss grimaces at the realization. "I apologize, sir."

Marcus leans back in his leather office chair. "It's a damned good thing you weren't on the payroll at the time, Alex. The foundation's legal team tells me that's the only detail of this shit storm that saved us."

Moss sighs. "Sir, about Seth and Mike—"

"This isn't about anyone but you Alex," Waverley interrupts. "I hold you personally responsible for all of this; those crewmen were following YOU, and if YOU hadn't decided to launch a rescue mission into a hostile, lawless country, none of this would have happened."

Moss straightens. "No sir, it wouldn't." He leans in closer. "As I stated in my written report, I accept full responsibility."

Marcus leans into the camera. "Good." He briefly reaches off camera for something. "Okay then," he says as he fumbles with a bulky file, "let's get down to business, shall we?" Marcus puts on his reading glasses, then he flips open the file and begins sorting through the documents inside. He glances back up at the camera. "I've been receiving some interesting correspondence on your behalf, Alex."

"Correspondence, sir?" Moss asks.

"Yes indeed . . . very interesting." Marcus adjusts his glasses, then he thumbs through the stack of papers before he stops and then pulls one out. "This one's from the Italian government."

Moss winces. "Yes sir, uh—"

Marcus stares at the document. "Says here, you've been awarded something called Ordine al merito della Repubblica Italiana."

Moss's look of surprise is more than genuine. "Sir?"

Marcus flashes a brief smile. "Oh it's legit, all right. Apparently the Italians would like to formally express their gratitude for the rescue and safe return of two of their citizens."

"I don't know what to say, sir."

Marcus smiles a bit more as he eyes Alex. "Oh, that's just the first one . . ." Sliding out a second document, he turns the formal letter around. It's decorated with an elaborate crest and ribbons. Marcus holds it up so Moss can see it.

"This one's an official thank you letter signed by the King of Sweden." Marcus draws the letter back from the camera before he lays it aside. He reaches back into the folder for another document. He holds it up for Moss to see. "This one is an official invitation for you to receive the Order of Merit of the Federal Republic of Germany."

Marcus grins again, then he lays the notice down and lifts up yet another document. "I think I like this one the best," he says as he flips the document around to face the camera. "It's got kangaroos on it," Marcus chuckles. "I love kangaroos."

He carefully lays the certificate back down on his desk. "It seems the Australian government would like to award you The National Medal, for your assistance in liberating three of their citizens taken hostage in Somalia."

A stab of guilt hits Moss in the gut . . . Trisha. Moss focuses back on Marcus. "I'm really happy to hear they got out, sir. I never found out what happened."

Marcus lays the last document down on his desk. "It was all thanks to your email, apparently. One of the girl's fathers has been in touch. We spoke on the phone, and come to find out, he's for-mer Australian SAS."

Marcus leans in as he folds his hands in front of him. "I'm sorry it took so long to brief you on this one, Alex, but I felt all of this was important enough that I needed to inform you personally. I knew you'd want to know what happened."

Moss leans back as his shoulders visibly relax. "Thank you, sir, I appreciate all of this more than you can know."

Marcus briefly smiles again. "After the girl's father read your email, he got on the horn and pulled some strings. He was able to convince the Australian SAS to coordinate with our Navy. Naval intelligence was able to track down the hostages. They were being held on the outskirts of Mogadishu. The SAS launched a night helicopter rescue mission from the deck of a U.S. Navy Frigate parked off the coast. It was successful, Alex, they got all three of the women out safe and sound."

Moss senses a wave a relief wash over him. "I don't know what to say, sir . . . thank you."

Marcus winks at the camera. "I've been pulling some strings of my own." He flashes a smile. "We just had our quarterly board of director's meeting, and if you agree to some amended bylaws regarding the command of Fearless, the board has voted unani-mously to reinstate you as ship's Chief of Operations."

Moss smiles. "Thank you, sir, I definitely accept your offer, and I'd like to say how much I appreciate you giving me another chance."

Marcus peers over his reading glasses at the camera. "You've earned another chance, Alex." He glances away as he momentarily reaches off camera. Then his hands reappear with another file folder. "Okay, so while we still have a good connection, let's go over your next assignment then shall we?"

Moss grins. "Absolutely, sir, let's hear it."

Marcus flips the folder open and then scans the first page. "Okay, so we've been coordinating by satellite phone with Malcolm Rafferty . . ." Marcus glances briefly back at the camera. "To say that he'll be relieved you're returning to command Fearless is an understatement."

Marcus looks back down at the file as he continues to speak. "He wasn't looking forward to the prospect of managing repairs and refit here in Cape Town on his own." Marcus looks up again. "It's going to be a big job." He then flashes a smirk. "But you already know that."

He looks back down at the file. "The ship's due to arrive here in port day after tomorrow." Marcus shuffles through papers as he speaks. "They had some mechanical issues that cost them time getting here; they had to lay up in Reunion Island for an extra week apparently." Marcus looks back at the camera. "So once the ship arrives, you'll have to get on this right away, Alex. Can you handle it?"

Moss looks straight into the camera. "Yes sir, I'll get in contact with Mr. Rafferty and begin organizing the trades before she arrives."

"Good, that's good . . ." Marcus answers before he stares back into the camera, "because the ship has to be ready; the new science team arrives in three weeks." Marcus looks back at the camera. "It's a team of great white shark researchers. How do you feel about sharks, Alex?"

Moss grins. "Sharks? Who doesn't like sharks? Sounds like a really interesting team to work with, sir."

Epilogue

Ten months later, Moss is alone on a Friday night. He sits at a small table inside the chic lounge of a trendy Los Angeles eatery and he waits. It's not normally the sort of place he would be, but Marcus Waverley's wife picked it. He takes a sip of his beer as he observes the crowd of stylishly dressed patrons mingling at the bar. Then his casual gaze suddenly sharpens focus at the sight of one woman in particular.

She's wearing a closely fitted black dress and high heels, while her long blond hair is loosely pulled up behind her head. Moss watches her, and he's pretty sure she is who he thinks she is. Then two more girls approach and when she turns to greet them, he clearly sees her face, and overhears her voice, and now he knows.

Moss stands up from his table and then he walks straight over to her. He's looking right at her, in fact, when she notices him. Her friends take notice too as they quickly size up the tall stranger.

"He's hot . . ." one of them whispers to the other.

"Where did Trish meet him?" the other girl answers. "He obviously knows her."

Moss walks up to the stunning blond Australian. "Excuse me," he says, "but I believe we've met before . . ." Moss then

269

catches himself. "Well, we kind of met, but we were never properly introduced."

Trisha smiles. "Is that so?" she says as she quizzically looks up at Moss with the pale blue eyes he has never forgotten. She stares at him for a few more seconds before something suddenly clicks. Then her cheerful expression goes blank as she whispers, "The Seychelles. . ."

As the words leave her mouth she briefly covers it in astonishment before allowing her hand to drop back to her side. "My god . . . how did I remember that?"

She smiles back at him. "It's Trisha actually," she says. She extends her hand. "But everyone just calls me Trish."

Moss gently grasps her outstretched hand. "It's a pleasure. I'm Alex, Alex Moss."

###

Books by T. R. Schumer

The Fearless Trilogy

Death Catch

Drone Catch

SEAL Catch

From the Author

The spark that ignited into the novel you've just read came from a short passage I wrote in Chapter 24 of *Death Catch.* In it the crew of *Fearless* aren't taking their nemeses too seriously, and the reason is because *they aren't men.* They are something else entirely— something that cannot possibly be real, but somehow is.

These are special operations forces veterans after all. They're battle-hardened survivors of multiple wars and dozens of covert operations carried out in countries all over the world. So it would take a hell of a thing to get them rattled. These are men who regularly clocked into a job that required them to face down an enemy very much like themselves—men skilled in the art of killing other men. When you give the reality of that workplace environment serious thought, it is truly a disturbing prospect.

A much more pleasant alternative, and far less dangerous, would be to leave all that behind and go to sea. Take a job that pays you to travel around the world while working amongst friends—fellow veterans who lack the need or desire to ask pointed questions about your past because they were there.

Why not go for a job that allows you to utilize your nonlethal skill-set for a change? Even better is the opportunity to work outside of the military spectrum. Why not crew aboard a state-of-the-art science research vessel? For Moss, Rafferty, Murray, and the

272

rest of the guys, it truly is a wonderful experience for the most part, but in the end, they're faced with some rather unique challenges.

I relished the experience of writing this novel. Each day the story progressed was exciting because, like you, I had no idea what was going to happen next. The whole process was tremendously fun, not only because it is the final book of the trilogy, but because all three stories seemed to breathe a life of their own.

Researching SEAL Catch was difficult, and also fascinating. The path rapidly developed into a disturbing journey to the darkest recesses of human nature. There are now numerous electronic files stored on my iPad, folders stuffed with articles, books, and PDFs. On one side lies a country that has fully descended into that hellish existence known as a failed state. On the other is how this reality would come to affect the story in ways that were totally unexpected. As a result, many aspects of SEAL Catch are actually factual.

The pirates are real, and I made every attempt to portray them, and their tactics, accurately. Somalia truly is overrun by various international interventions with a wide variety of motivations for being there. The references to AMISOM (African Union Mission in Somalia), the Kenyan Defense Force (KDF), South African mercenaries (Mercs), the United States Central Intelligence Agency's utilization of tribal warlords as proxy assets—all of this is actually real and well documented. Josh's training of "Lightning Force" is also based in fact. For further, nonfiction reading I recommend with confidence, Jeremy Scahill's 2013 book, Dirty Wars.

Dadaab is a real place, and the world's largest refugee camp. It's located in northwest Kenya just over the border from Somalia. Médecins Sans Frontières (MSF) really was forced to close their hospital at one point and relocate to Nairobi due to safety concerns within the camp. Al Shabaab is, in reality, only one of several jihadi groups operating within Somalia, but Dadaab is a documented base for the group. The infamous Westgate Mall attack in Kenya was carried out by the Dadaab terrorist cell. JSOC (Joint Special Operations Command) really has been, and still is, waging a drone war out of their base in Djibouti to wipe out the jihadis in Somalia.

All of this insane, and very real stuff, is taking place within a country only a bit larger than the U.S. state of California. Most of the smorgasbord of covert operations take place in the southern half. Given southern Somalia's limited roads and sparse population centers, the odds of these numerous player's activities overlapping each other is quite high and very real. Oh, and apparently, you really can, even today in 2017, purchase an AK-47 in Africa for about the same price as the average pizza. So when Mike tells Moss "You can pick your poison in this place," he means it.

I would be remiss if I didn't acknowledge, with tremendous gratitude, the contribution of a very dear friend. He also happens to be the person I dedicated this book to. The character of Murray is loosely based on a real guy. He is, in real life, a veteran of the Australian Special Air Services regiment, and chief tactical advisor for SEAL Catch.

Murray is highly detail oriented, as in, nothing gets past him. After he read Death Catch, for example, he pointed out that my backstory on Flip, the former SAS helicopter pilot, was pretty good, but not entirely accurate. Because, in real life, his regiment designations would read differently.

With that observation, I knew I needed to get Murray more involved. We fiction writers do try to breathe a whiff of reality into our stories as much as possible, but we don't always get it exactly right. So for SEAL Catch, I had to do better, which meant bringing Murray onboard during development.

After he read through the first draft of Trisha's rescue scene for example, I found out how much more work I would need to put in if I wanted it to ring true. So the first version got tossed and we started again from scratch.

We tackled the mission as if we actually had to pull it off. The first step was the recon of the building where the hostages were being held after our intelligence resources tracked them down. We needed to decide how best to enter the structure. From his own experience, Murray knew that a multi-story building on the outskirts of Mogadishu would present serious challenges for a manned, airborne assault.

For one thing, the rooftop of a building like this is a guaranteed mess. Our building turned out to be littered with all sorts of obstructions. Our Australian SAS troops ended up having to work around the rough, raw rebar that protruded from the structure's unfinished upper story, laundry lines, a rooftop-mounted water tank, a large cage housing live pigeons, an elevated access door—the situation was a real crapper.

With such limited space to work with, we split the guys into two teams. We fast-roped team 2 down to the roof from a hovering chopper. They had to avoid obstructions, injury, and getting shot, before they could force their way into the building through the rooftop access door and reach the hostages.

Meanwhile, team 1 had already been dropped outside on open ground. They reached the building on foot, and then fought their way up from street level. For everything to go well, the two teams needed to meet in the middle, with the baddies knocked out of commission, and all of the hostages collected up safe and sound along the way—easy-peasy, right?

So our two teams successfully pulled off the infiltration, bravo; now comes the hard part—exfiltration. This is where it really gets dicey, because our guys had to protect the hostages, while the hostages themselves had to be able to move, and I mean—*move*.

We used satellite images to select, then plot precisely, a patch of suitable waste ground where our chopper could land for the pickup. It had to be as near as possible to the structure. Which, in this case, would require an urban sprint, in the dead of night, of nearly four hundred meters. Doesn't seem like that far on paper, but when the enemy is trying to kill you along the way it might as well be a marathon.

Time is critical at this point—all of the well-planned elements of the mission had to come together with near perfect precision in order to bring everyone home alive. This was the part where my already high level of respect for what real special forces troops are capable of went parabolic. If anyone deserves the moniker of exceptional? It's those guys.

The next book is already in the works, and I'll be heading in a whole new direction with this one so I hope you're up for it, because you, my much beloved reader, are everything. Where's the boat, you ask? She's in Brisbane, Australia, and as I write this note, I find myself pausing regularly to enjoy a magnificent view of Lago Maggiore in Switzerland. Soon I fly back to Oz, and the around-the-world sailing journey will continue from there. What lies beyond the next horizon? I haven't a clue, but if you ever find yourself with the opportunity to go to sea, and with a chance to voyage across oceans, I highly recommend that you do, because the world is an amazing place.

All the best, and with much gratitude, T.R. Schumer